A Country Wedding
MURDER

BOOKS BY KATIE GAYLE

JULIA BIRD MYSTERIES

An English Garden Murder

Murder in the Library

A Village Fete Murder

Murder at the Inn

EPIPHANY BLOOM MYSTERIES

The Kensington Kidnap

The Museum Murder

Death at the Gates

A Country Wedding MURDER

KATIE GAYLE

Bookouture

Published by Bookouture in 2024

An imprint of Storyfire Ltd.
Carmelite House
50 Victoria Embankment
London EC4Y 0DZ

www.bookouture.com

ISBN: 978-1-83525-040-2
eBook ISBN: 978-1-83525-039-6

Around the world, people like Peter and Christopher are fighting for the right to love each other. This book is dedicated to them.

Julia couldn't take her eyes off her daughter. It made her so happy, seeing Jess there on the damask sofa in the sitting room of her Cotswold cottage, her legs tucked up under her, and Jake's velvety muzzle resting on her knee. The dog gazed at the young woman adoringly, with eyes like melting chocolate drops. Jess smiled down at him and blew gently on a mug of tea cradled in her hands.

It was her second mug of tea. They'd been sitting like this for well over an hour, talking. Jess had been exhausted when her father, Peter, and his partner, Christopher, had dropped her at Julia's cottage the previous afternoon, and headed to their B&B. The long flight from Hong Kong, a big time-zone change and the drive up from London had left Jess grey and uncommunicative. When she first saw her daughter, Julia had worried that this was how it was going to be for the three weeks of her visit– unnecessarily, as it turned out.

Jess had padded down the passage at 10 a.m., still in her pyjamas, some colour in her cheeks and her hair still mussed from bed, put the kettle on and said, 'Tell me everything!' They hadn't stopped talking since, and they hadn't done more than scratch the surface of what had happened in the two years since they'd last been together. Jess's studies in International Relations, her on-off boyfriend, her friends, her favourite dim sum shop in her Hong Kong neighbourhood. Julia's new life in Berrywick, her relationship with Dr Sean O'Connor, her work at the charity shop, her favourite walks along the river. They'd talked and listened, listened and talked, and the morning had flown by.

'Goodness, look at the time! We'd better get ourselves dressed. We're meeting your dad and Christopher for lunch at the wedding venue and it's on the other side of the village! And I haven't even fed the chickens.'

'Ooh, I want to see the chickens. Let's do it now.'

Julia grabbed a warm jacket from the hooks by the door and passed it to Jess. She took a long, shapeless jersey for herself, and slipped her feet into her garden shoes. 'Take the wellies, they'll fit,' she said.

'That's a stylish get-up, Mum.'

'Thank you. I do try to maintain high standards. You look very elegant yourself.'

'Why, thank you.' Jess pointed one wellie-clad foot in front of her, and bowed deeply.

Julia picked up a bowl of kitchen scraps from next to the sink and opened the door into the garden. She pulled the jersey closer and shivered. Winter was on its way. Fortunately, the weather forecast for the rest of the week was good, and Saturday – the day of Peter and Christopher's wedding – should be bright and clear. They crunched through the fallen leaves to the chicken coop. Julia opened it and called her 'chick chick chick' call.

The chestnut brown hens came running, bustling along in their officious way, eager for breakfast. Henny Penny, the biggest and bossiest, led the charge, shouldering the others aside to grab a length of potato peel which she swallowed in one gulp. Jake looked at her proudly, as if to say, 'That's my gal!'

'Would you like to get the eggs?'

Jess nodded, her eager smile so familiar that it transported Julia back to the girl's childhood. She remembered Jess's easy humour and her delight in the world. It had receded sadly, in the troubled teen years, and the shock of her parents' unexpected split had sent her into herself and then away to Hong Kong. But it seemed that the old Jess was back.

'Here you go.' Julia handed the now empty bowl to Jess, who tramped over to the nesting boxes in her too-big wellies and bent down, her hands feeling in the hay for the eggs.

'Five!' she said triumphantly, straightening up with the bowl held out ahead of her with its treasures.

'Good, let's pop them in the kitchen and get ready.'

Half an hour later, freshly showered and dressed, they looked less like country bumpkins and more like elegant 'ladies who lunch'. Jess's sea-toned wrap dress brought out the green of her eyes and draped elegantly over her long limbs. She'd inherited Peter's build, tall and slim, but her facial features were more like Julia's, to the extent that strangers recognised them as mother and daughter. Julia put on a dress for the first time in weeks, an elegant grey knit that she complemented with her mother's pearls.

'Are we meeting Sean there?' Jess asked, swinging a shawl over her shoulders.

'Yes, Sean and Tabitha. They will both be joining us for lunch.'

'Ah, I'm excited to see Tabitha. And to meet Sean...' she gave her mother a cheeky sort of smile and a little nudge. '*Very* excited. The mysterious country doctor who's swept my mother off her feet and captured her heart and—'

'Everyone's very keen to see you too,' Julia interrupted, not rising to her daughter's gentle teasing. She started the car, pulled out of her small driveway and onto Slipstream Lane.

'What do you think of Christopher?' Jess asked, after a few minutes.

'It was obviously strange at the beginning. But the truth is, I like him a lot. He was lovely when I moved here – they came down to help me settle in. He hung pictures, arranged flowers, and gave me advice on the garden.'

'Still a bit weird though, I guess. Dad's new partner. Soon-to-be husband.' Julia could hear that her daughter was struggling to get her head around these concepts – her father with a husband. It was a lot for any daughter to take in.

'He makes your dad happy. And I'm happy here in Berry-wick. That's what matters.'

'You're very sensible, Mum.'

Julia felt a tiny bit hurt, although she wasn't quite sure why. It was true, after all. She was sensible. And there was nothing wrong with being sensible.

'You know, Jess, it wasn't what I thought I would have wanted, but it's worked out well for everyone. I only hope it isn't still painful for you. The break-up.'

'I'm fine,' Jess said, perhaps a little too quickly. 'Getting away was good for me. I've grown up a lot in the last two years. I realise it's not about me, and not my business. We're still a family. I just want you both to be happy.'

It was Julia's turn to tease. 'You're very sensible, Jessica.'

'Yeah, guess who I got *that* from.'

2

Sean's car was already in the parking area outside The Swan. One of the things that worked well in their relationship was their shared belief in the virtue of punctuality, and sure enough, there he was, opening the passenger side door for Tabitha on the dot of twelve thirty. He looked up and waved to Julia. Tabitha exited and launched herself across the car park with a shriek, flinging her arms wide, her green and yellow kaftan fluttering brightly like a joyous flag behind her. She enfolded Jess in her arms, planting a kiss on each cheek and pulling back to look deeply into her face, as if searching for clues as to her well-being. She seemed pleased with what she saw, because she smiled broadly and said, 'Wonderful. I'm thrilled to see you, dear girl.'

'You too, Tabs, I've missed you!' Jess said, returning the hug. 'You look great. Just the same.' For a moment, Julia envied the ease of the affection between the two of them, untainted by the mother–daughter dynamic of love and expectation.

She let the momentary discomfort pass and introduced Sean, who had been standing rather awkwardly by, observing the reunion. He offered a hand, and spoke warmly, 'Hello, Jess.

Sean O'Connor. I'm delighted to meet you at last. Welcome home.'

'It's fab to be here. Good to meet you, too, finally. Mum's told me so much about you.' Jess gave a cheeky grin.

'Likewise.'

They laughed at that, and the handshake turned into a sort of hug, more of a shoulder bump really, which made Julia happy. 'Come on, let's go and find the men of the moment,' she said, leading the way into the big old ivy-clad manor house.

Kevin Moore, the front-of-house manager, came forward to welcome Julia. 'And you must be Jess,' he said, taking her hand. 'I'd heard you were coming for the wedding. You arrived yesterday, did you?'

'That's right. Landed Monday and drove up yesterday with my dad,' she said, shooting a glance at her mother.

'Welcome to Berrywick. Your dad's outside. Dylan will show you the way.' He beckoned over a young man in a black apron.

'Dylan! I didn't know you were working at The Swan,' Julia said.

'I was hired by the caterer for the wedding. I do gigs for them, and it's flexible so I can fit it in with my studies. But Kev needed some extra hands today, so here I am,' he said with a grin and a shrug. She could see he was pleased.

'This is my daughter, Jess,' she said. 'Jess, Dylan is in my book club. He's a very keen reader. He's studying English literature.'

'Cool,' she said. 'Hi.'

Julia couldn't swear to it, but it seemed like Dylan stood up a little straighter when he spoke to Jess.

'Yeah, hi. You are living in Hong Kong, right?'

'I am, I'm here for the wedding.'

'Cool. I'll show you where your dad is.' He smiled at Jess. 'Follow me.'

. . .

They walked through the restaurant to the covered terrace, already filling up with the lunch crowd. The Swan was popular with locals, and with the tourists who came from all over the country and the world to explore the Cotswolds. It was highly rated on all the travel websites, noted both for its charm and for its food. The gardens, with their bountiful planting and beautiful river, were frequently spotted on Instagram and Facebook, with holidayers smiling in the foreground, often raising a pint glass. High season was over, but the restaurant was still quite busy and filled with the sounds of good cheer – laughter and chatter, and the clink of cutlery on crockery.

Dylan pointed them at the big glass doors that opened onto steps into the garden.

'See you around,' he said, nodding to Jess. 'I hope.'

'Yeah, sure.'

'Cool.'

Julia noticed that the two of them had slipped into the brusque monosyllabic code of young people.

With Dylan gone, Jess reverted to her more loquacious self. 'Did you tell everyone in Berrywick about me?' she asked her mother, in a tone that held more affection than irritation – but only just. 'Did you hand out copies of my travel itinerary? Send round a photograph so they could recognise me if they spotted me in the wild?'

'I mentioned to a few people that you were coming to stay. I was excited to have you here, and for them to meet you.' Julia knew that she sounded a bit defensive, and tried to lighten her tone, make the whole thing into a joke. 'It's a village. Information moves in mysterious ways. People talk. People know things. It takes a bit of getting used to, I can tell you.'

Jess nodded. 'I can see that it would,' she said, sounding mollified.

Together, they walked down the steps onto the lawn.

'Oh isn't it lovely!' Jess exclaimed when she saw the deep flowerbeds that edged the terrace, the lawn that ran to the river, the stand of oaks in their autumn finery of red and gold.

In the middle of the lawn, Christopher seemed to be explaining something. He was pacing and gesturing towards the trees with a file of papers, while Peter stood by, arms folded, nodding. The couple stopped what they were doing when they spotted the new arrivals heading towards them, and came over for a round of hugs and kisses and handshakes.

'Come here, darling girl,' said Peter, opening his arms to Jess as if he hadn't seen her just the day before.

'Hello, Daddy,' said Jess, returning his hug.

Julia felt slightly voyeuristic watching the scene. It was strange to see Jess with Peter, now that she and Peter were no longer a couple. Their relationship was now something completely separate from Julia – she had no idea how often they spoke, or what they said when they did. She felt a bit jealous, and sad for all that had been lost.

Sean gently put his hand on Julia's back, as if sensing her complicated feelings.

When Peter released Jess, Chris hugged her – for a shorter time, and with less emotion. Still, he seemed genuinely fond of her, which pleased Julia.

Jess thoroughly greeted, Peter and Christopher turned to greet Julia and Sean. They had met Sean on their previous visit, when they'd come to Berrywick to look at venues and test out menus and decide on florists and caterers; an exhaustive and rather exhausting investigatory trip that was to come to fruition right here at The Swan on Saturday, when the two would tie the knot.

Certainly, thought Julia, as she embraced the two men and Sean shook their hands, this wedding had been carefully planned. Absolutely nothing could possibly go wrong.

3

'Is this where the ceremony is going to be held? Right here by the river?' Jess said, looking around with delight. 'Oh, it will be gorgeous!'

As if on cue, a swan floated past, huge and white and silent as a cloud. On the far bank, a woman sat on a bench while two little blonde children, a boy and a girl, both in striped dungarees, tossed bread to a duck and her ducklings. It was an idyllic scene that wouldn't be out of place on a postcard, or perhaps an advertisement.

'The ceremony will be over there by the flower garden,' Christopher said, looping one arm through hers and gesturing with the other, 'and the guests will be seated here. The beautiful, simple country wedding I've always dreamed of. Just us and our nearest and dearest.'

'Yes, Dad told me you're having a small ceremony for thirty or so, with drinks and food afterwards.'

'The guest list has grown a *leeetle* bit,' Christopher said with a chuckle, holding his thumb and forefinger an inch apart. 'Closer to eighty – but still simple and intimate.'

Julia noticed a microexpression cross Peter's face. They might have been divorced for two years, but they'd been married for twenty-nine, and she knew his face better than her own. The look suggested he had been happy at thirty guests but wasn't going to mention it. He saw her looking at him, and they shared a moment of recognition. He lowered his eyes, not wanting to be disloyal.

'Well, you couldn't wish for a prettier venue, and autumn is the most perfect time of year for it,' said Tabitha. 'Better than spring, if you ask me. Those oak trees are magnificent, with the leaves turning.'

'Aren't the colours magical? The golden leaves. That red... In fact...' Christopher paused and drummed the fingers of his right hand against his cheek thoughtfully. He squinted, as if looking into the future, 'I think we should move everything up towards the trees, and then reorientate the marquee, turn it around. Jess, did your dad tell you we're having one of those glass marquees?'

Jess shook her head. She caught Julia's eye. They both knew it would be very unlike Peter to describe the wedding tent. Although Peter had turned out to be significantly more unlike Peter than Julia could have anticipated, so who knew?

'Well, we are. It'll be like being in the garden, but no need to worry about the weather. We had planned for Peter and me to say our vows there by the flowerbed, but now I think we should be at the other end and have the oak trees behind us. They will be a stunning backdrop and lovely in the photographs. Don't you think, Peter?'

'I'm sure you're right, as you usually are about these things. I'm but a simple lawyer, happy to defer to you in matters of style and aesthetics.' While Julia had expected Peter to sound slightly annoyed at this last-minute change of plans – he was not a fan of spontaneity – he sounded completely calm and accepting of the plan to move the entire setting around.

'Well, I'm glad to hear that, my love,' said Christopher, 'because we will quite obviously have to change your tie.'

Sean gave a bark of laughter at that, but Peter looked momentarily pained. 'My tie? What's that got to do with anything?'

'The blue tie that you'd planned to wear won't work with this new set-up. We need something that will tone in with the trees. I'm thinking russet, perhaps. Or amber? Better with your colouring, anyway, come to think of it. Better all round. Right?'

'Well, it's just that I've already got the tie and it's a bit late to start shopping, I'd have thought. Is it really necessary?' This was the Peter that Julia knew, flustered by change.

'It is.' Christopher spoke simply and calmly.

'Maybe we can find something online and get it delivered before Saturday,' said Jess, playing peacemaker, as was her way. 'If you like, I'll have a look and send you some options.'

Christopher beamed at her, and clapped his hands together. 'Would you? Marvellous! Now if only the hire people were as can-do as Jess... The table napkins,' he shuddered. 'Honestly.'

'I'm sure Arabella will sort the table napkins out,' Peter said, patting his fiancé's arm in a soothing sort of way. Julia remembered being the recipient of the same calming attentiveness, and felt a pang. 'That's why we have a wedding planner.'

Christopher looked at him gratefully. 'So we can tell Arabella about the tent, Peter? That she must have them turn it around?'

'Of course. We'll ring her this afternoon. Now, shall we have lunch? I've booked us a table on the terrace.'

'And I must make sure that they remove all the snails. It would be terrible for a guest to stand on a snail as they walked to the tent.' Christopher sounded worried.

'I think you've mentioned that to her,' said Peter. 'Repeatedly.'

'Do you think that she'll have time to consult the feng shui person again?' said Christopher, his forehead creased. Julia felt Sean stifle a giggle next to her.

'I'm sure that Arabella's got it all in hand, darling,' said Peter. 'There's nothing for you to worry about at all.'

4

'What do you think of this one?' Jess asked, handing her phone across the lunch table to her father. He glanced at it, nodded, and handed it over the table to Christopher, who said, 'Yes, that's more like it. And it's silk, is it? I do love a silk tie.'

'Yes, it's silk. There's another option. It's a bit darker, and with a little dot. Also silk, of course,' She took the phone back, swiped the screen with the practised fingers of the younger generation and showed Christopher.

'Oh yes, even better.'

'Fifty pounds. Delivery in twenty-four hours.'

'Perfect!' Christopher said, waving it briefly in front of Peter. 'We'll take it. Thank you, Jess, you're a darling.'

'Done,' she said, laying the phone down on the table amidst the remains of their lunch.

'Thank you both for lunch. My trout was absolutely delicious,' Tabitha said, putting her knife and fork together on her spotlessly empty plate. Julia's pan-fried sole had been perfectly cooked, as had the little taste she'd had of Sean's pork chop with red cabbage.

'Isn't it? I was thinking, I might ask the caterer to source some trout for the canapés. Local, sustainable, and so on, you know,' Christopher said with a twirl of his hand. 'So it's on theme.'

'Isn't the menu all decided?' asked Julia. She remembered distinctly the many conversations about which caterer to use – The Swan's kitchen wasn't geared to catering functions – and the many additional conversations about what to serve. The theme was locally sourced and delicious, rustic but elegant, simple yet innovative, if she remembered correctly. Or was it simple but elegant, rustic yet innovative? Something like that.

'It is, but I don't think a tiny tweak will be a problem. I'm sure they will be able to source the trout.'

'You're right. They probably won't mind,' said Julia brightly.

She regretted even mentioning the menu. She was determined not to get involved in the arrangements unless explicitly asked, and in particular not to voice anything that might possibly be construed as the slightest criticism. Her role, as she saw it, was to be pleasant and quietly supportive from a distance.

Christopher pulled his phone from his pocket. 'If you'll excuse me, I think I should phone Arabella right now. I'll tell her about the trout and the tent.'

'Who is this Arabella?' Jess asked.

'Arabella Princeton is the wedding planner. She's *the* planner in the Cotswolds.' Christopher leaned in and spoke in a stage whisper, as if the paparazzi might be lurking behind the pot plants: 'She has done royal weddings.'

'*Minor* weddings for *minor* royals. Royals by association, rather than actual royals. Not Harry and Meghan,' Peter said.

'Minor ones, yes. A great niece of Prince Phillip, I think she said, which still counts as royal. And a good few lords, or their daughters. Anyway, she's very highly regarded and very busy. We were lucky to get her for a small wedding.'

'Christopher was at his most persuasive and charming,'

Peter said, smiling at his daughter. 'The woman didn't have a chance.'

'Oh, Peter,' Christopher looked pleased, but batted Peter with a napkin. He turned to Jess. 'So Arabella is in charge of the whole look and feel of the event. She works with Desmond Campbell, who is the caterer – she doesn't generally use The Swan's kitchen; they can't cope with the additional load – and with Angela, the florist.'

'Angela from Blooming Marvels?' asked Julia. 'I know her work. I bought flowers from her for a friend who was in hospital. They were lovely.'

'She is an absolute genius with flowers.' His eyes shone when he spoke about the flowers – he was a landscaper, after all. 'Arabella says Angela is the sweetest in the business – she won't use anyone else, because her arrangements are incredible. She's been featured in *Country Life*, and on one of those television programmes about celebrity weddings. *Marrying for Love*, I think it was called. And her fiancé is a well-known potter, Ben Roberts. He makes vases for the smart affairs, but we decided on glass and antique silver, for a simple rustic look. Anyhow, as I was saying, the food, the flowers, the table settings, they all work together to tell a seamless story across the event. As Arabella puts it.'

He got up from the table and bent to kiss Peter on the head as he passed him on his way to the edge of the terrace. Julia felt an unexpected surge of something – sadness? envy? – but it dissipated almost as soon as it arrived.

'Christopher wants things to be perfect,' Peter said, looking at his intended, who was now talking earnestly into his mobile phone.

'No harm in that,' said Sean. 'It's a special day, you might as well have everything just the way you want it.'

Christopher came back, looking cheerful. 'Arabella said she'd take care of everything. The trout, the marquee, the table napkins, the feng shui. Thank heavens for her. This is why we're paying a professional, Peter. To have someone take care of things, and to think about every detail.'

'Right, well I'm pleased it's all organised and Arabella is on top of things.'

'But I did message Desmond, the caterer, to be on the safe side.'

Peter raised an eyebrow but didn't comment.

Christopher laughed. 'Oh, Peter, you know me. I can't help that I'm a micromanager. This is going to be the first day of the rest of our lives. I want everything to go off smoothly, exactly as we want it, without a hitch.'

Tabitha raised her wine glass with its last half-inch of wine and said, 'Here's to a smooth and lovely wedding. To getting hitched without a hitch.'

'Without a hitch!' Christopher said, tapping his glass against hers.

5

As the wedding march started up, and the guests rose to their feet, Sean reached for Julia's hand and gave it a light squeeze. She looked at him and smiled. It was a wordless conversation, a gesture of love and support on his side, and on hers, reassurance that she was fine, that all was well.

It wasn't without its awkwardness, watching one's ex-husband get married, but she hadn't found the ceremony at all painful. She didn't want to be married to Peter. And she didn't want Peter not to be married to anyone else. Julia was, in fact, pleased that Peter was happy and settled and had found someone as nice as Christopher. With Jess on one side of her and Sean on the other, she was happy. With an open heart, she wished the couple well. She listened as they made their vows – they'd written their own, and both men spoke with great love and sincerity. The guests all cheered when the celebrant announced them 'husband and husband' and invited them to 'kiss the groom'. Even Julia had a tear in her eye.

Peter and Christopher turned and walked arm in arm down a short aisle between the rows of guests. Peter beamed, his face flushed with pleasure at the whooping and clapping that greeted them. Christopher grinned and waggled his fingers, showing off his wedding band. Behind them, through the glass of the marquee, the autumn oaks glowed red and gold in the late afternoon light, and she had to admit that Christopher had been right – it was a splendid backdrop to a beautiful ceremony.

Julia was pleased to see Christopher looking relaxed. Jess, who had come over to The Swan early to be with her dad, reported that poor Christopher had spent most of the morning fretting about the arrangements, with his ear glued to the phone, or popping down from their hotel room to check on things. At around lunchtime, when a spat erupted between him and the lighting designer – yes, there is such a thing, Jess assured her – followed soon after by another altercation with the caterer, Peter had finally put his foot down and banned him from the venue until it was time for their entrance.

The guests followed them to the other end of the marquee where canapés were being handed round. Julia took a pancake topped with a grilled prawn. It was warm and spicy, with a hint of lime, and she had to restrain herself from falling on the tray and tossing the delicious morsels into her mouth like smarties. It had been hours since she'd eaten. She had left early to drive to Sean's house with Jake, who would be spending the night with Sean's Leo and a dog-loving young neighbour who was house-sitting. They'd settled the dogs and the sitter, and headed for The Swan where they would be staying for the night, so as not to have to drive home after the wedding. No sooner had they arrived than it was time to get dressed and ready. Somehow, lunch fell by the wayside, and she was surviving on the morning's bowl of oats with honey.

Dylan appeared at Julia's elbow with a tray of champagne. She could see that he was concentrating hard on keeping it horizontal and avoiding knocks from stray elbows and shoulders.

'Thank you,' she said, taking a glass.

'Jess?' he said, holding the tray towards her.

'You are an absolute *lifesaver*, Dylan,' Jess said, grabbing a flute with unseemly eagerness. 'Thank you.'

The young man smiled and blushed.

'I must say, everything's lovely,' Julia said. 'Are you enjoying the work?'

'Yeah. Events are stressful though, weddings especially.'

'I'm sure. There are a lot of moving parts to take into account.'

'You get used to it, I suppose. That Arabella has nerves of steel. The caterer fellow, Desmond Campbell, threatened to walk out this morning. Still looks pretty sour about things. That's him over there.'

A thickset black-haired man in chef's whites stood in the service entrance, looking over the guests and the servers. His arms were crossed over his chest, the white sleeves riding up to reveal thickly tattooed wrists, the ink almost as dark as his hair.

'Ooh you're right, he doesn't look very cheerful,' Jess said with a laugh, taking another swig of the bubbly.

Dylan continued. 'I know, right? He was in a proper state. First there was some kind drama with the florist, Angela. Lord knows what about, I couldn't hear, but they seemed to be having *words*, and there was some flinging about of hands. And then there was another drama, something to do with the trout. I don't know how you can get into a fight about trout, but he and the groom – Christopher, I mean, not the other groom, your... um...' The sentence stammered to a close.

'Just the usual wedding jitters, I'm sure. It's a big day. Lots of emotion in the run-up. But it all seems to be running smoothly now,' said Julia.

Consulting the table plan on a chalkboard at the entrance, Julia found herself standing behind a couple she and Peter had socialised with occasionally.

'Nice service, wasn't it?' said the woman, Janet, who worked with Peter.

Her husband, Richard, a banker whose name Julia had remembered in the nick of time, said, 'Short and sweet, and very convenient to have it all in one place. I suppose you and Peter did it in a church the first time round, hey?'

Janet looked aghast and mumbled an apology which Julia brushed off.

'Oh yes, we did the whole thing, the local church with a full slate of bridesmaids in yellow satin and then lunch in my parents' garden. I must say, this is lovely though.' She was pleased with her calm response, and even more pleased when Sean appeared beside her and draped his arm around her shoulders.

'Can I introduce you to Dr Sean O'Connor? This is Janet and Richard.'

Janet gave Sean the full once-over, head to toe and up again. 'Ah, I see, well no worries there, then,' Richard said, nodding knowingly at them. Janet blushed furiously, murmured her goodbyes and led her husband briskly away.

'Old Richard's in for it, I'd say,' Sean said, when they were out of earshot.

'He's probably used to it. I remember now that he's one of those people who blunders in without a shred of a filter, saying one rude or stupid thing after the other and not even noticing. And she's constantly stammering apologies. Here we are, Table 2. Oh good, Tabitha is with us. Jess is at the main table with Peter, of course.'

The tables were wood, carefully distressed to look as if they'd been languishing in a barn until last week, each with a burlap runner down the centre. Unmatched silver vases and glass jars of flowers were carefully arranged, to look as if armfuls of blooms and wild grasses had been gathered from a meadow and simply tossed into the closest empty vessel and placed randomly on the table. White candles of all sizes and shapes threw a soft glow over scattered lavender and tiny white flowers, and reflected off the glass walls and roof. It all looked loose and rustic and natural, but earlier Julia had seen Angela, the florist, fussing with the flowers, gently moving a sprig or stalk a little to get precisely the effect she intended. And she was certain that Arabella, the wedding planner – no doubt under the eagle eye of Christopher – had made sure that each candle and vase was set out just so. Outside the sun was dipping to the horizon, setting the clouds on fire and illuminating the autumn trees.

Richard gave them a friendly wave as they passed his table on the way to theirs. He was making his way through the rustic bread selection heaped in a basket on the table, that a blonde spiky-haired waiter was filling as fast as he could empty it. 'Bread's good,' Richard said helpfully, slathering a roughly cut chunk with the herbed butter, and popping the crust into his mouth.

The *ting ting ting* of a knife against glass called the guests to their tables. Tabitha was already seated. They barely had time for a hug and a hello when Jess stood up to welcome the guests. Julia's heart gave a little squeeze when she saw her daughter push her shining auburn hair behind her ears in a gesture she'd made since childhood and start, 'Welcome, to this beautiful celebration of love and life...' Jess spoke for a few minutes, making it clear that she supported her father and was happy for him, and that she welcomed her new stepfather with an open heart.

'Jess, my darling girl, thank you for that introduction.' Peter's eyes were damp when he took his place at the microphone – in fact, there were more than a few tears at Jess's words, as well as some laughter at her quick wit. Peter looked over at Christopher, and started to speak, 'I must say that this day has been quite the most wonderful—'

Before he could finish his first sentence, there was a crash of glass and a woman's voice rang out, 'Help! We need help. Is there a doctor?'

Sean stood up and turned to the source of the cry – it was Janet. Richard had collapsed onto the table, knocking over a vase. He groaned, clutching at his throat.

'What happened?' Sean asked, addressing the woman calmly, while lifting the man's torso against the chair, and leaning his head back to keep his throat open.

'Nuts. He's allergic,' she said. 'There must have been nuts in something. We did mention the allergy when we sent the form to say we were coming, but... Oh dear, and we didn't bring his pills.'

'I see. Julia, could you fetch the bag from our room please?' Sean asked. She felt the urgency underneath his low and measured tone. 'The brown one. Quickly, please.'

By the time she came back from their room – fortunately, it was not far – she was panting from exertion and stress. Richard was white as a sheet, but he was conscious. Peter was still at the microphone, looking dazed. Every guest, and all the staff, were gathered around, looking on. Sean grabbed the bag, pulled out a bottle of pills and shook two into his hand.

'Take this,' he said, handing them to Richard, who popped them into his mouth, grabbed a glass of water and swallowed hard.

'You'll be all right in a few minutes. Try to breathe normally.'

'The bread,' Janet said. 'I think it must have been the bread. But I did tick the box, when we RSVP'd.'

'Yes, it was noted,' said Christopher, who was almost as white in the face as Richard. 'It was on the form – nut allergy – I checked with Arabella, it was on the file.'

All eyes were on the wedding planner, who – along with almost all the guests and most of the waiters – had been drawn to the table by the commotion.

'It was, and I passed that information on to the caterer,' said Arabella, her arms crossed, and her face stony. There would be no shifting of blame on to *her*. 'I was very clear. Wasn't I, Desmond?'

The eyes followed hers to the man in chef's whites. 'Yes. Which is why there are no nuts on the menu,' Desmond said, glaring back at her, his chest puffed out, his shoulders square. 'I didn't use anything with nuts.' Behind him, the spiky-haired waiter who had been manning the bread baskets nodded vehemently.

'The bread? The butter?' Janet said. 'He'd just eaten a slice when...'

Desmond's aggressive stance softened slightly. 'No, that can't be it,' he said. 'We made all the bread ourselves, because of Mr Carter's very specific requests. We used this mix. Seeds... for the bread. But...' Desmond didn't get a chance to finish what he was saying.

Christopher looked at him with nothing less than hatred. 'You did it on purpose. You did it on purpose because of the trout. And now you've *ruined* our wedding, you horrible man. I would like to feed you peanuts until you swell up and DIE.'

And with that, he burst into tears.

6

'It's too tight. I don't think you can get past it,' Sean said, looking from Julia's car to the van and back again. The white refrigerator van was parked at an odd angle, its back door facing the service door to the hotel, half blocking the driveway to the exit. Because Julia and Sean were spending the night, Peter had asked Julia to park her little Peugeot by the service entrance, to leave more room for guests in the hotel parking. But this morning they were blocked in. Julia had tried to squeeze by. Sean had even got out to see if he could guide her through the gap. But it was too small, by inches. They were stuck.

'What a stupid way to park,' Jess said crossly, emerging from the back seat and slamming the door.

'I'm sure we can find the driver,' Julia said in a conciliatory tone.

'It has Candy Catering on the side. It must belong to the caterer. What was the guy's name? Desmond. The nut murderer. Remember?'

As if anyone could have forgotten, thought Julia. She ignored her daughter's bad joke about last night's drama, and said mildly, 'I'm sure he'll be out in a minute. He's probably collecting something.'

'Well, that's no excuse for parking like a selfish prat. Where's he?' The warmth and good humour that had accompanied the three of them when they'd arrived at The Swan the day before had vanished. 'Never mind. I'll go in and see if I can find out what's what.' Jess stomped off in the direction of the kitchen, grey-faced and grumpy.

After the nut incident, Richard had gone to hospital for observation and Christopher to the honeymoon suite to 'freshen up' and calm down. Meanwhile, the guests had chatted awkwardly over their starters, knocking back the wine to ease the discomfort.

When both grooms were present the rest of the speeches were delivered, at least an hour behind schedule and in rather a subdued manner. And then there was the cake and some dancing. Everyone had done their best, but the wedding had limped along rather. Even the weather seemed determined to wreak havoc. The heavens had opened, rain clattering down on the glass marquee. There was a brief moment of panic when the electricity went off for a moment, and the music stopped and they were plunged into gloom, with only the candles for light.

Jess had felt it her duty to save the day by being super *jolly*, and had too much champagne, laughing loudly and pulling reluctant guests onto the dance floor to do the Macarena. Tabitha was her enthusiastic partner in the jollying and in the dancing, quickly picking up the moves and executing them with grace and vigour. Her curls and her beads and bangles seemed to take on a life of their own.

Breakfast had been a sombre affair. Sean and Julia were eager to get away. They told each other they needed to get back to the dogs – it was Jake's first sleepover, after all – but really, they were tired and wanted to be home with a cup of tea. And now they and Jess were stuck in the service parking with the dustbins and the gardening tools. And an immobile refrigerated catering van had put a chill on things, dissipating any residual good humour.

Jess arrived at the kitchen door as Kevin came out with a pile of metal serving trays.

'What's going on?' he asked, surveying the scene – the car and the van, Sean and Julia, grumpy Jess.

'Some idiot's blocked us in. I think it must be the caterer. Can you call him?'

'It's Desmond Campbell's van, all right – Candy Catering. I don't think he's here, though. I saw him doing clean-up last night but there's still stuff lying around. The breakfast shift aren't happy about it. They asked me to move his stuff out of the way.' He held out the serving trays, by way of demonstration. 'I was going to put them outside.'

'So he's not here?'

'Haven't seen him. More likely he left in a hurry last night. Such a pity, really. He's been so much better the last few months. On the wagon, so I heard.'

'Great,' said Jess. 'So he went off on a bender and left his van in the driveway?'

'I'm not saying that's what happened,' said Kevin. He looked as if he'd like to swallow the words. 'Once or twice he had a tipple and left poor Cynthia, his partner, to clean up his mess.'

'Ppfft,' Jess said dismissively.

Julia cut in. 'Well, can we move the van? We only need to move it a couple of inches and I can get my car out... Could we push it?'

'The keys are in the ignition,' said Sean, peering through the window.

'Good idea. I'll put these trays in the back and then I'll

move the van. Strange that he left the keys there. Presumably he wasn't drunk when he left. *Presumably.*' Kevin gestured with his full arms to Jess, who was standing scowling at the back door of the van. 'Open up, will you?' She tried the door. 'Locked. Sean, can we have the keys?'

He pulled them out of the ignition and gave them to Julia, who walked to the back of the van, unlocked and pulled down the back door handle. Jess came over to the van's back door, ready to help Kevin with his trays. Julia was pleased that Jess wasn't letting her rather grumpy mood stand in the way of good manners.

Julia opened the door crack, releasing a cloud of cold mist into her and Jess's faces. The cloud cleared to reveal Jess's face staring into the back of the truck, a distorted mask of horror, half covered by her hands. Julia followed her gaze.

There was something dark and spiky and icy in the gap of the door. Julia pulled the handle and the door swung further open. The object shifted, then gathered momentum, tumbling out of the door and hard onto the ground in a flash of white, and with a sickening scraping thump.

For a moment, Julia didn't know what it was. But then her eyes and brain focused, and took in the full horror of what had landed at her feet.

It was Desmond, the caterer, frozen solid.

He was dressed in his chef's whites, his black hair frozen into stiff spikes. His blue-grey face was contorted into a scowl, his eyes shut and his lashes laced with ice. He was very cold. And very stiff, his knees bent up to his chest.

The little group stood still, as still as the man lying on the ground before them. Nobody said anything for a long moment.

Then the sound of the metal trays tumbling from Kevin's arms and clanging onto the tarmac brought them back to life.

Jess dropped to the ground and began to shake the frozen man by the shoulders, shouting wildly, 'Wake up! Mum, is he dead? Come on, someone help him, please. Sean! You're a doctor.'

Sean knelt down next to her and gently pulled her away. He leaned over the man and felt for a pulse, or any sign of life. His manner was thorough, but Julia knew he was going through the motions, not expecting to find a flutter of pulse, or rise of the chest. It was clear that Chef Desmond had been in the cold truck for a long time. He was frozen rigid, and was well and truly dead.

But Jess was still holding out hope. 'Is he alive?' she asked tearfully. 'Sean, can you feel anything? Can you help him? You're a doctor. Make him be alive.'

Sean straightened up and shook his head. 'I'm sorry, Jess. He must have got himself shut in last night. He'd have been in there for six or seven hours – too long at that temperature. It's likely he died of hypothermia.'

Jess started to cry in earnest, big gasping sobs, wiping her eyes and nose with the back of her hand. 'The poor man. Imagine how cold he was. And probably banging on the side of the truck, hoping for someone to come and help him.'

Julia held her daughter tight, comforting her as she'd done through any number of childhood hurts, disappointments, and teenage heartbreaks. 'I know, love, it's so awful. The door must have blown shut on him. A freak accident.'

Kevin stood by, his phone in his hand. He stared at it, befuddled and in shock. 'What should I do?' he said. 'Should I phone?'

'Call 999. An accident like this is termed an unnatural death, which means they'll need to send the police, and possibly forensics, to the scene before the body can be moved,' said Sean.

Jess was shaking and gasping for breath. Julia looked at Sean in desperation.

'Jess, come and sit down here with me,' Sean said, taking her arm and leading her away from the body on the tarmac. He sat her down on a low retaining wall, put his hand on her back and bent her forward so that her head was cradled in her hands, her elbows on her knees. Julia couldn't hear Sean's words, only the comforting rumbling burr of his voice.

Relieved that Jess was in good hands, Julia turned her attention to Kevin, who still appeared to be in a shocked stupor, staring at the phone as if it were an exotic object he'd never come across before.

'We could call Hayley. She always knows what to do. She'll notify the right authorities, or tell us what the procedure is for something like this.'

'Right, Julia, good idea,' Kevin said gratefully. 'Will you do it?'

Julia took her own phone from her handbag and dialled Hayley's number while Kevin stared down at the body curled on the ground with wisps of vapour coming off it.

'I'll go inside and get something to cover him with,' he said, finally coming up with a practical task he could attend to. 'And then we'll keep the kitchen exit closed. We don't want staff or guests coming out and stumbling on a dead man.'

He was back moments later with a white tablecloth which he shook out in a billowing cloud, letting it settle over the body like snow on a mountain range. A strange peace settled on them at the same time, a moment of quiet, broken seconds later by the sound of the kitchen door being opened hard and fast, crashing back into the wall.

'Kevin, what's with the door? Why are you—' A young woman in The Swan's retro black and white waitress uniform, and her hair dyed a matching jet-black, appeared in the doorway. She took in the scene in an instant, the white shape, the worried faces of the onlookers. 'Who's that? What's going on? Kevin, what happened?'

'There's been an accident,' he said.

She took a step closer and caught sight of the hands, with

their swirling tattoos, emerging from the sheet. 'Is that... Is that Desmond?' Her voice came out in a hoarse whisper.

'Yes, I'm afraid so.'

The woman let out an ear-piercing scream, bringing the staff of The Swan running.

There was no keeping things quiet after that.

7

DI Hayley Gibson didn't seem to observe Sunday rituals and practices. That, or she'd changed her clothes after she got Julia's call. She was in the same uniform she wore on weekdays – an interchangeable set of trousers (she had black, grey and navy, presumably multiple pairs), and button-up shirts (white, blue, green, black, plain and striped), which she wore with a jacket, or a coat, as appropriate to the season. This morning, it was black trousers and black-and-brown striped shirt, with a black jacket. Suitably funereal, thought Julia. As well as her work clothes, Hayley wore the same expression of deep concentration, verging on suspicion, her eyes narrowed and searching.

'The mortuary van is on its way,' she said, by way of greeting, and squatted down next to the body. She lifted the top edge of the sheet, examined the dead man's grey face and then pulled the sheet back over his head.

Jess and Sean walked over. Jess was still pale, but she was calmer.

'This is my daughter, Jess,' Julia said. 'Jess, this is my friend, DI Hayley Gibson.'

It was an awkward situation, and 'pleased to meet you'

hardly seemed the right response, with a dead body between them. The two women nodded at each other in grim silence. Hayley moved the little gathering away from the van into a patch of warm autumn sun.

'So,' she said. 'Who is he?'

Kevin answered: 'Desmond Campbell, from Candy Catering.'

'Does he work here?'

'He's probably the top caterer in the business around here. He does a lot of weddings and other sorts of parties here at The Swan and all over the area. Him and another crowd – In Good Taste, they're called – they're the top two. Desmond was catering a wedding here last night.'

'Peter and Christopher's wedding,' Julia said.

'That was last night?' Hayley asked in disbelief. Julia nodded. 'Well, that explains what you're all doing here.'

'We found him.'

'You did?' Hayley looked at her in astonishment. Unspoken between them was the fact that this was not the first body that Julia had come across in Berrywick. Nor, in fact, the second. Or even the third.

'Me and Sean and Jess. And Kevin. It was a completely strange— I mean, we didn't expect... we were just trying to get out of the parking lot.'

'Take me through it from the beginning.'

Julia told Hayley the story of the van, their efforts to move it, and the awful discovery. Jess and Kevin chipped in from time to time with additional information.

DI Hayley Gibson let them speak, and then walked back to the body. She took a pair of gloves from her pocket and lifted the sheet again, freeing his hands one by one, examining them, and replacing them without a word. She patted him down and felt his pockets.

'No phone,' she noted.

'It might be in the van,' Julia said, taking a step towards it, reaching for the handle.

'Let me,' Hayley said quickly, holding up her gloved hands. It hardly seemed necessary, given that Julia's prints were already all over the handle and door, and besides, it was an accidental death. But Hayley was a consummate professional who played everything by the book.

Julia lowered her hand from the handle. Hayley opened the back door and there it was in the centre of the stacked platters and bowls lined up at the far end of the van. Along the right-hand side two square tubs held lettuce leaves that had wilted and then frozen, hard and glittering. Another tub held sliced cucumbers, similarly cryogenically preserved. It was a creepy sight.

'He would have tried to phone,' said Julia. 'I suppose the insulation blocked the signal.'

Hayley smacked the sides of the van. They gave off a solid muffled thud. 'He would have shouted, too, I'm sure – not that you would hear much through these panels.'

'I doubt there would have been many people about, anyway. Not after the party. Poor man.'

Hayley looked at the phone and sighed. 'I'd better try to find his family.'

Taking a notebook from her pocket and freeing the pen that was clipped to it, Hayley turned her attention to Kevin. 'So do you know anything about Desmond's life? Wife or family?'

'There's a wife.' Kevin shrugged and shook his head, 'We live near them, actually, but we haven't been there long and he wasn't one to chat much. I could ask my Nicky. She always knows these things. In fact, she told me...'

'She told you what?'

'The marriage seemed a bit rocky. He moved out for a bit. Or she did. Nicky had the whole story.' He looked briefly at Julia when he said that, knowing that she would know Nicky's

'whole story' would have been an overwhelming deluge, and
one couldn't be expected to remember it in its entirety. 'Anyway, they're back together now. Or were.'

'Did he have a business partner?'

'That's Cynthia. She's the "C" in Candy Catering. C and D
– Candy, get it? She's top-notch. She wasn't working here last
night, she was managing another wedding they were catering.
Somewhere at Edgeley, I think, early in the afternoon. He
mentioned that they had two events, that it was a juggle. *She*
would be the one juggling, if I know Desmond.'

'Her full name?' Hayley held her pen poised over her
notebook.

'Cynthia Skipper. And, um, another thing...'

They turned to look at him expectantly.

Kevin stammered. 'It might not... I mean, I don't think...'

'What is it?'

He sighed and then spoke, with some reluctance. 'Desmond
liked the booze. Never while he was cooking, but, after an event,
he liked to throw a few drinks down. He managed it, mostly.
But once or twice... Not recently, but once or twice things got a
bit out of hand at clean-up. Cynthia had to bundle him into his
van to sleep it off and do all the work herself. I don't like to spec-
ulate, but it could be that he had had a drink and went to sleep.'

'Thank you, Kevin, you've been very helpful. The toxicology report will look into that as a matter of course.'

'Right.'

'And have you got Cynthia's number?'

'I can get it.'

They were interrupted by another van pulling into the
parking area. It was eerily similar to the caterer's van – white,
with a double door at the back – but this one was kitted out for
the transportation of dead bodies rather than cakes. Hayley
walked over briskly and conversed with the driver and the man
who had arrived with him. Julia heard her say, 'As soon as foren-

sics have done their work...' The men nodded and leaned against the van, arms crossed.

She strode back to Julia and led her away from the others to a quiet spot near the gate, then jumped right in with a question. 'I want you to take me back to the moment you opened the door. Was it definitely locked? Could you not just open it?'

'Jess tried it first, and she said it was locked. We took the keys out of the ignition to open it.'

'Those big handles can take a knack and a bit of muscle to open. I want to be sure. Did you actually unlock it?'

Julia thought back to earlier that day. She was pretty certain she'd unlocked the door, but could she be absolutely sure? The whole incident was a blur of horror. And she realised what the question meant: if the door was locked, someone must have locked him in. But if the door was merely closed, it could have slammed shut accidentally.

'Are you saying that Desmond's death might not have been an accident?'

Hayley gave her a warning look, touched her finger to her lips and lowered her voice. 'I'm covering all the bases, Julia. The first thing is, it's not easy to shut yourself inside the back of a van. The door has to swing closed quite hard.'

'The wind, maybe? That storm came up, remember.' Julia badly – with all her heart – wanted to believe that Desmond's death was an accident. A terrible accident.

'There's also a safety catch inside the truck,' said Hayley. 'Unless it was faulty, he would have been able to get out if the door wasn't double-locked.'

'He'd had a rough night, what with the nut situation. Maybe he had a few, and passed out or fell asleep – from what Kevin said, it wouldn't be the first time – and someone closed the door, not knowing he was in there. And he didn't wake up. Froze to death in his sleep.'

'It's a very long shot, Julia. About as unlikely as the wind, in my view.'

'Well, I suppose that's why a freak accident is called a freak accident. The circumstances are particularly unusual.' Julia felt herself clutching at straws.

Hayley's eyes narrowed, and glinted a hard steely blue. 'That's the trouble with being a police officer – "unusual" tends to mean "suspicious".'

'Of course, it's how you're trained. It *would* be unusual for him to get shut in accidentally, but that's not to say it's impossible.'

'True. But if the door was *locked*, locked from the outside, then it's... well... I'd say it's almost impossible to imagine how that might have happened accidentally. Which is why I'm asking you. Was the door locked?'

Julia closed her eyes and played the moment over in her mind. She felt the resistance of the key entering the lock, the pressure as she turned it, the tumble as the inside mechanism turned over. She heard the rasp and the click.

Julia shivered, and sighed.

'The door was locked. Definitely locked.'

8

Julia woke up feeling as if she'd emerged from a coma. Her head was fuzzy with the tail end of a mad dream playing out, something to do with her old maths teacher, who for some reason – explaining fractions, perhaps? – was cutting a chocolate cake into big wedges, which he was feeding to a swan, who was also, inexplicably, Julia's father. The dream vanished before she could grapple with its meaning. Probably for the best, she thought.

Her phone was vibrating silently next to her. That must have been what woke her. It stopped as she picked it up.

Missed Call Hayley Gibson.

Hayley could wait a few minutes. Julia needed to wake up and clear her head before she answered a barrage of follow-up questions about the previous day's gruesome find. She shook her head from side to side to loosen her neck, which was stiff from the odd angle she'd been lying at. Almost every morning there was something, she thought. A crick or a crack or an ache.

She looked at her bedside clock – nine thirty! She never slept that late. For a start, Jake would never let her. Why wasn't he prodding her rudely with his damp nose, eager to be outside with his morning snack?

Julia pushed her feet into her slippers and went into the passage.

'Jake?' she called in alarm. 'Where are you, Jakey boy?'

'He's in here with me,' came Jess's voice from the open door of the spare bedroom. 'We're having a chilled pyjama morning.'

Julia went in to find Jess in bed, propped up on two big, colourful Indian print pillows, a down duvet in its white cotton cover pulled up to her chest. She had an open book resting against her knees, and a cup of tea was cooling on the bedside table. Jake was sitting on the floor beside her, his shiny choco-late-coloured head and one paw resting on the bed. Julia had splashed out on all the new linen to make the room up prettily for her daughter's arrival, and it made her happy to see it in use in the comfortable little scene – even if Jake shouldn't really have his feet on the new bedding. 'I took him out early for a walk round the garden and gave him one of those biscuits from the tin. He said he was allowed. You were dead to the world – I didn't want to wake you.'

Without moving his head, Jake swivelled his eyes guiltily to Julia and snuck the paw back to the ground, then returned his adoring gaze to Jess.

'Thank you. Gosh, I can't believe I slept so late. I was exhausted. But you two seem to be happy and cosy as can be.'

'I love Jake, Mum. He's such a darling. I've missed having a dog. I really wanted one.'

'Daddy and I didn't want another dog after Charlie the Spaniel died,' Julia said. Within their family, Charlie was always referred to as 'Charlie the Spaniel'. Julia couldn't remember why. 'The idea of training up a puppy was too much, especially with you almost ready to leave for uni, and us working long days. I thought my dog-owning days were over. But then I moved here and met Jake. We fell for each other.'

'Ah, poor Jakey Wakey, naughty doggie getting kicked out of guide dog school. But now we've got you, haven't we, my good boy? My goodie goodie boy.' Jess spoke to him in baby talk, playing with his floppy, silky ears. Jake's melting expression made it clear that he had longed for a sister, too, and was equally delighted with this outcome.

'Well, I'm glad you're getting along so well. And I'm really happy to have you home. No need to get up. I'll make us all breakfast when you want it, and if you two are prepared to get out of your pyjamas at some point, let's talk about what we're going to do today.'

The vibration came again. Hayley was nothing if not determined. Except it wasn't Hayley. The name on the phone screen flashed *Peter Bird*. She hadn't expected to hear from him, and certainly not so early. She took his call.

'The police have taken Christopher in for questioning!' he said, sounding cross, with an undercurrent of panic. 'I've never heard of anything so absurd.'

'*Christopher?*' she repeated idiotically. 'What questions? What do you mean?'

'Julia, please. Don't be vague.'

'I'm sorry, I've just got up. My brain is still half asleep.' As she said this, finding herself apologising for something that wasn't really her fault, Julia realised how very little she had missed Peter in a bad mood.

He sighed. 'They're asking Christopher questions about the dead caterer.'

'Well, I suppose they will need to talk to everyone who was there at the time.'

Jess was performing an elaborate pantomime, something to do with a phone and her ears.

'Hang on, Peter. What, Jess?'

'Put him on speaker so I can hear! Hi, Dad.'

'Hello, darling. I was telling Mum what's been going on. So, the police came yesterday to ask questions about the poor caterer who accidentally shut himself in the fridge van.'

Hayley had asked Julia not to mention her suspicions to anyone – 'No one,' she'd said emphatically. Julia had kept her word but wondered now whether she should spit it out. While she hesitated, Peter continued. 'We were having a late breakfast on the terrace, and this chap – Farmer, his name was – came and asked us if we'd answer a few questions.'

'DC Walter Farmer, I know him,' Julia cut in.

'You do? And DI Gibson is some kind of friend of yours too, isn't she?' Peter managed to make this sound like an accusation.

'Yes. I've helped them both on a few investigations. Just in an unofficial capacity.'

'Well, he was there yesterday, asking all the guests the same questions. Did we know Desmond Campbell? Had we seen him? And so on. Very basic questions. Of course, we had nothing useful to say. We'd seen the poor man at the wedding, under not the best circumstances, what with the nut disaster – which Christopher has still not got over, by the way. He was very upset. We saw the caterer that night and then glimpsed him again the following morning, you know – dead, under a sheet. That's all we know.'

'You told all this to DC Farmer?'

'Yes. We answered what we could, and he made notes. He thanked us and went on to the next table. And then this morning DI Gibson asked if Christopher would come into the station and answer a few more questions.'

'That's strange,' said Jess. 'If you had already been interviewed.'

'That's what I thought. Christopher doesn't know anything more than what we told Farmer – which was nothing.'

'It's odd that they asked him to come in and not you,' Julia said. 'I wonder why?'

'I've no idea. But no one here will tell me anything.'

'Who? Where? Where are you now?'

'I'm here at the Berrywick police station. I drove Christopher in, of course. I couldn't let him go alone.'

'Dad, you're a lawyer,' Jess said loudly in the direction of the phone. 'Why don't you tell them what's what? Stomp around like those lawyers on television, muttering about probable cause and human rights.'

Peter gave a gruff laugh in spite of himself. 'You don't really get much experience of that sort of thing when you specialise in international tax law. I've put in a call to a friend in London who deals with criminal matters; he might be able to advise. But I haven't heard back. A bit early, I suppose.'

'I doubt you'll need a lawyer,' Julia said. 'They probably have some sort of follow-up questions. Or clarification of DC Farmer's notes.'

'Julia, can you come? You know the police here, you could have a word.'

Julia had planned nothing more demanding than tea and a bowl of oats for the next hour or so, and a walk with Jake and Jess at some rather later point in the day. The last thing she wanted was to rush off for a fruitless drive to the police station.

'They will probably have finished their conversation by the time I get there. It's not as if Christopher knows anything that will help with the investigation.'

'Julia, please... I'd feel better with you here, Mouse. I need a friendly face, at least.'

Peter's now soft and plaintive voice, and his old affectionate name for her, stirred up her old tenderness towards him, and her habit of trying to fix things. She hesitated.

Another call was coming through on her phone. She took it away from her ear and looked at the screen.

Hayley Gibson.

'Peter, I'll phone you back.'

She ended one call and answered the next.

'Hello, Hayley.'

'Julia, I have a few more questions about what happened yesterday. Can we talk?'

'I've just had Peter on the line. He says he's at the police station, and that Christopher is with you, answering questions.'

There was a pause.

'Hayley, what's going on?'

'I was going to tell you about that too. Julia, I think you'd better come to the station.'

Christopher and Peter were in the waiting area when Julia and Jess arrived. Christopher was ashen, his eyes rimmed red. Peter looked quietly furious, but trying to hide it.

'I'm sorry, Julia, I brought you over here for nothing. You're right. He's come out from the interview.'

'Not to worry, Peter. Christopher, I'm glad everything's sorted out.'

'Thanks for coming,' he said. 'I'll be okay.'

'Come on, we'll go out for a good breakfast, that'll cheer us up,' said Peter, putting his hand on Christopher's shoulder. 'Where's good around here?' he asked Julia.

'The Buttered Scone. It's on the main street, about three blocks down. You can't miss it. Good coffee, and Flo's full English is legendary if you're feeling properly hungry.'

'Join us?'

'Not for me. I've had breakfast, and I'm going to pop in for a quick chat with Hayley, while I'm here.'

'Jess?'

She looked at Julia with a tiny frown on her face, as if she was wondering whether her mother would mind her leaving.

'Go on, love, I'll come by and join you for a coffee when I'm finished here.'

It was one of the incongruities of DI Hayley Gibson that, in contrast to her incisive and well-ordered brain, her good organisational skills, and her neatly professional appearance, her desk was a terrifying maelstrom of unbounded chaos. Files and ring-bound notebooks spread horizontally and vertically across its surfaces, sprinkled with coloured Post-its, and peppered with scrawled notes on scraps of paper. In addition to being messy, it was strangely anonymous. Not a photograph, or a personalised coffee cup, or an amusing magnet or a cartoon cut out of the newspaper adorned the space.

Julia hadn't been into Hayley's office for some months, and it seemed, if anything, even more chaotic. She focused on the DI's face and tried to block out the rest.

'Hayley, what is going on? Poor Peter is in an awful state, and as for Christopher...'

'I'm sorry I had to disturb the wedding couple. It's unfortunate timing, but I have to do my job. Which is to investigate the suspicious death of Desmond Campbell.'

'Yes, but what has Christopher got to do with anything? Why was he brought in?'

There was a pause. Hayley must have decided to share what she knew, because she said, 'We had a phone call saying that Christopher had threatened to kill Desmond just hours before he died.'

'Threatened to kill him? Christopher? Now that's ludicrous!'

'Is it? Well, I might have agreed with you. Except that I received this.' Hayley picked up her phone, and pressed play on a video already on the screen. There was Desmond, in his chef's whites, as alive as anyone ever was, and there was Christopher, in his wedding suit, his face contorted with fury, his voice screeching from the tinny phone speaker: '*You did it on purpose. You did it on purpose because of the trout. And now you've* ruined *our wedding, you horrible man. I would like to feed you peanuts until you swell up and DIE.*'

He did indeed look murderous. Julia felt a flutter of fear. 'I wouldn't say Christopher *threatened* him. And he didn't mean what he said. He was very upset and angry. It was his dream wedding, and the incident with the nuts derailed everything. The speeches were interrupted—'

'So he told me. At some length. I understand that he was likely angry and sounding off. It doesn't mean he actually did anything to harm the man. But as I said to Christopher, I'm sure you understand that this video requires investigation and an explanation.'

Julia nodded. 'Of course. But if it wasn't an accident, and it wasn't Christopher – which it certainly wasn't – then who?'

'DC Farmer is speaking to the deceased's family, and the people who worked for him. Just to see if there are any skeletons to be shaken out of the closet.'

'I've been wondering, how does a van like that stay cold?'

'I asked the same question. There's a refrigeration unit, much like in your domestic fridge. The fridge runs on the van's power, and the body of the van is well insulated. The insulation does a good job of keeping the interior cold once it's cooled. In this case, it turns out the engine was actually running. The petrol tank is completely empty. Walter will look into the petrol situation, when the van was last filled up, where he'd driven that day, but my theory is that the tank was close to full and the engine was running all night, keeping the cooling unit on.'

'It's tragic. Just think – if the petrol tank had been half full, or quarter full, Desmond Campbell might have lived.'

'That sort of philosophising is beyond the scope of my job, I'm afraid, Julia. The fact is, he's dead.'

'You're right. It's a sad and awful situation and nothing can change that. But I can tell you right now, Christopher had nothing to do with it.'

Hayley's response was a gruff, noncommittal grunt.

9

The Buttered Scone was buzzing with a lunchtime crowd of late-season tourists and regulars from Berrywick and the neighbouring villages. Julia's family – it felt odd to say it, but that's what they were – had secured a table in the corner by the window overlooking the street. Jess caught sight of her mum and waved her over, patting the empty chair next to her.

'We've ordered already, Mum. We decided on full English all round. When in Rome, as they say.'

'A bold move,' Julia said. 'Many's the man who has fallen before the might of the full English.'

'I back my chances,' Jess said, and handed her a menu. 'Do you want to have a look?'

Julia waved it away. 'I know the menu off by heart. This is my regular, remember.'

Flo arrived with three plates, each the approximate size of a bicycle wheel, each with two fried eggs and great heaps of accompaniments – sausages, bacon, tomatoes, mushrooms and baked beans. A big slice of fried bread glistened golden and oily at the edge of each plate.

Flo put a plate in front of each of the three of them. 'There you go. Three full English breakfasts. Hello, Julia.'

'Hi, Flo. This is my daughter, Jess. And this is Peter and Christopher.'

'Ah yes, the newlyweds. Congratulations to you. And welcome to Berrywick, Jess, I hope you enjoy your time here. You'll find it a bit of a change from Hong Kong, I'd imagine.'

Of course, Flo would know all about Jess's studies, and all about Julia's ex-husband's wedding, and, no doubt, all about the dead caterer. The Buttered Scone operated as a kind of vortex, drawing in all Berrywick's information – gossip, if you prefer the term – at improbable speed. It paid to be a little careful, as any information you let slip would be pulled in and just as rapidly disseminated, and before you knew it, your own careless comment or whispered confidence would be all over the village. Most times, there was no malice in it, but even so, the smart approach was to receive more information than you contributed in the transaction.

'Thank you,' said Peter. He looked down at his breakfast and said in a tone of deep admiration, 'My goodness, I don't think you could get more calories on that plate if you tried.'

'I wouldn't think so, but I could bring you a small jug of clotted cream if you like,' Flo said, deadpan, her hands on her hips.

'I shouldn't think that will be necessary, thanks, Flo,' Peter said with a laugh, picking up his knife and fork. 'But we'll see how we go.'

'What'll you have, Julia?'

'Just coffee for now, thank you, Flo.' She felt mildly queasy at the sight of so much breakfast.

'Coming right up,' Flo said, and headed over to the next table, pen and pad at the ready.

'I haven't even had a bite and my belt is feeling tight already,' said Christopher, patting his non-existent belly. 'I'm so bad. I should have ordered the health breakfast, but I couldn't resist.'

'Nonsense! You deserve this. I've seen the movies. This is the perfect meal for a man who's been sprung from jail,' said Jess, drawing raised eyebrows from the dads. 'Sorry, too soon?'

'I think so,' said Julia. 'Maybe wait an hour or two for the jail jokes.'

'Okay,' said Jess cheerfully, spearing her egg with a fork. She cut off a slice of sausage and dipped it into the runny yolk. 'Yum.' She popped it into her mouth.

Julia was relieved that Flo hadn't been there for the jail comment, given that her own husband, Albert, actually *was* in jail and would be for quite some time. An additional element of awkwardness was that Julia had played a part in solving the mystery behind the crime that had put him there. It had shocked Berrywick and devastated Flo and their daughter, Fiona. Although they didn't exactly blame Julia for what happened to Albert – that was his own poor judgement – relations had been strained for a while. Julia decided to push on through the awkwardness, and she and Jake continued to make their visits to the Buttered Scone. Things between Julia and Flo were back to normal, but she saw in Flo a deep underlying sadness that hadn't been there before, and felt distressed for her.

'Here, have some of my breakfast, I'll never eat all this,' Jess said, reaching for a side plate. 'Piece of bacon?'

'Okay, one rasher, and a tomato.' She watched as Jess scooped from the large plate to the smaller. 'Thanks, it does look good.' The modest serving looked just right – together with the coffee Flo brought – and it had hardly made a dent in Jess's breakfast.

'What are your plans for the day?' Julia asked the honeymooners. She had been surprised by their decision to honeymoon in the Cotswolds, until they'd told her that they intended to go to the Bahamas for the whole of December as their 'official honeymoon'. Just as well, perhaps, given the way things had turned out.

'Christopher and I are going for a little drive to Stow-on-the-Wold. Apparently there are some super antique shops there, as well as very nice cream teas – which I doubt we'll be eating after this breakfast.'

'Oh goodness, yes, Peter, you'll love it there. It's a charming village and an antique shoppers' heaven! It'll be like being on one of the television shows you love. It would be fun if you spot some hidden gem, previously unrecognised but, as it turns out, madly valuable. Although it's often the other way round on your TV shows, as I recall. The poor things discover that the precious family heirloom is worthless.'

'Peter's guilty pleasure. He still watches them, you know,' Christopher said, patting his husband's shoulder affectionately. 'I've never got into them myself.'

'Me neither.' Julia and Christopher smiled at each other. It was nice finding these strange points of connection.

'They're relaxing,' said Peter defensively. 'And they are actually very educational. I've learned so much about Georgian silver, you'd be surprised.'

'No, I wouldn't,' Julia and Christopher said in unison, and then burst out laughing.

'Christopher and I decided we'd each be in charge of choosing the outing for a day. Today, we're trooping around the antique shops for me, and tomorrow we're going to something called the Old Arboretum.'

'Have you been, Julia?' She shook her head. Christopher got a dreamy look and said, 'It's a Grade I listed site on the Register of Parks and Gardens of Special Historic Interest. Over eighteen thousand trees!'

'Jess, do you fancy either of the outings?' Peter asked. 'Come with us, I'd love to introduce you to English antiques.'

'Thanks, Dad, sounds tempting, but you go and enjoy your day. Mum is going to take me and Jake on a very long walk, to give me a proper feel for the layout of the area. We'll go along the river, and then on the public footpaths over the countryside, to the lake. And I might even be brave enough to do some wild swimming.'

'Heavens!' said Peter. 'It's autumn!'

'It's all the rage,' Julia explained. 'Rain or shine, summer or winter. People are hurling themselves into murky lakes and freezing seas all over Britain. You often spot them in the Buttered Scone afterwards, damp and shivering over a hot chocolate. Sean has once or twice had to treat some overenthusiastic cold swimmer who's almost frozen himself to death.' Julia mumbled the end of the last sentence, suddenly remembering its relevance to recent events, and ended cheerily, 'It's very good for you apparently, and exhilarating. So they say.'

'Sounds delightful. I can't see it would be more exhilarating than looking for treasure in antique shops, Jessica, but if you want to swim in a freezing pond, I can't stop you,' Peter said, shaking his head in bewilderment. 'But make sure there are no submerged logs or rocks, or a strong current. You can't always tell with lakes and rivers, they can be deceptive, you know. And don't dive headfirst, rather push off from the bank—'

'Thanks, Dad, I'll be fine.' Jess cut him off in the clipped, irritable tone Julia recognised from her daughter's teen years, when Peter's anxious caretaking had driven her mad.

Jake fell upon Jess with a degree of eagerness and delight ordinarily reserved for a pork sausage. After a suitable period of whining and patting and cuddling, they broke up the love fest, and Jake looked guiltily at Julia as if to say, 'Oh, there you are too! Sorry, couldn't help myself.' Henny Penny, his other fave, looked on from the shrubbery. In so far as a chicken was capable of expressions, hers was what Julia would describe as disgruntled. Jake's clear enthusiasm for the interloper was noted.

Julia rattled Jake's lead, 'Come on, you faithless hound, we're going on an adventure. And yes, Jess is coming too.'

They had made their way along the footpath by the river on Julia's usual daily walking route. Julia raised a hand in greeting to the bouncy jogger with her AirPods in her ears and her two well-behaved border collies at her heels. Aunt Edna came tottering towards them, dressed in black and swathed in layers of scarves and shawls, one of which looked like it might be a chenille bedspread.

'The apple falls next to the tree,' she announced, pointing from Julia to Jess and back again.

'Hello, Aunt Edna, and yes, you're right, this is my daughter, Jess.'

The old woman looked into the young woman's face and pronounced, 'Fair's fair. Love is in the air. You mark my words, there.' She turned her attention to Jake, resting her hands on her knees and bending down until her face was inches from Jake's worried one, and said solemnly, 'Bark my words.' She straightened up creakily and walked off at a surprisingly brisk pace, cackling at her own joke.

'Who's she, the local fortune-teller?' Jess asked.

'The funny thing about Aunt Edna is that she talks a lot of what seems like inscrutable nonsense, peppered with some weirdly perceptive gems from time to time. So maybe love really is in the air, Jess.'

'Yeah. I'm going with inscrutable nonsense on the love thing, Mum.'

'Could happen. Bark my words.'

They crossed the bridge at the very end of the village and joined a good footpath. They were quickly in open countryside, walking at a steady and comfortable pace past fields of sheep and hedgerows busy with birds.

'It's hard to believe that we're on the same planet as Hong Kong,' Jess said, as they entered a small wood, the ground already golden with fallen autumn leaves. 'I love it there, it's beautiful in its own way, but it's so full of people and buildings that you're never alone and there's hardly any space for nature. But this... The green. The trees. The sky.' The landscape was beyond her powers of description. She said simply, and inadequately, 'It is just so beautiful.'

'Did you know that the Cotswolds is an Area of Outstanding Natural Beauty? Capital letters. AONB. It's an official designation.'

'I didn't, but I'm not surprised.'

Jess insisted on carrying their small daypack – 'in deference to your age, Mum' – with a water bottle, a flask of tea, a swimming costume, two apples, two pieces of shortbread and a Good-Dog-Go Fair Trade Organic Beef and Barley Treat for Jake.

After an hour's walk they arrived at a clear, glittering lake, fringed along one side with reeds. On the far side, a grass bank sloped gently towards the water. A heron stood silently at the edge, poised for a strike. A pair of ducks paddled by, breaking up the reflections of the clouds on the water.

'I'm going in,' Jess said, pulling the backpack from her shoulders and dropping it on the grass. She grabbed her swimming costume from the pack and changed quickly. Once they'd stopped walking, it felt quite chill, but she was clearly determined. She walked down the grassy slope and launched herself into the water with a shriek. She took a few strokes towards the middle and stopped.

'It's divine!' she called in between gasps. 'Come in.'

'I didn't bring a swimming costume!'

'There's no one here, swim in your undies.'

Jess flipped onto her back and floated like a star.

'And it looks cold.'

'YOLO, Mum!'

'What does that mean?'

'It means You Only Live Once, so don't be a ninny.'

'The acronym for that would be YOLOSODBAN.'

'Hilarious, Mum. Now get in!'

Julia had promised herself that she would embrace new experiences when she moved to the country, and here was one presenting itself. Wild swimming. And she was with Jess. A promise is a promise, she thought and, without further hesitation, pulled off her hiking shoes and socks, and then her fleece and long-sleeved T-shirt, and finally her walking trousers. She tried not to think about the condition of her bra and knickers as she ran down the slope and hurled herself into the lake.

It was breathtakingly, gaspingly cold when she hit the water. She yelled out the air in her lungs, and immediately feared for her next breath, but it came, and then another.

'You did it!' Jess yelled in delight. 'Big ups, Mum!'

Julia managed to swim a few jerky breaststrokes. It was icy, but somehow not unpleasant. Her breath soon returned to almost normal. She wasn't going to die after all. In fact, she felt brave and fresh and invigorated. All those endorphins, or was it dopamine? Serotonin? Whatever it was that exercise was meant to give you, it was sloshing around in her veins and saturating her brain with good feeling. Jess was laughing, and swimming an inelegant crawl towards her mother, her hair streaming behind her.

'Best. Swim. Ever!' she said.

'Absolute best.' Julia flipped onto her back to survey the sky, a pale wintry blue with flecks of small puffy clouds. She felt wild and free and happy, her skin tingling, her daughter bobbing next to her.

Minutes later, they were out, and clamouring for their clothes, shrieking with a mixture of joy and pain. Julia's teeth chattered audibly as she pulled on her socks with shaking hands. She pushed away thoughts of Desmond, and how cold he must have been, and for so long.

Jess was nimbler and was already dressed. 'Tea,' she said, between gasps. She pulled out the flask and poured them each a cup. The heat thawed their fingers, and the hot, milky tea warmed them from the inside.

'God, imagine that poor Desmond's last hours.' It was as if Jess had read her mind. 'How cold do you have to be to freeze to death?'

'I don't know. Very cold, I suppose, and for quite some time.'

The question and its answer niggled Julia as she bit into the shortbread Jess passed to her. Why *was* Desmond *so* cold? How was the truck cold enough to freeze a man to death?

Julia had a thought.

A frightening thought.

10

Julia didn't like to spoil a supper date with talk of death. Instead, Julia and Sean chatted easily about everyday matters while he made the salad and she stirred the tomato sauce, which she had made from the last of the summer tomatoes and basil, and frozen. He told her about a patient who had come in with a sprained wrist which he suspected might be broken, so he'd sent them for an X-ray. She told him about the wild swimming with Jess, and the fun they'd had. She told him about Peter and Christopher's day out, which she'd heard about briefly when they'd come by to fetch Jess. 'They had such a lovely time. They trawled the antique shops and bought themselves a wedding gift – a little oil painting that may or may not have been painted by... I forget who, but someone well known. I haven't seen it, but I'm sure it's lovely. Peter has a very good eye. The important thing is, they had the happiest day.'

'Excellent. Take their minds off all the disasters and disappointments at the wedding.'

'Exactly. And they're taking Jess out for supper at that gastropub over near Edgeley this evening. The one that was in the paper last week? They do all sorts of things with local ciders and sheep's cheese and so forth. Peter invited us to join them, but I thought...' She let the sentence hang there, between them.

'Yes. Good call.' He smiled at her. 'I'm pleased to be having a quiet supper, just the two of us.'

'Me too. It's very nice.' She dropped the bundles of linguine into the boiling water – 'salted like sea water', as instructed by an Italian friend.

When the linguine was cooked and tossed in the sauce, and the salad was dressed and on the kitchen table, they sat down to eat. Sean put his phone down on the table next to him. 'Excuse me for leaving the phone on at supper. I told my patient to phone me once he's had the X-ray and to let me know the result. I'll take his call, if you don't mind; it won't be long.'

'Of course, that's fine.' She appreciated Sean's dedication as a doctor. Having been a social worker most of her life, she knew that in their lines of work you didn't leave everything behind when the clock struck five.

'The pasta smells delicious. Much better than cider and sheep's cheese and so forth, I've no doubt.'

'Well, until we've tried sheep's cider, we can't say for sure,' Julia laughed. She enjoyed Sean's dry humour. He had a keen eye for the ridiculous, and not a drop of malice – the best combination for humour, in Julia's view – and the fact that it was delivered in his rumbling burr made it all the more attractive.

Once they were settled in, Julia found she couldn't keep her suspicions and questions to herself any longer, and the conversation took a darker turn.

'Sean, I've had a thought about Desmond Campbell's death. A thought that I fear points to murder.'

'And what would that be?' Sean spoke patiently, calmly, as if Julia had said she thought it might rain later, and he didn't pause in his task: grating parmesan over his bowl of steaming pasta.

'It was too cold in the van.'

'Damn right, it was too cold. Too cold for the poor man to live. Cold enough to kill him.'

'That's exactly it. It *shouldn't* have been cold enough to kill him.'

He looked at her, a small frown wrinkling his brow.

'Sean, Desmond wasn't transporting frozen products. He had vegetables and salads and fruits and cheese and meat in that van. Desserts and cakes. I saw the lettuce and tomatoes when we opened it. They were frozen. The inside temperature must have been close to freezing. He wouldn't have set the temperature in the van so cold.'

Sean thought for a moment, then nodded.

'You're right, Julia. The van should have been at fridge temperature, not freezer temperature.'

'Fridges are set at four or five degrees. Freezer temperature would be around zero.'

'How do you know that?'

'Google. How else?'

'Of course.' Sean grinned.

'We don't know how long he was in the van, but if we assume he was shut in there for six or seven hours, at four or five degrees, would he have died?'

She could see Sean's mind working out the variables as he twirled his fork in the linguine. When he answered, it was in his usual measured way. 'It's hard to say. Seven hours is a long time to be so cold, but it was at least dry, and out of the wind. Being wet brings down the core temperature very quickly and is a big determining factor for hypothermia. If I had to offer a professional opinion, it would be that a young, healthy man would have a good chance of surviving. One thing I can say – if the van was refrigerating, not freezing, he wouldn't have been frozen stiff.'

Julia shuddered at the memory of the sound the frozen body had made when it hit the ground in the car park. Her mind was already moving on to the next question: 'Why was the thermo-stat set so cold?' but Sean's phone rang before she could voice it.

'Excuse me,' he said, and took the call. She pondered the next obvious question, the million-dollar question – Who had set the thermostat at that temperature, and why? – while he murmured comfortingly in the background. 'Yes... yes... A plate, yes, well if that's what the orthopaedic surgeon recommends, it sounds like that's for the best... Oh yes, she's a very good surgeon. You're in good hands.'

Julia looked at her watch: 7.30 p.m. She tossed up whether or not it was too late to phone Hayley. On one hand, it was after most people's working hours. But Hayley usually worked late and would most likely still be at the station, so Julia made the call.

Hayley answered in two rings, and came straight to the point, 'What is it?'

Julia answered in the same vein. 'The van. It was too cold. The fresh produce was frozen and it shouldn't have been. Not to mention Desmond. The thermostat wouldn't have been set so cold for lettuces. Someone must have reset it. Deliberately.'

There was a moment while Hayley thought about what Julia had said. One of the good things about Hayley was that she seldom spoke without thinking.

'Good logic,' she said eventually. 'You're right, it shouldn't have been so low. Should've been like a fridge, but the man was frozen like a block of ice.'

'Sean says he would likely not have died if it had been regular fridge temperature. Hayley, I think your suspicions are correct. Desmond's death was no accident.'

'You've definitely added to the evidence pointing that way, Julia.'

Julia had felt a little spark of self-satisfaction for working out a clever bit of information, but it quickly left her, and she felt suddenly very down. 'I hoped it would turn out to be accidental. What Kevin said about the drinking, and Desmond perhaps passing out, and there was the wind that came up... I thought that an accident sounded plausible.'

Sean had finished his call and came over to sit next to her, his hand on her knee. He sat quietly while she listened to Hayley speak:

'Yes, I know, I'm sorry too. The toxicology report came back this afternoon. There was no alcohol in Desmond's system. And no drugs. He didn't pass out in the back of the van.'

'So it seems. And even if he had fallen asleep, and even if someone had somehow accidentally shut him in...'

'Which is a heck of a big if.'

'Yes, but even then – there's no explaining the locked door. And there's no explaining how the setting of the thermostat could have been accidental.'

'No, none.' Hayley's voice came grim and certain through the phone. 'Someone locked Desmond Campbell in that van, and then turned down the temperature on that thermostat with the intention of freezing him to death. There's no doubt in my mind: Desmond Campbell was murdered.'

11

It had come as a surprise when Julia looked in her little red leather pocket diary – she had not succumbed to digital just yet – and discovered that it was book club at the Berrywick Library that night. Last month, Tabitha had asked if they could move it from the usual Wednesday and Julia had completely forgotten about it. It is always a shocking thing to be reminded that ordinary life goes on in the face of tragedy, and while Desmond Campbell was in the local mortuary, the book lovers of Berrywick were arranged in comfortable chairs in the reading area, discussing their favourite reads of the past month.

Curled on Jess's lap was the library cat, Too – so named because she was called Tabitha, too, like the librarian. She had slunk through the assembled book clubbers with studied disinterest, stopped in front of Jess, and jumped up, presenting her tiger-striped back for a stroke. It seemed like every animal in Berrywick was going to fall in love with Julia's daughter.

'I just don't know about speculative fiction. I've tried,' Jane said with a little frown, to indicate that she really was *trying*. 'But it always seems so... so made up.'

'It's all made up, though, isn't it? Fiction?' said Dylan, in his gentle drawl. 'Those romances where there's a misunder-standing and they, like, lose each other and find each other. The crime mysteries where some schoolteacher manages to find the killer when the police can't.'

When Dylan finished what was undoubtedly one of the longer speeches he'd made at book club, to Julia's surprise, Jess jumped in, 'You're right. Those characters are no more or less real than the robots or the plagues or the dystopian overlords.'

'Probably *less* real than the dystopian overlords,' Dylan said, uncurling a little from his customary position, which was slouched in the chair, well on the way to horizontal.

'And we know all about the plagues. Far too real,' Jess said with a shudder. She should know, she'd been stuck in Hong Kong for the lockdown.

Julia was pleased and surprised to see the lively interaction between the two of them, both younger than the next youngest member by about fifteen years. After some indecision, Jess had agreed to come along to book club, but without very much enthusiasm.

'When you put it that way, I do see your point. Okay then, I'll give that a proper try,' Jane said gamely.

She held out her hand for the book, which Dylan gave to her with a smile. 'Keep an open mind.'

'Promise.'

On that friendly note, they broke for tea. Pippa stood proudly at the tea table, doling out large squares of carrot cake onto plates.

'Ah, go on,' she said with a wink to Tabitha, who was dither-ing. 'It's a vegetable, really. Mostly carrot. Excellent for the eyesight. And you can be good tomorrow, instead.'

Tabitha held her plate out. 'You make a sound point.'

Tea was allocated fifteen minutes, and conversation at tea was, by tradition, about general village news, rather than books. Gossip, some might call it. To this end, people drew closer to

Julia, the most likely source of intelligence about the big news of the week, 'that awful accident with the van,' as Jane put it, in a hushed tone.

'It must have been horrible,' she said encouragingly. 'You and Sean found him, didn't you?'

'We were there. The poor man.'

'Well, what happened?' asked Pippa, rather more directly, when it became clear that Julia was not going to provide more detail without a push. 'How did he manage to shut himself in his own van?'

It was clear from the way they were discussing the incident that no rumours of foul play had leaked out into the general population. Julia intended to keep it that way, answering briefly, 'I don't know how it happened. There's going to be an investigation.'

'That must have put rather a damper on the wedding,' Diane said, putting her fork down on her plate to concentrate on the story she was about to tell. 'I was at a wedding too, on Saturday afternoon. My boyfriend's cousin's son. No one died, fortunately. Although I came close when I saw what the groom's mother was wearing.' She bowed her head into her hands dramatically, so her red hair fell forward like two fiery shining curtains, and sighed, 'Lordie, what a sight!'

All eyes were on her now, as the assembled company awaited further details of the fashion abomination. Diane paused for full effect, and said, 'White. White! Well, off-white, or perhaps cream, but still. Only the bride wears white, as everyone knows.'

There was no argument to that. On the contrary, there was nodding and murmured agreement.

'But there she was, the mother-in-law, in a dress as close as can be to white and – believe me or don't – it was *above the knee.*'

Diane took encouragement from the audience's gratifying

gasp, and continued: 'Good pins, I'll grant her that. She does Pilates, apparently. Oh, and I almost forgot, she had a corsage!'

There followed some brief discussion about appropriate etiquette and styling as regards wedding parent attire, followed by some remarks as to the relative merits of a corsage. A smile and a flicker of an eye roll passed between Dylan and Jess, who – Julia noted – were now sitting next to each other. She suspected it was the word corsage that caused the eye roll, or perhaps it was a shared acknowledgement of the ridiculousness of old people's concerns and conversations.

As Pippa offered seconds of cake, Diane came and sat next to Julia. 'Funny coincidence – it was the same catering company, Candy Catering, that did the wedding I went to. Not the Desmond fellow himself, obviously.'

There was an awkward moment of silence at the mention of the dead, and Diane continued, 'The other caterer, his partner, did ours. Funny thing. I heard this woman – Cynthia, was it? Yes, Cynthia. I heard her and one of the waiters talking about how her partner was doing the posh, bigger budget wedding for a gay couple down from London. I thought it must be your ex-husband and his new husband. I mean, what are the chances? Anyway, she wasn't happy that she got the afternoon tea and champers. The food was good. Delicious little filo quiches and a magnificent cheeseboard... But still, nothing terribly fancy compared to the other wedding.'

'There wasn't much to envy at Peter's wedding, as it turned out,' said Julia.

'I suppose not. But she didn't know that at the time, did she? She was awfully cross about it.'

Julia really didn't want to be talking about the wedding and the death and the petty disappointments of Cynthia the caterer. 'I suppose she's not so cross any more,' she said, hoping to bring the conversation to an end.

'More than cross, I'd say,' said Diane, as if it wasn't she

herself who had used the word 'cross' in the first place. 'I saw her a bit later in the afternoon, she was having a smoke outside, and I was keeping my friend Grace company – she can't kick the habit, poor Grace, she's tried everything acupuncture, patches – anyway I heard the caterer on the phone saying, "Well, Desmond, you gave me the second-rate assignment. Again. You can do your own clean-up. I'm not coming to help you this time." Oooh, she was telling him! Livid, she was. I bet she feels bad now.' Diane sounded rather triumphant about this, as if she had some stake in the caterer's guilt and shame.

'Poor thing, she probably does,' said Julia, more kindly. 'But none of us know what might happen at any moment.'

'Well, you're not wrong about that. We should mind our words, I suppose.' There was a brief moment to contemplate the degree to which Diane herself had not minded her words. In fact, she'd been full of scurrilous gossip. She had the grace to flush slightly.

Julia's mind was already making a leap. 'Oh my heavens. Think about it. If Cynthia had gone to The Swan to help Desmond clean up, this whole thing might never have happened. She might have arrived before the murderer. Or she might have found him and unlocked the van. Desmond might still be alive.'

'You're right. Isn't that awful to think about? Oh, and it's even worse!' Diane, who had been having a good time of it, sharing the gossip and acting out the scene, looked suddenly pale. 'I remembered what she said on the phone. Before she rang off, she said something like, "You've pushed me around for the last time. Whatever happens from now on, it's on you. You can't blame me." Imagine those were your last words to someone.'

. . .

An hour later, Sean, Julia and Jess stepped out onto the road. It was dark already, the first stars glimmering above, and the road glimmering below, fresh with a sprinkling of rain.

Sean rubbed his hands together to warm them. 'I should have brought gloves. Winter's on the way.' He took Julia's basket of books from her and hitched it onto one arm. His other hand reached for hers.

'It certainly feels like it. I must get some more wood in. Please remind me to put in an order tomorrow, Jess.'

'Will do, Mum.'

Julia and Sean started to walk in the direction of home, but Jess didn't move. 'I thought I'd go down to the pub for a bit,' she said with deliberate casualness.

'The pub?'

'There's a singer, apparently. Dylan says he's not awful – that's a direct quote.'

'High praise indeed,' Sean muttered.

'I know, right? Who can resist? So, we're going to go for a quick drink.'

Julia did her best to sound unsurprised, but her words came out weirdly high-pitched and chipper. 'Oh, yes, of course. Dylan. The pub. That'll be nice.'

Dylan came out of the library with his backpack over one shoulder, laden with books. He nodded to Jess and said, 'You ready to go?'

As the young couple and the old parted ways, Julia called back, 'Oh, and Jess—'

'I'll walk her home, Mrs Bird,' said Dylan.

'Good. Thank you, Dylan. Have fun.'

When Jess and Dylan's footsteps had died away, Sean and Julia turned to each other with their eyes wide in exaggerated astonishment, a spontaneous silly moment that made them both laugh.

'He's a good chap, Dylan,' said Sean.

'He's a very good chap, I've always thought. And I'm pleased that Jess has got someone closer to her own age to hang out with. I was worried that she'd get bored with just her old mum for company.'

She took his hand, and they walked on.

'Well, she seems very happy to be with her old mum, from what I can see. And it's hardly been boring. The wedding, and then poor Desmond, and the wild swimming.'

'And now book club, and the not awful singer. Thrills and excitement all round.' She paused. 'Honestly, though, it's been lovely. I was worried that we'd struggle to find our connection, but it's been so easy. Better than when she left, even. She's grown up, and I'm less annoying.'

'Are you then?' He laughed. 'In what way?'

'Not trying to control things and make everything right. More relaxed. Able to trust that things will work out. We've been able to have fun without me working so hard at it. I realise that my two years in Berrywick have really changed me. I wanted to change my life and I did. For the better.'

'I'm glad for you, Julia. And glad for me.'

They walked on, each in their own thoughts, with only the sound of their footsteps breaking the contented silence.

12

It had been years since Julia had slept the lightened sleep of the parent waiting for a child to come home. It was an oddly familiar feeling, the unconscious worry keeping her alert even in sleep, and then the sound of a door or a footstep signalling the safe return, and finally the deep slumber of a mother whose chickens had come home to roost.

Jess's door was firmly closed, and remained so for some hours after Julia got up and started tending to herself and her animals. It was a pleasant entry into each day, a gentle routine that she enjoyed, but this morning she was preoccupied, her mind running over what she'd heard about Cynthia's last conversation with her partner. Diane said Cynthia was angry. She had said that, whatever happened, it was on Desmond. But what did she mean? What sort of happenings? Did they include murder? It seemed a stretch.

Julia had come home last night eager to share what she knew with Hayley, but in the cold light of day it seemed rather less like information relevant to the case, and rather more like village gossip.

The dog and hens fed, Julia made a pot of tea and two slices of toast. She spread one with honey and the other with marmalade, and settled at the table with her iPad. The daily Wordle was both soothing and stimulating. It would take her mind off murder for a few minutes at least. Lots of people had a favourite first word, carefully worked out to use the maximum number of vowels, or the most frequently used consonants, but Julia always let something float out of her brain.

'CATER' she typed into the five available blocks.

The tiles turned over on the screen. Yellow, yellow, yellow, yellow, yellow, yellow.

Every single letter correct! But in the wrong place.

After a moment's grappling for the anagram, she typed, 'REACT'. Green, green, green...

Solved! And in only two goes. It was a record for Julia's Wordling, and a sign, for sure, that she should react to her instincts regarding the caterer. She picked up the phone and called Hayley Gibson.

'I'll add her to the list,' Hayley said, once Julia had recounted the evening's conversation. There was rather less eagerness than Julia had expected.

'Okay, good.'

'It's quite a long list. I'm talking to Desmond Campbell's family and friends. There's the trouble between him and the wife – Goldie, her name is – but I don't think there's anything there. I was a bit suspicious that she hadn't reported him missing, I must say, but she says with his work he's often back late and gone early, so she didn't realise he hadn't come home.'

'I suppose that makes sense,' said Julia. 'I had a friend in London married to a chef, and she often complained that she could go all week without seeing him. Who else is there?'

'DC Farmer is talking to the staff at The Swan, and people

who were at the wedding. They're all possible witnesses, even if they don't know it. Those are our priorities right now, and there are a lot of them. And there's some CCTV tape to look at. But we'll get to Cynthia, once we're done with all of them.' Hayley gave a deep sigh, clearly feeling overwhelmed by all she had to do.

'But don't you think it sounds ominous, what Cynthia said? "Whatever happens from now on, it's on you. You can't blame me."'

'It sounds like someone angry sounding off at a business partner, Julia. It's a long way from a murder threat, if you ask me.'

'I agree, it's hard to tell without knowing the context, hearing the tone, but it's worth—'

From Hayley's side came the sound of footsteps, voices, and a door closing. 'Listen, Julia, I've got to go. There's new evidence come in, it seems. Sorry I can't go rushing off on your tip. I know you're trying to help.'

Julia poured the last of the tea from the pot into her mug and took a sip. It was only just hot enough, and so strong as to be verging on bitter. Sean would be horrified to see her drink such a brew. He was a stickler when it came to tea, and adhered strictly to 'proper' process, from the warming of the pot, to the milk-before-tea rule. He would definitely have tossed this mug of tea out and started again.

She put down her mug and picked up her iPad. Her research/snooping skills were first-rate after her recent crime-solving experience, and within minutes she'd found Cynthia Skipper, partner in Candy Catering, marathon runner, and half owner, with her husband Tim, of the Village Pie Place in Edgeley. Julia didn't hesitate. She dialled the number Google had so helpfully provided, and asked for Cynthia.

'She's not here right now. Is there something I can help you with?'

'Ah, thank you, no. I'll try her later. When will she be in, do you know?'

'Hang on a mo.'

The woman didn't bother covering the phone while she shouted, 'Tim, is Cynth coming in? I thought she said she'd be here this morning.'

'She had a bad night's sleep and wasn't feeling too well this morning. But she said she'd be in by noon.'

The voice spoke into the receiver. 'We're expecting her at about lunchtime. Give her a ring then.'

'I'll do that. Thanks for your help.'

As Julia finished her phone call, Jess came into the kitchen, still in her pyjamas, her hair mussed from sleep and dark smudges of mascara under her eyes. In monosyllables, she reported back on her evening ('fun'), Dylan ('good guy'), the pub ('hilarious') and the music ('not awful'), as well as her return time ('way too late'). A shower and giant vat of tea perked her up, and she professed herself eager to accompany her mother to Edgeley to check out Cynthia Skinner.

Jess fiddled with the music console, her fingers running quickly through the touch screen to connect her phone via Bluetooth. A jazzy female voice came through the speakers and filled the car with its soft smokiness. It was a relief. Five years ago her car music of choice was shouty rap music peppered with words so deeply offensive that Julia felt compelled to deliver small lectures about the dangers of drugs and misogyny, which invariably ended in a fight on the way to school.

'Nice music choice, Jess.'

'Something chill for the drive. I'm pretty excited to be on an investigative mission to a pie shop. Me and my mum in the depths of the Cotswolds. Two bad-ass women, out for justice. At the pie shop.'

'Don't get too excited, Jess, we're going to have a nice drive to the next village and get pies for lunch – they're rated 4.9 on

Tripadvisor, you know. "Possibly the best pies in the world" according to a woman from Buffalo, New York. I hope Cynthia's there. If she is, I will—'

'Hold her under water until she confesses?'

'Heavens, Jess, what an awful thing to say. No! I only want to get a sense of her, and see if anything comes up that might be useful.'

'What's my job?'

'To order the pies.'

'No, I mean, in terms of the investigation. Distract the husband maybe? Or soften up Cynthia by flattering her pastry?'

'Just the pies, I think, love. And of course you can see if you get any instinct about her.'

'On it, Mum.'

Julia slowed, looking for a parking place on the Edgeley main road. 'Oh my goodness. Look!' said Jess. Julia's gaze followed her daughter's pointing finger. 'It's the van. The Candy Catering van. It's outside the pie shop.'

'Well, I guess that means Cynthia is here. Ugh, I can't imagine what it must feel like driving the van, knowing her partner died inside it.'

'Awful. Just awful.'

'Come on. Let's go in.'

Inside, the tiny shop was warm and cosy, and smelled delightfully of fresh baked goods. There were three little tables, each with a red checked tablecloth. At the service counter was a gleaming coffee machine. Under the glass counter were rows of shiny, golden pies. An old chap stood in front of the counter, surveying the pies and trying to make up his mind.

'Ah, my Helen does love the lamb and mint, but I'm wondering if I shouldn't get her the pork and apple for a change.'

'Both excellent, of course, Fred,' said the woman behind the counter. 'But you can get the lamb any time, and the pork is a special, it's not a regular menu item, so there's that to consider.'

'Well, let's get the pork and apple for Helen, then, and the rosemary chicken for me.'

The woman put two pies into paper bags and handed them over. She had the slim, wiry build of a long-distance runner, and the dark ringed eyes of someone who'd had a bad night's sleep. Cynthia, presumably.

Jess clearly thought so too. She nudged her mother and flicked her eyes in the woman's direction. Her expression assembled into a *meaningful* look. She'd always had one of those faces that told you everything. Even as a little girl, she couldn't tell a fib.

Jess and Julia inspected the list of available pies on a chalkboard behind the counter, and discussed their choices while watching her serve the customers ahead of them. Julia thought about how she might engage her in conversation. She could hardly say, 'Did you kill Desmond because he always took the good jobs and expected you to clear up?' But what *would* she say instead? The matter was helped along – and the woman's identity confirmed – by the old chap at the counter who said, as he left, 'Thanks, Cynthia. And I'm sorry to hear about your business partner, Cyn. What a terrible thing.'

'Ah, Fred, yes. Terrible. A terrible freak accident. We're all gutted.'

Her face didn't contradict her. Her eyes glistened, and she pursed her lips tight, as if keeping back a sob.

Fred patted her hand and moved aside, letting Jess and Julia to the counter.

'I couldn't help but overhear. I'm sorry for your loss,' Julia said gently.

'Thank you.'

'By strange coincidence, we were at the wedding at The

Swan. The one that Desmond catered. The night he got shut in the van.'

'You were? Goodness, that *is* strange.'

Jess chipped in. 'It was my father who got married. I met Desmond when we were setting things up.'

'His food was wonderful, I must say,' said Julia.

Which was true, if you discounted the Great Nut Disaster.

'I'm glad to hear it, although I'm not surprised. Desmond was a perfectionist. Who could have known it was the last meal he would ever make.' Cynthia paused for a moment, as if considering her next words. 'How did he seem to you?' she asked.

'Well, I can't say, really. I only saw him in passing at the function. He seemed...' Julia thought for the right word. 'He seemed focused. Concentrating on the job at hand.'

'That's Desmond,' Cynthia gave a little smile. 'He could be incredibly focused when it came to the food, the flavours, the plating. Now, what'll you have?'

'One vegetable, one beef and mushroom please.'

Cynthia served them up. Julia thanked her and was turning to leave when Jess said, 'What you said about the last meal, the last day... A school friend died when we were in our last year. I always wished I could remember our last conversation. What we talked about. How we left it. Do you remember your last conversation with Desmond?'

Julia was surprised and a little annoyed at Jess's intrusive question, but Cynthia leaned forward, her elbows on the counter. A minor storm of emotions flitted across her face, and she took a slow breath before answering. 'I'm sorry about your friend. Since you ask, yes, I remember our last conversation well. I called him that very evening – we talked about the business, our roles. I offered to come and help him with the clear-up after my function was finished, but he told me to get an early night for a change. That's what we were like, me and Des,

we wanted the best for each other. It was an excellent partnership.'

'An excellent partnership...' echoed Julia, her eyes catching
Jess's. Was this the same woman whose last words to her
partner had been steeped in anger and resentment? Jess raised
her eyebrows at Julia.

'Yes,' said Cynthia. 'Never an angry word. And that's a fact.'

13

'Finally!' Julia muttered when she saw Hayley's name pop up on her phone screen. She'd left a message for the detective inspector the day before, eager to report back on her conversation with Cynthia, and get her take on it. Cynthia's version of that last phone call was completely at odds with what Diane had overheard. By Diane's account, Cynthia had fought with Desmond and refused to help him clear up. Yet Cynthia had said she had offered to help and he had told her to take the night off. Why would she fib to a complete stranger? It did seem odd, but Julia also knew from her social work that humans have an enormous ability to self-justify, to deny their bad feelings and actions to themselves and others. Did Cynthia massage the facts to create a story so she could feel better about herself now that Desmond was dead? Or was it more ominous than that?

That was what she'd wanted to talk to Hayley about, but Hayley hadn't called her back. Three or four times Julia had stopped herself from phoning again in her impatience, and now here was Hayley, twenty-four hours later.

'I need to take this, if you don't mind,' she said to Wilma, who was behind the till at Second Chances charity shop. It had been a busy morning, but the afternoon was shaping up to be quiet. There were at that moment only two customers, a multiple-pierced girl in her late teens, and a scruffy young man a year or two older. They were looking at a rack of old coats and jackets, which they would likely describe as vintage, not secondhand.

Julia stepped out of the shop onto the pavement.

'Hey, Hayley, thanks for getting back to me. Do you have time for a coffee? I wanted to tell you about—'

'No time for coffee, Julia, sorry. I've got a lot going on here. But there's something new... Hang on a sec.'

There were steps and then silence, as if Hayley had covered the phone with her hand. She came back a minute later and said brusquely. 'Listen, I've got to go. The boss has arrived for a meeting about the Desmond Campbell situation. I'll try and call you, but I don't know when.'

'I'm at Second Chances,' Julia said quickly. 'It's not busy, so I'll be leaving early. I can come by the station on my way home.'

'That won't work. I don't know when I'll be out of the meeting,' Hayley said.

'I'm passing. I'll pop by anyway.'

'Julia—'

'Got to go. See you soon.'

Fortune favours the brave, Julia's dad used to say, and so it was that afternoon. Julia begged off the rest of the afternoon shift, and walked into the police station at the very moment that Hayley walked out of the door that separated the front of the station from the offices behind. She looked at Julia, hesitated, and then nodded, wordlessly leading the way to her office.

Five minutes later, they were at Hayley's desk. Julia finished recounting her odd interaction with Cynthia, and awaited Hayley's response. Hayley didn't speak. She looked tired and deflated.

'Long day?'

'Yes, but it's not that.'

'What is it?'

'It's Christopher. There's new information. I'm going to have to bring him in again.'

'Hayley, why? He's told you everything he knows.'

'That's just it, Julia. He hasn't. The CCTV footage shows him outside.'

'Outside? Well, that's possible. That's not a crime.'

'He was outside, at the service entrance. Right next to Desmond Campbell's van. There's no reason he should have been there on his wedding night.'

'Hayley, it *can't* be Christopher who killed Desmond. I know him. He wouldn't hurt a fly.'

'If you had seen the tape, you might not be so sure.'

'Well, let me see it then.'

'Absolutely not. You are his...' Hayley was briefly flum-moxed by the question of what to call Julia in relation to Christopher, but whatever it was, it was compromising.

Julia cut in. 'It doesn't matter. Whatever is on the tape, there's got to be an explanation. Christopher is many things, but he's *not* a murderer.'

'He'll have plenty of time to make that explanation when we talk to him. DC Farmer has gone to ask him to come in.'

Hayley stopped, distracted by the sound of a door slam-ming. Footsteps. Raised, indistinct voices.

'If I'm not mistaken, Hayley,' said Julia, knowing she sounded angry, 'your suspect has arrived.'

All eyes were on the monitor mounted in the corner of the meeting room when the screen fizzed to life. It was matched by the crackle of anger emanating from Peter Bird. Julia knew him to be slow to anger, but on the rare occasions when it took him over, it burned with a white-hot intensity. She could almost feel its pulse. Next to him, Christopher was grey and shaky. Peter had told Hayley he wanted Julia to stay with them, and Hayley hadn't argued. Julia wasn't sure if this was because Peter had a right to have whoever he wanted there, or because he'd dropped several heavy-handed references to the fact that he was a lawyer, or because Hayley wanted Julia to see the video.

The snowy screen resolved into a greyscale image of the back of The Swan. It was mounted so as to cover the back delivery entrance that led to the kitchen, and the parking area beyond. Rain was falling, showing as thin white streaks in front of the camera. The tarmac glistened. There was her own car, Julia realised. And there... she felt a prickle race up her spine to her scalp... there was Desmond's white van, just where Julia had found it on that fateful day.

'The time stamp in the corner shows 10.01 p.m.' Hayley gestured with the remote control. The seconds ticked over, and Christopher appeared in the upper right of the screen. He came round the side of the building, from the direction of the garden, keeping close to the wall. He stopped when he came to the end of the wall, and peered round, towards the kitchen door. Desmond came out of the kitchen door and Christopher shrank back, out of sight. When Desmond disappeared between his van and another one, Christopher emerged at a tiptoeing trot, and dashed into the kitchen. He was gone for not more than a few seconds, and trotted out again, this time in the direction of the suppliers' vans.

Julia could hardly believe what she was seeing. She *knew* that Christopher was innocent of murder, but what was he doing there? He looked so furtive, ducking and diving between the building and the vans, making sure that Desmond didn't see him. As he got to the vans, the image on the screen froze, broke into a series of horizontal stripes that flickered and flashed.

'What happened?' Julia asked.

'Apparently a fuse blew, taking the cameras out,' Hayley said.

'Oh yes, there was a bang and the lights went off for a minute or so, remember, Peter?'

He didn't answer her. He was still staring at the screen, now grey and snowy. He looked at Christopher and back at the screen.

'Here's the same scene from another angle,' Hayley said, typing into her laptop. There was Christopher again, this time seen from a camera that must have been mounted at the entrance to the service area of The Swan, pointing towards the parking area. Again, the furtive ducking and dodging between the vans. He stopped behind one of them and reached out for the handle. Again, the image froze and fractured into lines and snow.

'Look at the angle. That's a different van,' Peter said. 'That's not the van Desmond died in. It's the florist's van, if I'm not mistaken. Your so-called evidence proves nothing.'

'It puts him at the scene. And why was he trying to open the van?'

Christopher cleared his throat and said, 'I can explain.'

'No. Don't say a word until Scott Lillifield gets here.'

'But, Peter, I can explain.'

'Christopher, please.' He put his hand over his husband's, and spoke calmly. 'This is all going to be sorted out, but I'm asking you to please be patient. I'm not a criminal lawyer, but I am a lawyer, and I am pleading with you not to speak without representation. Scott will be here tomorrow and you will have your say.'

'All right.' Christopher looked from Peter to Hayley and back, then lowered his eyes to the desk and said miserably. 'I'm sorry, Detective. I *can* explain, but I... I'm going to wait until my lawyer gets here.'

Hayley looked deflated. 'You are within your rights to do that. But don't leave the area until we've had our conversation, please.'

Jess had just put the kettle on when Julia arrived home, so they made tea and she relayed the events of the day over tea and biscuits. Quite a few biscuits. Jess was reliving her childhood through the Great British Biscuit Project (GBBP), which entailed eating all the biscuits of her childhood, and then moving on to sample any newcomers. The two of them had been to the supermarket on Jess's first day in Berrywick, and purchased an exhaustive selection of the classic favourites. A packet of Hobnobs lay open on the coffee table. Julia, who did not have a twenty-six-year-old's metabolism, tried to keep to one biscuit per session of the GBBP, but was not always successful.

'Poor Christopher,' Jess said with a sigh when her mother finished recounting the conversation at the police station. She dipped a Hobnob into her tea. Jake's head followed the biscuit's progress into the steaming liquid, and back up to her mouth. Jess swallowed, and continued. 'He must be so scared and worried. I wish we could help him prove his innocence.'

'I know. I feel the same. But you mustn't worry about Christopher. He didn't kill anyone and the truth will come out. Daddy has a big shot criminal lawyer coming down from London tomorrow. He'll sort things out.' Referring to Peter as Daddy felt strange now that Jess was grown, but it was a hard habit to break.

'You're right, it'll be sorted out.'

She continued with the dipping and sipping, Jake's head bobbing up down, up down, in time with her hand, his eyes fixed on the biscuit. 'Still, I wonder who did kill Desmond.

Mum, what sort of person would kill someone in that way? Lock them in a van to freeze to death?'

'That's an interesting question, Jess. I've been thinking about that. It's a very hands-off way of killing someone. The murderer didn't have to lay a finger on him, or wield a weapon. He – or she – didn't have to see the victim suffer, or see him die.'

'Just slam the door, lock it and walk away.'

'Yes. It seems like something done on the spur of the moment. Not planned.'

'Someone he knew? Maybe in the heat of an argument?' Jess tilted her head to the side, thinking.

'Perhaps. That's true of most violence, you know. It's mostly committed by someone who knows the victim. Often someone close to the victim, like a spouse or a partner.'

They both pondered that sad fact for a moment, but the young can't hold death in mind for very long. Jess popped the last of the biscuit into her mouth and changed the subject.

'Mum, could you give me a lift to the village? I said I'd meet Dylan at The Swan when he gets off work at five.'

Jess looked mildly embarrassed delivering this information, although there was no reason to. She was a grown woman, entitled to make her own arrangements. Julia didn't enquire further about their plans, or the nature of their friendship. She said casually, 'Sure. If we leave now, we can take Jake and have a walk. We can park at The Swan and go across that lovely big field to the woods.'

Jake might not be an excessively brilliant dog, but he did recognise his name and all variations on the word 'walk'. Hearing the two words together in a sentence caused him to leap up and start spinning in circles like a lunatic, bunching up the rug with his feet, while his tail swept dangerously over the table where the tea tray sat. It caught the Hobnob packet on one pass, lifting it up and sending the last biscuit flying. He wheeled round, snapped it out of mid-air and swallowed it in one gulp. It was pretty impressive, it must be said.

'Jake!' the two women said in unison. 'Sit.'

He was so surprised by the stereo instruction that he obeyed it, plonking himself down on the carpet and looking from one to the other, expectantly. His whole body quivered with anticipation, but he stayed in place, his expression that of a dog trying his very hardest to be A Good Boy.

'You're a good boy,' said Julia, with a laugh. 'Well, goodish. Some of the time. Come on, let's get your lead on you.'

14

The main road was chock-full of traffic as they entered the village. Rush hour in Berrywick was short, but it could be brutal. The narrow, winding roads hadn't been designed for commuters and tourists and parents on the school run in their big cars. Julia drove a block at roughly the pace of an elderly snail, and turned off the main road in frustration as soon as she could, intending to wind her way back to the main road and The Swan on the other side of the village.

'Look, Mum' – Jess was pointing at a small shop on the side of the road – 'that's the florist from the wedding! Blooming Marvels, remember? Who could forget such a great name? Weird, we were talking about them and the van.'

Although she had once bought flowers there, Julia had forgotten that the florist was situated on this side road. But there it was indeed. The shop occupied an ancient cottage that managed to be both charmingly authentic, with its swayback roof and its golden stone, and meticulously renovated and maintained.

'Let's go in!' Jess said eagerly. 'If the florist van was in The Swan parking that night, like you saw in the security video, that must mean the florist was there. Maybe she saw something. Let's pay her a visit and see what we can find out. Like we did with the catering lady, Cynthia. That was so cool. Detectiving our way to the pie shop, picking up clues. Getting a sense of things, as you call it.'

'We can't go around randomly calling on the wedding suppliers of the Cotswolds looking for clues to a mystery that's none of our business. That's the job of the police, Jess. They will have interviewed everyone who was there and, if she saw anything – which I doubt – she would have told the police.'

'I guess you're right.' Jess slumped down in the seat, disappointed.

Julia glanced back at the shop. 'Well, what do you know? There she is – Angela, the florist, herself.'

Angela, still in her blue denim apron, stepped out of the sage green front door, pulled it closed behind her, and locked it. She dropped the keys into her bag and paused for a moment to survey the shop. She looked up at the hanging baskets and down at the arrangement of pots of varying sizes artfully planted and arranged along the shopfront with the casual stylishness that Julia had come to realise was the florist's trademark. Angela reached down and snapped a dead leaf off a bush. She straightened up and gave a little nod of quiet satisfaction, as if to confirm that all was in order. A long, angry blast from a car hooter made them all jump. Angela swung round to her left, in the direction Julia was headed, her peaceful moment shattered. The noise had come from a small delivery van, pale sage green, with the words Blooming Marvels and a daisy in loose, looping style in black across the side. Julia was almost in line with the parked van now, her window next to the open passenger window.

'Come on then,' the driver shouted to Angela, his handsome face screwed up with irritation. 'I haven't got all day.' She hurried towards him, her pretty face pale and pained.

'What a very rude man,' said Jess.

'Horrible. I hope he's not her husband. He looks like an aggressive prat.'

'Weird. We were talking about the van and there it is.'

'But that's not the van on the security camera,' Julia replied with a frown. 'The van that was parked by the service entrance in the video, the one Peter thought was the florist's van, was plain white. It was bigger, too – about the same size as the Candy Catering van. And it definitely didn't have a daisy. The other white van must have belonged to someone else.'

'Hhhm. Well, no point in questioning her then. Pity.'

'Sorry to disappoint you,' said Julia, with a laugh.

Julia parked at The Swan and she, Jess and Jake walked across the field and into the woods, carpeted in fallen leaves. She enjoyed the crunching of leaves under her feet, and the way Jess kicked them up as she walked, just as she'd done as a child. Jake gambolled about in delight. He hurled himself into drifts of dry leaves and rolled around, twisting and turning to scratch his back, then leapt up and set off after the scent of rabbits, or some other tempting beastie. Julia didn't bother to call him back, happy to let him play, knowing he'd be back at her heels between adventures. He never went far.

The fresh autumn air soothed her, and the beauty of her surroundings distracted her from thoughts of Christopher's current troubles, and Desmond's more permanent predicament. She stopped under a massive horse chestnut tree, its leaves turning dramatically, one side of the tree darker and redder, the other still gold. The ground beneath it was thickly carpeted with leaves and the prickly outer cases with shiny, brown conkers bursting out. She picked one up and felt the familiar heft of it in her palm.

'Remember these?' she said, handing it to Jess.

'Of course! The hours we spent looking for the best and biggest conkers. Dad used to make the hole with a skewer and hammer to thread the string through. He wouldn't let me do it, he was always scared I'd lose a finger.'

'Yes, your dad could be a bit overprotective, but to be fair to him, you do still have all ten fingers.'

'I did almost lose an eye though, remember? A particularly cut-throat game, and Susie Jones' conker flew off its string and smacked me in the face. I've still got the scar.'

Jess traced her left eyebrow with her finger, where a tiny silver scar could be seen, if you really looked. She tossed the conker she was holding hard into the distance, and Jake took off after it. He screeched to a halt, ploughing through the leaves, only to discover that the thing he was chasing was one of a hundred identical not-very-interesting hard round things, and stopped looking.

The sun was setting when they got back to The Swan. Every day was a little shorter and every night longer than the previous one, as autumn headed towards winter. Jess walked across the lawn towards the front door, giving her mum a wave. 'Not sure when I'll be back. Don't worry about me for supper,' she called over her shoulder. 'Bye, Jakey love.'

Julia watched her walk away. She looked strong and confident, with her long strides, and her shining auburn hair swinging side to side. She seemed happy, Julia thought with simple gratitude, and got into her little red Peugeot parked in the main guest parking area. She was pleased not to be in the service parking, not to have to revisit the scene of the gruesome discovery. The traffic had cleared by the time she left, and it was an easy drive home in the dusk, with Jake sitting regally at the back like a royal who unexpectedly finds themselves in an Uber.

The house was in darkness. She opened the door and walked around switching on side lamps and drawing the curtains. In just a few minutes the place looked cosier and more

welcoming. Soon it would be cold enough for a fire. Not tonight
though.

She moved through the house and out the back door to feed
Jake and check on the chickens. They had already settled into
their nesting boxes for the night, making contented little
creaking clucks. 'I'll be doing likewise soon enough. I'm going to
turn in early. It's been a long day,' she told them conversation-
ally. She had resigned herself to being the batty old lady who
spoke to her hens. 'What a day. First the shop, then the police
station. And we had a lovely long walk.' Henny Penny, the
premier chicken of the group, raised her head and fixed her
beady little eyes on Julia as if to indicate that she should
perhaps pipe down. 'Sorry, girls, you're ready for bed. Good-
night. See you in the morning.'

She'd become used to quite a lot of her own company, and
much as she loved having Jess staying, it had been a busy time
and she was all peopled out. It was very pleasant to be home
alone with only a cheese toastie and a glass of Chardonnay for
company. As she opened her mouth to take the first bite of the
sandwich, her phone buzzed on the kitchen table. Ordinarily
she would ignore it, but Jess was out. She felt the fizz of anxiety
she recognised from Jess's teen years, when she lay awake,
awaiting the girl's safe homecoming. It was completely ridiculous. Jess was a grown-up, and this was Berrywick, where
people didn't even lock their front doors. But still. Julia knew
better than most that even Berrywick had a dark side.

Julia put down the toastie and looked at the phone. It was
DC Walter Farmer. Her finger hovered over the green button.
Her toastie would get cold. And *The Great British Bake Off* was
due to start in ten minutes. She looked from the phone to the
toastie, the toastie to the phone. The ringing continued. She
sighed and answered. He was a policeman, after all.

'Hello, Mrs Bird. Sorry to phone so late, it's been a heck of a
day. I didn't have a second to call.'

'No problem, Walter,' Julia said, eyeing her toastie wistfully. 'What's up?'

'Would you be able to come in for fingerprints tomorrow? Forensics has lifted a lot of prints from the van, and they need to eliminate yours. And Jess too, please. I'm sorry to make you come in, I know you were here earlier today, but no one thought to ask you.'

'That's okay. I can come in. What time?'

'Would ten thirty be convenient? Desmond Campbell's funeral is at eleven thirty tomorrow, and DI Gibson wants me to go with her. The fingerprinting only takes a few minutes, and I'll leave for the funeral as soon as we've finished.'

'Right. That's fine with me. Jess isn't here, but it should be okay with her. See you tomorrow, Walter.'

'Good evening, Mrs Bird.'

The next morning, DI Hayley Gibson came into the station as Walter had finished with Julia and Jess. The fingerprinting process had been quick and a lot less messy than they'd expected. No more rolling your finger in ink and pressing it onto paper, it was all digital now. A quick scan and you were on your way. The pocket-sized container of wet wipes in Julia's bag went unused.

'Oh hello, Julia, Jess. Thanks for coming in,' said Hayley. 'That's the end of the forensics, I think. They'll wrap it up now and release the van to the victim's family.'

'Did you find Christopher's fingerprints?' Jess asked.

Hayley looked at the young woman, taken aback at her directness. 'I'm sure you understand that I can't comment on what the forensic team found.'

'Well even if you did, it doesn't mean he killed the caterer. Doesn't Desmond have a wife? Mum says that in most cases it's someone close to the victim. And Christopher isn't—'

'Speaking of which...' Walter cut in. They followed the direction of his gaze to see Peter and Christopher walking into the police station, accompanied by a small dishevelled-looking fellow with tufts of wiry steel-grey hair emerging from his head like a pot scourer.

'Oh!' said Peter, surprised to see his daughter and his ex-wife. 'What are you doing here?'

'Fingerprints.' Julia waved her fingers in demonstration.

He looked from her to Hayley and back, and frowned. 'But they don't think you...'

'No, no. For elimination.'

'Oh. Good. Detective Gibson, this is Scott Lillifield. He'll be representing us going forward.'

The fancy London lawyer was anything but smart – to look at, at least. But it had to be said that he got promptly to work. 'Mr Bird and Mr Carter won't be speaking to the police without me present,' he said, without so much as a hello.

'I want to explain what I was doing,' Christopher said. 'Tell you my side.'

Hayley responded briskly: 'I'm afraid this will have to wait. I only came back to the station to fetch DC Farmer. We are going to Desmond Campbell's funeral.' She looked at her watch. 'We have to leave now, I'm afraid. It starts in fifteen minutes.'

Lillifield looked mildly irritated but didn't protest.

'Can we go, too?' Jess looked at her mother. 'We did find him. I'd like to pay my respects.'

'Yes, I suppose we could go.'

Julia was hardly concentrating on the conversation going on around her. She was still mulling over what Hayley Gibson had said a few sentences ago. That the van would be released to the victim's family.

'Hayley, a moment?' she said, gesturing in the direction of the door. 'It's about the van.'

'Drive with me. You can explain. Mr Bird. Mr Carter. Mr Lillifield. Can we meet later? I should be back here at two.'

'I suppose we will have to wait.' Lillifield looked at his watch and made a bit of a show about being inconvenienced by the country ways, but nodded. 'We'll be here at two. I feel certain that will be the last time you need to speak to my client.'

15

Jess rode the short distance to the church in DC Walter Farmer's car, while her mother drove DI Gibson.

'It's about the van,' Julia said as she started the car. 'Or I should say vans. I've realised that there are two Candy Catering vans. You have Desmond's van, the one he died in, in the police pound. His business partner, Cynthia has another, identical van. I'd thought that it was the same van, but it's not.'

'Okay. But what about it?'

'I was thinking about that footage of the service parking, when Christopher came out. There was Desmond's van and another van there. A very similar-looking van, although we couldn't see the number plates or the side, where the logo might be.'

'I thought it was the florist's van?' said Hayley.

'It's not the florist's van. I've seen it. It's smaller, and it's sage green. And it has black line drawings of daisies on it.'

Hayley gave Julia a long look, and decided not to push the question of where and under what circumstances she happened to have seen the van.

'Are you suggesting the van in the parking lot could have been Cynthia's?'

'That's what I'm saying, Hayley. Or at least, it's worth checking out.'

'She told us that she wasn't there that night,' said Hayley.

'Well, someone was there. Someone with a white van.'

'I'll look into it, but white vans are pretty common. It's a bit of a leap to assume it's hers.'

'Except that there's something else. She lied about what happened that evening. I happened to meet Cynthia...' Julia stopped.

'You what?' Looking over to the detective inspector, Julia saw that her face was stony, her eyes narrowed in anger. 'Have you been interfering again, Julia?'

'Her husband has the pie shop over in Edgeley, and she was there when Jess and I went in for pies.'

'Well, that seems an unlikely coincidence.'

'Let me get to the point,' Julia said, keen to move on from the question of how she actually came by this information. 'People in the shop were talking about what happened to Desmond and I heard Cynthia saying how kind he was, that she'd spoken to him that evening, and he told her not to come and help him clear up, that she should get an early night. That they had such a great partnership, and she was so sad.'

'So?'

'Well, we know that's not how it went. From what Diane said, Cynthia was furious with him and said all sorts of horrible things. She refused to go and help him clear up. And she wanted to end the partnership.'

'She wasn't on the witness stand under oath, Julia. She was chatting to a customer in the shop. She might massage the truth a bit so as not to speak ill of the dead.'

'Or, perhaps she *did* go over there, not to help clear up, but to kill him. And she said otherwise because she wants it known about the village that she wasn't there.'

'The one thing that is consistent in what she's telling everyone is that she didn't go there that night. It's what she told us, and on both versions that you've heard, that remains the same.'

'That's what makes me think,' said Julia. 'It's like she's so intent on communicating that she wasn't there that she's lost track of what she has said about it.'

After a moment's thought, Hayley said brusquely, 'I'll look into it.'

Julia slowed down outside the church. There were quite a few cars parked along the road, and people walking towards the church. She drove on. 'Desmond Campbell was a popular fellow. Although clearly not with everyone, given the circumstances.'

'And my job is to find out who hated him enough to kill him.'

'Well it won't be Christopher,' she said, slowing and pulling into a parking space some way from the church. 'Someone else killed Desmond Campbell. If you don't like Cynthia as a suspect, what about the wife? Have you spoken to her?'

'Of course. She was the first person we spoke to. It seems to be one of those marriages full of separations and reconciliations. The food business isn't easy on relationships. He worked all hours, he was obsessed with food, with trying new recipes. He wasn't ready to have a child, which she wanted. She didn't even try to hide the fact that their marriage had been through some very rocky patches. But as it happens she was at a book club weekend in Gloucester on the night he died. We checked it out. She was there.'

'Oh. Well. Not her then. Unless she got someone else to do it?' Julia glanced at Hayley to see her reaction to this idea.

Hayley shook her head. 'Unlikely. It's not the sort of thing you get someone else to do. More of an opportunistic situation, I'd have thought. Besides, he was bringing home the bacon with that catering company. It was doing well, and provided her with a good lifestyle. She said she didn't know what she was going to do without him to run it. She didn't know if she could manage, even with Cynthia as a partner. She doesn't know about food, apparently, which is quite a disadvantage in a caterer, I would have thought. I'm of the opinion that she didn't kill him.'

'What about a girlfriend? Or a rival? There must be other suspects.'

'Well, there's nothing like a funeral to bring out all interested parties. Let's go and see what we can find.'

Hayley strode off to the little grey stone church, looking like a woman on a mission. Julia looked around the pretty grassy churchyard of ancient graves, their headstones worn and leaning at odd angles, like wayward teeth. A few had crosses, or statues of angels. Some were well tended and planted with flowers, but Julia preferred the ones that had sunk into the earth, covered in dandelions visited by bees, the names of the dead erased by time and weather. Some were double burial plots, husband and wife, together for eternity; Julia hoped they were happy with that arrangement. Eternity is a long time. She averted her eyes from the tiniest graves, and the heartache they must have held, looking, instead, at the crowd that was gathered at the door of the church.

Jess was talking to Dylan and Kevin. She spotted her mother and waved her over. As Julia got there, the crowd began to move into the little church, as if by some silent signal, and their little group followed, filing into a pew about halfway down.

There were other familiar faces. Angela the florist sat near the back, without her denim apron for a change. A man –

possibly her husband; Julia recognised him from the van – was next to her. Arabella Princeton, the party planner, was in the row in front of Julia, Jess and Dylan. Cynthia came in, looking thin and drawn, arm in arm with a lanky fellow who Julia recognised from her Facebook stalking as her pie-maker husband, Tim. Cynthia nodded to Dylan, who murmured an awkward hello. She sat down next to Arabella, who placed her hand on her arm and spoke to her in a stage whisper. 'Not to detract from the terrible tragedy, but I think it's wonderful how you're soldiering on, Cynthia.'

'Thank you, Arabella. I have to, don't I? It's what Desmond would have wanted.'

'Oh, he would! The show must go on.'

A rustle of movement, a craning of necks. An older couple came unsteadily down the aisle once everyone was seated. It was impossible to know whether she held him up, or he held her. They seemed to lean into each other, like those trees and creepers that entwine until you can't tell which is which, but you know that if one went, the other would go with it. They walked to the front of the church, to the first pew, their faces glazed with shock and disbelief. The grieving parents. A few steps behind them were two younger women. One was the spitting image of Desmond, the same black hair, the intense hawkish face. She even had the tattoos, albeit a lighter smattering and more delicate designs. The other woman couldn't have been more different – a chubby, cherubic little person with freckled cheeks and long waves of golden hair, who might have been lifted from a Renaissance painting. They followed Desmond's parents into the family pew. Julia took them to be Desmond's sister and wife, respectively.

The service was short and filled with ambiguity. The cause of death was unspecified in the priest's address, and hovered delicately in the air as 'a terrible thing' and 'an awful tragedy'. There was no mention of ill intent, only that Desmond was 'taken too soon'. Julia wondered if the investigation into his suspicious death had somehow been kept a secret – it seemed almost impossible, given the efficiency of the Berrywick gossip mill – or if it was not being mentioned as a matter of courtesy.

The priest intoned that 'we know not when death may come', which came over as rather threatening, Julia thought. Sympathy was extended to Desmond's parents, to his younger sister Anna, and to his wife, Goldie. There was no mention of the couple's troubles, of course. Goldie looked stunned, but shed not a tear.

The congregation sang 'Amazing Grace' surprisingly tunefully, and the priest gave a blessing and invited them into the church hall for tea. They all stood as the grieving family passed back down the aisle, and in the row in front of Julia, Arabella loudly picked up her conversation with Cynthia where she'd left off.

'Now, are you sure you can manage Lady Wellmouth's daughter's bridal on Thursday? I hate to ask, but I do need to be certain.'

'I am one hundred per cent sure. Penelope Wellmouth's bridal shower will be perfect. It will be the talk of the town.'

'It's just that if I'm going to have to ask In Good Taste to step in – and I would only do this to save you the pressure – I should let Henrietta know today. She's already offered—'

'Do *not* phone Henrietta. Desmond would *hate* that. You know how awful she has been to him. You have nothing to worry about. It's all organised.'

'Is it? Are you absolutely sure?'

Cynthia started counting things off on her fingers with a slightly manic air, while keeping her voice to an acceptable level. 'I've briefed the pastry chef. The cakes are going to be astonishing. As for the sandwiches, the Scottish smoked salmon has been flown in. Farmer Brown will deliver his organic free-range eggs. The cucumbers will be picked fresh from the greenhouse the afternoon before. Couldn't be fresher. Lady Wellmouth will be delighted with everything, I promise.'

'You know I'm not one to speak ill of the dead, but I have to say, that business with the nuts at the wedding was—'

'A terrible mistake. It won't happen again.'

'If you're absolutely sure.'

'I am. Arabella, this is entirely my business now, and Desmond's legacy. I'll do whatever it takes to honour his vision and his hard work, and the company we built together.'

Arabella patted her arm and said in a voice dripping with sympathy, 'That's terribly brave of you, Cynthia. I do so admire you. You have my support.' She paused, and added ominously, 'Just don't make me regret it.'

16

Julia found Jess with Dylan at the tea table outside the church. The young are very resilient, she thought, watching her daughter's strong, straight teeth bite through the strawberry jam and whipped cream, and into the scone beneath. The girl chewed and swallowed eagerly, her appetite unaffected by the presence of death. On a bright autumn day, and with a new flirtation afoot and a good tea in the offing, it was easy to overlook the brief and transient nature of human life and the inevitability of its end. Jess wiped a blob of cream from her lip and licked it off her finger.

A cup of tea, thought Julia, and then she would leave. It wasn't like she was a great friend of the deceased. If she was honest with herself, it was curiosity that had her at this funeral, and even Julia had to admit that this wasn't the most laudable motivation. She picked up a cup, and teabag, and joined the inevitable queue to the urn. Standing in front of her was Angela, the florist.

'Lovely funeral,' said Julia, wanting to speak to the woman who created such beautiful arrangements. 'Did you do the flowers? They were lovely.'

Angela smiled at Julia. 'I did, thank you,' she said, unsurprised to be recognised. 'It was the least I could do.' Her eyes filled up with tears.

'Were you good friends with Desmond?'

As Angela opened her mouth to answer, the man that she had been with in the church seemed to step out of nowhere. 'Darling,' he said, gently touching Angela on the shoulder. 'Have you got my tea?'

Instead of pointing out that he could clearly see she was in the queue still, as Julia was tempted to do, Angela just smiled. 'I'll have it for you in two shakes, love,' she said, and her partner smiled and kissed her on the cheek.

Honestly, thought Julia, as she watched the couple get the tea together, she could maybe learn from the lovely Angela. A very peaceful person to be around. As lovely as her flowers.

She sighed and followed them to help herself to tea, the chance of any small talk about Desmond lost.

'Jess,' Julia called, once her tea was finished. 'I'm going home. Do you want to come?' Her daughter looked over to her and said, with a wave, 'No thanks, I'll walk. See you later, Mum.' She quickly turned her gaze back to Dylan, whose eyes were already waiting for hers.

Julia checked her phone when she got to the car and saw a missed call and then a text message from Peter, asking her to phone when she could. She hit dial before she turned the ignition.

'Thanks for getting back to me, Julia. I wanted to update you on what happened with the police and the lawyer. Are you home?'

'I'm in the car, about to leave the caterer's funeral. But I can talk now.'

'Why don't I come round a bit later? We can talk in person.'

'Okay, yes, that's fine. Come over. Give me a few hours. I've got some errands to run, and Jake needs his walk.'

'I'm dropping Christopher somewhere at five. I'll come after that.'

At five fifteen he was on her doorstep, peering over the top of a large paper bag.

'I was starving,' he said, wiping his feet and walking through the front door. 'I got us a few odds and ends from the deli. A late afternoon snack or early supper, however you want to look at it.'

'I'm starving too, actually,' she said, leading the way into the kitchen. 'I had a giant cream scone at the funeral, which meant I wasn't hungry for lunch. I had an apple at about three.'

'Well, you won't be starving after this, I got rather carried away. They do have lovely local delicacies, don't they? I can't resist the Cotswolds cheese. I'd be the size of a house if I lived here.' He put the paper bag down on the table and looked around. 'Where's Jess?'

'She's out. There's a young man, his name is Dylan. She met him at The Swan when we had lunch there the day before the wedding. He was at the funeral and she stayed to chat to him. I think they... like each other.'

Peter raised his eyebrows in surprise. 'Well, I never. A holiday romance in the Cotswolds.'

'I'm not sure if it's a romance. Yet. But she could do worse – he's a good chap. I know him a bit from my book club.'

'I have to wonder, what kind of fellow would join a village book club with a lot of middle-aged ladies?' Peter sounded judgemental.

'Rather a nice young man, actually. And we're not all women. There's Sean.'

'Noted. But even so.'

'Dylan's the quiet type. He did spend a couple of months slumped silently in a chair, but now he's started talking, it turns out he's clever and interesting. He's studying English literature, and he works for Candy Catering. He works – worked – for Desmond.'

'One of the young chaps who was at the wedding? Not the spiky-haired one, the other, darker one? I noticed him chatting to Jess.'

'That's him.'

'Heavens, that's all rather close to home.'

'That's what it's like in a village. Anyway, they're just friends, as far as I know, but there does seem to be a bit of a spark. Anyway, she phoned earlier and said she'll be back soon. You could text her, let her know you're here, she might hurry back.'

'I don't want to bother her. Let's you and I eat.'

They put the food out, falling into the casual routine of decades. She fetched a wooden board and a bread knife. He unpacked a loaf of rye bread, a few tubs of pâtés and spreads, a jar of olives and a wedge of cheese, and began to arrange things nicely on the board. She put two plates on the table. Two knives. Two forks. It was a familiar feeling, except that they were in her kitchen in the Cotswolds, rather than their shared kitchen in London. It was her space. He was a guest.

'So where's Christopher? Where did you drop him?' Julia spoke from the fridge, where she was rummaging for a tub of baby tomatoes that she knew was in there but couldn't see.

'At the spa down the road. I booked him a massage as a treat.'

'Ooh, how lovely. A massage,' Julia said, automatically rolling her own neck and shoulders, feeling the stiffness, the clicks and pulls that seemed to arrive in increasing numbers post-fifty. A massage would be exactly the thing to sort out those sore, tight muscles, but she wouldn't spend that sort of money on herself.

'Poor thing. He's been so stressed with all that's happened since our wedding. And before that, the organisation, which was really mostly his doing. Then the poor caterer's death. I thought a nice massage would be good for him. Christopher does love a good spa, and this one has all the facilities. He's going to use the steam room and whatever else they have. He'll be there for ages.'

She remembered how thoughtful Peter could be. She'd been the beneficiary of similar small acts of kindness. She felt momentarily sorry for herself – the non-recipient of the massage – and then pulled herself together. She had a good life, a life she had made and chosen. She had a kind and clever new lover, and good friends. She had a devoted dog. Her daughter was staying. And she could simply pay for her own massage at any time.

The enumeration of her many blessings was interrupted by Peter's continuing explanation of Christopher's woes. 'And of course this morning, we were with the police and the lawyer. I must say, we've spent far too much time in the Berrywick police station, which does not feature on any list of Ten Things You Must Do in the Cotswolds.'

'Let alone, Ten Must-Visits for Honeymooners,' she said with a laugh. This was the sort of banter she and Peter had been good at when they were married. It felt familiar, and also strange.

She put the tomatoes in a bowl on the table and sat down, more serious. 'Is that at least sorted out now the lawyer is here? Christopher said there was an explanation for his being in the parking area. What was it? What did he tell the police?'

Peter blushed – he had always been quick to flush at the slightest awkwardness. 'He was planning a surprise. For me.'

'So what was the furtive sneaking around for?'

He cleared his throat and reached for a knife to cut the bread, using it as an excuse to turn his face – now a colour approaching cerise – from her gaze. He focused on cutting that rye loaf with the deep concentration of a surgeon operating on a patient's brain.

'He wanted to... ahem... pretty the room up.'

She waited.

'The bedroom.'

'Oh.'

'He was looking for flowers. Some petals. Ahem. For scattering, I believe. Hhhhmmm. For the, um, bed.'

Julia felt her own cheeks growing warm in response to the surprising and embarrassing turn the conversation had taken. 'Ah, I see,' she said brightly. 'Well, that explains why he was wandering around looking at the vans.'

'Yes. Apparently he went out there thinking he might find the florist and she might have something in the van, some flowers he could use. Or perhaps find the caterer and get some chocolates. It wasn't very well thought through, by the sound of things. More of a spur-of-the-moment thing.'

'An impulsive romantic gesture. Well, it was a kind thought.'

He smiled at her, grateful for her understanding. 'Yes, he's very kind. And a bit impulsive. The trouble is, he does look rather guilty in the video.'

She reached for a tub of hummus and fiddled with the plastic lid, trying to remove it without tearing a hole in her thumb. 'I suppose it did look suspicious, under the circumstances. All that skulking around in the dark, trying the doors of the vans. One can see how Hayley might have thought the worst.'

'Yes, especially after everyone had seen him get cross with Desmond.' The word 'cross' was rather an understatement, Julia thought, but didn't say. 'And then when Desmond turned up dead in the van, well...'

'But now Christopher has explained it to the police, and his lawyer was there to smooth things along, surely that's all been cleared up?' Julia said hopefully. She finally freed the lid from the tub and put them both down on the table. She reached for a jar of olives and recommenced battle.

'Well, it's been cleared up, to an extent. But not entirely. He has explained what happened, but it's really only his word.' Peter took the jar from her and opened it with a satisfying snap.

'Well, what about the florist? Can't she vouch for him?'

'No. He didn't find her. She wasn't there. It seems he poked around for a bit, trying to find someone who might help, but he didn't come across anyone, so he gave up on the idea and came back to the party.'

'I see the problem. There's no proof, no evidence, no witness to corroborate, no video footage after the fuse blew. They have to take Christopher's version of events on his say-so.'

'Exactly. DI Gibson asked us not to leave the area until she's looked into it further. Hopefully they'll find some corroborating evidence quickly.'

'Or,' said Julia slowly, 'better yet – find the murderer.'

Jake, who had been lying quietly in the kitchen doorway with Henny Penny tucked in between his neck and his front legs, leapt to his feet, sending the chicken flapping furiously out. Peter nearly jumped out of his skin at the sudden commotion and the hysterical squawk. Penny headed out grumpily to the garden to join the fowl, and Jake ran to the front door, which opened that very minute to reveal Jess, followed by Dylan.

Jake welcomed Jess as if she were a soldier returning from a perilous three years on the frontline. He howled and barked and jumped and spun around. She bent down to stroke him, speaking calmly as he settled down to some gentle whimpering and whining.

When Jake had finished his performance, Julia was able to

get a word in, 'Come through to the kitchen. Your dad's here. We both missed lunch, so we were about to have a snack.'

Jess gave her father a hug, and held on to him, while beckoning Dylan over. Seeing them side by side, Julia was struck by the similarities between father and daughter which had become more pronounced in the years Jess had been away. While Jess looked like Julia, she had Peter's long-limbed build and his mannerisms – the way they held themselves – the little tilt of the head to the right, the way they crossed their arms when they had to stand for a while.

As Jess did the introductions, Dylan shook Peter's hand, ducking his head but meeting the older man's eyes.

'Pleased to meet you, Dylan. I recognise you from the wedding. I saw you working there, didn't I?'

'Yes, I work part-time for the caterers.'

'I'm sorry, Desmond Campbell's death must be hard for you and your colleagues,' said Peter.

'Yeah. Very sad. He was a hard taskmaster, a perfectionist, you know. Intense. Some people didn't like him, but I did.'

'But at least the business isn't going to close,' Jess said. 'So people will still have work.'

'Ah, that must be a relief,' said Julia, who already knew this from her eavesdropping, but was interested to hear the official version.

'Yeah. Big relief. That job has been good to me. I would be in trouble without it,' Dylan said with a frown. 'But I spoke to Desmond's partner, Cynthia, at the funeral.'

'I saw her there,' said Julia. 'I recognised her from the pie shop.'

'That's right. She helps her husband out at the shop sometimes. You might have seen her at the wedding, too. Anyway, she says she's going to keep Candy Catering going, which is good. I mean, it doesn't help Desmond, poor guy. But...'

'But it does mean Dylan and the rest of the staff still have jobs,' Jess said.

'Yeah, a couple of things on the weekend, so I'll be all right for the month, at least. And I help out at The Swan when they're short-staffed. So there's that.'

'Good for you, Dylan,' Peter said. 'It sounds like you've got yourself well sorted.'

17

'Thanks for coming in at such short notice,' Wilma said, bounding up to the front door of Second Chances at precisely 9.01 a.m., her blonde bob swinging side to side like a glossy metronome keeping time to some cheerfully efficient waltz.

'No trouble,' Julia said. 'I managed to rearrange things quite easily.'

Wilma dug into the pockets of her cerise puffa she had on over her customary leisure/athletic wear, and pulled out the keys to the glass door.

'Diane had to take Mark to the hospital. He hurt his ankle badly and he needs an X-ray to see if it was broken. And of course he can't drive himself. Because of the ankle. Ah, there we go.'

She turned the lock and opened the door. Julia followed her in.

'Mondays can be busy, so I appreciate the extra pair of hands.'

'Yes. I imagine there's a certain type of person who does a big clear-out over the weekend and then loses no time in offloading the offending items.'

'Exactly. Can't wait another minute to get rid of those boxes! Not that I'm complaining, mind you. We always need new stock.'

'As long as it's not ancient yellow paperbacks,' Julia joked, referring to the great boxes of dated books that seemed to reside in every elderly person's home in the entire county, and that every charity shop received in huge numbers, and that not a single person wanted to buy.

'We'll get those whether we want them or not,' Wilma said with a roll of her eyes. 'Thank heavens for the charities that still want them.'

They hadn't even got to their first cup of tea when their observation about the Sunday clear-outs and the busy Mondays was borne out. The bell at the front door tinkled merrily, heralding the arrival of a large cardboard box with two short denim-clad legs staggering under it.

'Let me help you with that!' Julia said, leaping up from her chair and bounding across to the door. She got her hands in under the box as it started to slip from the bearer's grasp. It listed alarmingly, but between the two of them, they managed to hang on to it and manhandle it down to the floor. It fell the last inch or two, landing with a thump, and a lot of metallic clanging and clattering. Julia straightened up and found herself face to face with Desmond's pretty freckled wife, who, it turned out, was holding the other side of the box.

'Thank you. You got it just in time,' said the woman. Goldie, that was her name. It suited her looks so perfectly that Julia imagined it must be a nickname. 'You're welcome. It's a big heavy box. Far too unwieldy for one person.'

'I did a big clear out on the weekend and wanted to get it out of the house as soon as I could.'

Wilma shot a smug 'you see?' look in Julia's direction.

'Well, thank you for bringing it to Second Chances. Your

donation will contribute to a good cause.' Julia spoke gently, in the assumption that this clear-out wasn't your average overdue spring-cleaning.

'Now, what do we have here?' Wilma asked, who had made no such assumption.

'Cooking things, mostly. Utensils, baking trays, cake tins, and so on.' She sounded vague, almost as if she didn't know or care what they were.

'Kitchenware is always in demand. I think it's because of the television. The celebrity chefs,' said Wilma, who was clearly unaware of the identity of the donor, and thus oblivious to the fact that the donations were likely the possessions of the murdered and recently buried Desmond Campbell. Julia gave Wilma a look intended to encourage her to calm down a bit, but either Julia wasn't very accomplished at non-verbal communication, or Wilma was hopeless at taking a hint. She reached in and took out a fistful of whisks and spatulas, waving them about. 'Oh, these will be snapped up. Everyone thinks they're Jamie Oliver these days, don't they? They're all making their own gnocchi. And preserves. What's with preserves? Everyone makes them, but no one eats them.'

'I don't cook, myself. These are my husband's things.'

'Well, lucky you!' Wilma said, completely ignoring Julia's attempts to bore into her brain with her eyeballs and shut the chatter down. 'I wish I had a husband who could cook. It must be marvellous.'

'Believe me, it's not all it's cracked up to be,' said Gloria. The poor young woman looked as if she was poised between fury and weeping. 'Not by a long shot.'

'Oh.' Wilma finally read the atmosphere of the room and stopped her wittering. 'I'm sorry. I have been going on a bit.'

'That's all right. It's not your fault. He's dead, my husband. I don't want any of his stuff.'

Julia stepped into the awkward moment. 'I'm very sorry for your loss. We'd be glad to take it, if you're sure you're ready to give it all away?'

'I'm sure. There's more in the boot of my car. I don't want any of it.'

'Let's make you a cup of tea, and you can sit quietly here while we get everything out of the car. How does that sound?'

'I'd like that, thank you,' she said meekly, taking the seat that Julia offered at the sales counter. 'It's been a rough few days. I've hardly slept. I'm Goldie, by the way.'

'I'm Julia and this is Wilma. Wilma, if you do the tea, I'll get the boxes.'

Wilma nodded in agreement, and disappeared into the back room, looking somewhat shamefaced at her succession of blunders.

When Julia came back with two big bags of clothing, Wilma had produced three mugs of tea and a plate of biscuits, and was sharing her own story.

'My Nigel died two years ago, so I know how hard it is. Lung cancer, it was. Terrible.'

'I'm sorry, that must have been awful for you.'

'It was, but it's true what they say, the pain does get better. You think it won't, but it does. It comes in waves, and it takes time, but you won't always feel this bad.'

'Right now I'm mostly furious, to be honest.'

'Grief affects us in strange ways,' Julia said, dropping the bags heavily on the floor. 'It's not unusual to feel angry. Or to go into "sort things out" mode, and clear out the cupboards. You can't bear to look at the person's things.'

'Those are Desmond's chef's whites. He was a chef.'

'Desmond Campbell?' Wilma asked. 'Oh goodness, I'm sorry. I heard. What a terrible thing.'

'It is. Terrible. We had been having some troubles the last

while. He even moved out for a bit. Things had been difficult, but we went to couple's counselling, and things were so much better. I hoped we might start a...'

Goldie's words wavered and caught in her throat. Julia laid a hand on her shoulder, but said nothing.

'Well, we won't be starting a family, of course. And now it turns out I've not only lost my husband, but the business, too. He left it to his business partner. Not a thought for me.'

'Oh my goodness, I'm so sorry,' Julia said. 'So Cynthia will have the whole company?'

'How do you know Cynthia?' Goldie asked, her freckled, cherubic face suddenly hard and suspicious. 'Is she a friend of yours?'

'No, I don't actually know her. I knew that they were partners in the catering firm though. My ex-husband used Candy Catering for his wedding.'

Goldie looked mildly confused by that statement, so Wilma added helpfully, 'His wedding to someone else.' She handed Julia the third mug of tea, already lightly milked as Julia liked it. She smiled her thanks, while Goldie went on, bitterly.

'Bloody men. Got himself some pretty young lass, did he? I bet it was someone at work, that's where they find them.'

'No, actually, it wasn't like that. Not at all.'

Wilma gave a snort of amusement.

'Well, if you're expecting anything to come your way when he goes, you'd better check his will is all I can say,' said Goldie, glaring at Julia as if Julia might disagree. 'Turns out Desmond changed his will a couple of months ago, when we separated, even though we were having the couple's counselling! And it looks like he never got round to changing it back. Or he didn't really care.'

She paused for a moment, but it seemed she wasn't yet done. 'I'd been working at the company too, doing the books and the ordering and all that. Running the show, really, the back end at least. But I left when we had our troubles. It was too stressful, us both being there. I needed some distance from him. And from all the girls, you know – the waitresses, the sous chefs, the suppliers. They all had their eyes on him, and he liked the attention, didn't do a thing to stop it. So I got another job, and they found an office manager for Candy Catering.' She stopped again to take a long breath and then a long slurp of her tea. 'I didn't know until the will was read after the funeral that I'd been cut out, and Cynthia was cut in. She got his half of the catering company when he died, and I got a few bob and a cupboard full of chef's whites and cook books.'

They sat for a minute thinking their own thoughts. Julia's were whizzing about her head like pinballs in one of those old-fashioned machines, careening about hitting buzzers, lighting up lights, disappearing into hopeless holes only to reappear from some other corner. What, if anything, did all this mean, in terms of the murder investigation? She needed to tell Hayley. She needed to find out more from Goldie. She was trying to frame an acceptable question for the angry woman, when the door opened and a young couple came in and the moment was lost.

'Looking for a coat?' the girl said. 'Something for winter?'

Wilma got up with some reluctance – it seemed a pity to leave a good story halfway through – and went over to show them the relevant rails.

'I'll get the rest of the boxes from the car,' Julia said and headed back out to the road. Two more trips and the boot was empty. The teacups too.

'Thank you for the donations, Goldie. It's much appreci-ated. I'm sorry that the circumstances are so difficult and painful.'

'That they are. That they are. And you know the worst part?' She brought her face close to Julia's and lowered her voice so that the customers couldn't hear. 'The police believe that Desmond was murdered. They say it wasn't an accident at all. Can you believe it? That means someone's walking around, free as you please, having killed my husband.'

'I'm so sorry, Goldie. I hope the police find who did this.'

'Only if I don't find them first.'

18

The house was richly fragrant. There was ginger, garlic and a whiff of something sweet in the air that greeted Julia.

'I'm in the kitchen,' Jess called, when she heard the front door open. 'Dylan's coming for supper. I made enough for Sean, I thought you might want to invite him.'

'Wow, Jess, this smells incredible!' Julia said. 'What are you making?'

'A hot sour soup. I did a cooking class in Hong Kong and this was my favourite dish. And so easy. I thought I'd get it started, it's quick to finish right before we eat. 'I've turned it off. What's the time now?'

'Three o'clock.'

'Dylan will be here soon. He's coming early so we can have a walk before supper.'

'I'll ring Sean, see what his plans are.'

Sean, as it turned out, had a light afternoon at the surgery. His last patient was at three fifteen. He would fetch Leo and join the walk and the supper.

'He will be here before four. Let's have tea and biscuits to tide us over. I didn't have much of a lunch,' said Julia.

'Tea we can do, but I'm afraid I finished the biscuits,' Jess said. 'I can't help myself. It was the Jammie Dodgers. What am I, five years old?'

'Don't worry. I'll have a piece of toast. We'll get more biscuits tomorrow. See if there's some long-lost flavour you haven't found yet. Oh, that reminds me, I've got another treat for you! Another blast from the past. How could I forget? We'll go there this very afternoon, as soon as the chaps arrive.'

'Where? What is it?'

'Not telling. It's a surprise.'

An hour later, the two couples and two dogs were in front of a little shop with a red-and-white sign saying simply 'Sweeties'. 'Oh, Mum, look at it, it's adorable. I love it!' Jess said, her hands clasped in delight as she surveyed the tiny shopfront with its lead-paned front window.

'Wait till you see the inside,' said Dylan, regarding her with a smile. 'You're gonna faint.'

A little sign said, 'Dogs with well-behaved owners are welcome!' Jess squealed again, and made Sean and Julia pose next to it with Leo and Jake, while she took a picture on her phone.

'Try and look well-behaved!' she said, which made them both laugh. She took another pic of them laughing, and said, 'One for the Gram.'

'Instagram,' Dylan said helpfully, seeing the blank looks.

'Come on then,' said Julia, leading the way. They went in.

'Hello. Oh, Dr Sean!' the old lady behind the counter exclaimed in delight at the sight of the doctor. 'Well, this is a nice surprise. And your family.'

'Friends,' he said. 'Good friends. And how are you, Dora, have you been keeping well?'

'Oh, very well!' she said. She did indeed seem in excellent health and spirits, with her peaches and cream complexion and a halo of soft white curls. She was small and round, like a chubby cherub, Julia always thought. Maybe all the sugar kept her sweet-natured.

'Oh my word, dolly mixtures! I haven't seen those in years.' Jess was in ecstasies, peering into the glass jars ranged along the counter and exclaiming. 'Ooh, and humbugs. And sherbet lemons!'

Dora watched her with a smile.

'Jess has been out of the country for a few years. It appears they don't have sherbet lemons in Hong Kong,' Julia explained.

Dora handed her a couple of small paper bags. 'Here you go, love. Help yourself.'

Jess reached into the jar, picked up the scoop, and scooped up a generous helping of sherbet lemons.

'And what do you fancy?' she asked Dylan.

'I'm a pear drop man myself,' he said. She reached into another jar, dug in and popped a few of the green pears into a bag, which she handed to him.

'Sean?'

'Liquorice, please.' She scooped again.

'And, Mum, I know you love your toffees. Here we are, something for everyone!'

Once sufficient variety had been achieved, and everyone's favourites included, Jess handed the packets over for weighing. There was a brief dispute as to who should pay, but Sean won that round. The young took their packets and the two dogs outside. The little shop was bursting at the seams with the four humans and two canines, and there was only so much good behaviour and patience one could reasonably expect from a dog in a sweet shop.

'You're a good man, Dr Sean,' Dora said, taking his money. She had clearly worked out the relationships by this point, because she turned to Julia and said, 'You've got a good one there. He was such a wonder when my dear Fred was ill with the cancer. Even came to the house to check on us. You don't see that these days, you know. A good man and a good doctor, he is.'

Sean, who wasn't comfortable with compliments at the best of times, blushed and said gruffly, 'Ah well, Dora, glad I could be of assistance. I was only doing what I was trained to do.'

'More than. You helped us right to the end, Dr Sean. You knew what I went through, your poor Annie having been through the same, not so long before. Ooh, I was fit for nothing with all the stress and the sadness. I lost my Fred, and then I nearly lost our shop, you know.' This last comment was addressed to Julia. 'Couldn't find the will. And then all that business with the bank and the insurance. Oh, it was terrible. I didn't feel at all well, remember, Dr Sean?'

'I do, Dora. It was a hard time. I'm pleased to see you looking so well, and the shop is obviously flourishing.'

'Ah, people still like the old things, you'd be surprised.' She handed him his change and reached for a Fry's Chocolate Cream. She slipped the bar to him with a smile and a wink, as if he were a little boy. 'A little something extra for you, dear.'

Julia and Sean exited the shop to find the young deep in conversation with Aunt Edna, who was swaying in the light breeze, her long scarves fluttering. She was so tall and thin that she looked like a maypole with ribbons, but minus the dancers, of course.

'Didn't I tell you?' she asked Julia triumphantly, raising a bony finger to point at Jess and Dylan. Julia had no idea what she was talking about. 'Love is in the air. All's fair in love and walks, I always say. Don't you?'

This last question appeared to be addressed to Jake, who didn't seem to know what response was required of him. He looked at Julia pleadingly, as if she might assist.

The breeze caught one of Edna's scarves and lifted it off her shoulders. Dylan grabbed at it, but the wind whipped it out of his hand. It skittered along the pavement remarkably nimbly. He chased after the purple scarf, but as he got to it, the breeze snatched it from his grasp. After a few failed attempts, grabbing and missing rather comically, he caught it.

'Got it!' he said, waving it triumphantly as he walked back in their direction. 'Here you are, Aunt Edna.'

'It's the wrong one,' she said. 'Mine's purple.'

There was an awkward moment, Dylan looking down at the purple scarf, and then up at Jess and Julia for ideas. Jake looked away, determined to have nothing to do with it. Everyone was stumped.

'Sorry. My mistake,' Dylan said, and turned back the way he'd come, the scarf tucked into his hand. He reached into the box hedge and pretended to pull the scarf out. 'Here it is! Is this the one?'

He handed it to Edna, who inspected it carefully and said, 'That's the one. Thank you. You're a good boy.'

'No trouble, Aunt Edna. Can I offer you a pear drop?' She reached her bony fingers into the packet he held out to her.

'He's a keeper,' Edna said to Jess in a stage whisper so loud that Dora must have heard it from inside the shop. 'A lighthouse keeper,' she added cryptically, winding the purple scarf around her neck. 'A flame, aflame. Keep the flame alight.'

And she popped the pear drop into her mouth.

'They say virtue is its own reward, but a chocolate is a nice bonus,' Julia said, accepting the Fry's Bar from Sean and taking a bite. 'Yum. It pays to be a good chap.'

'Ah, well,' Sean said, embarrassed. 'It wasn't much. Poor Dora. She was in a bad way for a while.'

'She always looks so sweet and cheerful, it's sad to imagine it.'

'Well, death and its administrative hurdles are enough to take the good cheer out of anyone. The shock of it all knocked her sideways. Luckily they found the will, and sorted out the insurance issue – I forget now exactly what it was – and she kept the business, and she has managed it without him all these years.'

They walked slowly, enjoying the chocolate and the late afternoon light that illuminated the golden-hued stone of the cottages that they passed. The trees along the river were in their full autumn finery. The air was clean and crisp.

Ahead of them, Dylan and Jess walked so close that their shoulders touched and their hands brushed as they walked. Julia noticed that they were almost exactly the same height, now that Dylan was walking tall and not slouching, and their hair was almost exactly the same colour. Which was, in fact, almost the same colour as Jake, a deep chocolatey auburn, all three of them glowing richly in the last of the afternoon sun.

Jess had Jake on a lead and Dylan had Leo, each dog trotting along ahead of its human, both behaving impeccably, tails wagging in time with each other like windscreen wipers. The young couple were oblivious to the pretty light, it seemed, and to the fiery autumn leaves and the fine quality of the fresh country air. They were concerned only with each other, their heads turning to each other as they spoke. Snatches of words reached Julia on the breeze, but she couldn't hear what they were talking about. Whatever it was, they certainly had a lot to say. Chat, chat, chat. And every now and then they'd break into laughter at something one of them said.

They looked so happy and carefree. So *young*. They weren't talking about death and wills and sadness, that's for sure.

Julia thought about poor Goldie's recent discovery on the subject of death and wills and sadness. She filled Sean in on the young widow's visit to the shop to dump Desmond's belongings, and what she'd said about the company and the will. 'Poor woman, can you imagine? She buried her husband, and a few hours later, when the will was read, discovered that his half of the catering company had been left to his business partner, not to her, his wife.'

'She didn't know?'

'Apparently not. They were having problems, she and Desmond. She'd stopped working there, and she'd moved out of their house for a bit, but was back, according to Goldie. She had no idea until Saturday afternoon that the will had been changed.'

'Makes you wonder why and when it was changed...'

'Oh my lord, why didn't I think of it!' she said, interrupting him, struck by the realisation. 'Goldie didn't know the company wasn't hers, but someone else did.'

He stopped too, and turned to face her. 'Who? And how do you know?'

'Cynthia, his partner. I was sitting behind her at the funeral. The way she was talking, she knew the business was hers.'

'And that was...'

'That was on Saturday *morning*. The will was only read that *evening*. Sean, Cynthia knew *before* the reading of the will that she owned the company.'

19

Julia had phoned Hayley as soon as she got home, and the detective had taken the new information seriously, at least.

'He left the business to his partner?' she'd asked, incredulous.

'Yes. And she knew about it, even before the will was read.'

'Cynthia didn't mention it when we spoke to her today. Not that she was asked directly. She was too busy trying to explain why she'd lied about being on the scene.'

'So she was there?'

'Now she says that they *did* have a fight and she said she wouldn't go and help, but then she felt bad. When she got there, he apologised to her and said he'd do it himself. So both versions were true. There was a fight, but their last conversation was amicable.'

'Except for the part where she lied to you about it in the first place.'

Hayley sighed. 'Yes, except for that. She says she panicked. It happens.'

Rather unexpectedly, Julia had a lower tolerance for lying to the police than Hayley did. 'It happens if you've got something to hide. And now it turns out that she inherits the business and she knew she would. She might have been worried he'd change the will back,' she said.

'So she murdered him?' Hayley sounded sceptical.

'I've heard of stranger reasons for a murder. We both have.'

'True,' said Hayley. 'I'll get her in for a follow-up interview. I must say, you do manage to stumble upon a lot of information.'

'I keep my ears open. It's my training,' Julia said. 'Also, I'm naturally nosy.'

Hayley gave a snort of a laugh at Julia's honesty. 'Well, thanks for the info.'

'You're welcome.'

Julia dug a cup of dog pellets from the big bucket at the kitchen door. Jake sat waiting, as he'd been taught, but with every nerve and muscle straining in anticipation of his supper. The pellets clattered into the metal bowl. A strand of saliva dropped from the side of his mouth.

She poured a second cup of pellets for Leo, who was sitting patiently at his bowl, his tail brushing the floor.

'All right,' she said.

Jake fell upon the pellets like a starved stray who hadn't eaten in days, his eager snout pushing the bowl across the bricks of the patio, his tongue sending stray pellets flying. Leo ate his supper with a more restrained enthusiasm, pausing every now and then to savour the meal, or admire his surroundings.

Julia let her mind wander while she watched them. It wandered, of course, to the murder investigation. Had Hayley brought Cynthia in again, or would she wait until tomorrow? Was she there now, perhaps, spilling the beans? If there were beans to be spilled. Or had Hayley dispatched DC Walter Farmer to have a chat with her? Much as Julia liked Walter – he was a good chap – she rather hoped Hayley had gone herself. She was smart, Hayley. Perceptive. She had good instincts. Walter was... Well, he tried.

'Supper's ready, Mum,' Jess called from the kitchen.

A happy, domestic scene greeted her. Dylan was setting the table, the cutlery lined up evenly. Sean was opening a bottle of wine he'd brought with him, a Pinot Noir, which he knew she liked. Jess was dishing up bowls of a deliciously aromatic soup. Julia felt a deep sense of contentment, seeing her loved ones gathered at her dinner table. 'Wonderful, darling, thank you. It smells absolutely delicious.'

The soup tasted even better than it smelled. Julia detected ginger, chilli – of course – pepper, and something tangy that she couldn't identify.

'Rice wine vinegar,' Jess said, in answer to her question. 'It gives it that sharp taste.'

There was a gratifying volume of slurping and appreciative groans. Jess looked quietly delighted at the display.

'I forgot to tell you, I got a call from a lawyer today, asking about the incident with the nuts at the wedding,' Sean said.

'A lawyer?'

'Yes. Richard, the guest who had the nut allergy, plans to sue the company that supplied the seed mix – Seedy Business, it's called. Quite an amusing name, I thought, although there won't be much laughter around their boardroom. From what I understood, there might even be a criminal case – endangerment or negligence or something. I'm not sure. They wanted a statement from me, as the doctor on the scene.'

'The wedding drama just never ends!' Jess said.

'Well, I couldn't help them much. I told them what I knew – that the man appeared to be having an allergic reaction, and responded to the antihistamines. My assumption at the time was that he was reacting to nuts, as he has a known allergy. I still believe that to be the case, but I have no way of saying for sure. And of course, if it is a nut allergy, it's not possible to determine where the nuts came from.'

'I suppose they'll have to analyse the seed mix and see if there are traces of nuts in it,' said Julia. 'If not, the nuts must have come from elsewhere, perhaps introduced in the kitchen.'

'Was the lawyer's name Mr Bidman or Birdman, something like that?' Dylan asked.

'Birdman, yes.'

'I think he came to see Cynthia today. I went to the office to collect my uniform for tomorrow's fancy kitchen tea – there's a special apron thing we have to wear for the occasion. It's pink. Pink stripes.'

He sighed, no doubt pondering the indignities visited upon him in the food service industry. 'He arrived when I did, asked me about the company as if he was just chatting. But he had a funny way with him. Beady little eyes. And then he asked all of us that were there about the nut incident. He freaked out poor Braydon.'

'Who's Braydon?' Jess asked.

'The other waiter. He was at your dad's wedding, too.'

'The tall blonde guy? Spiky hair?'

'Yeah, him. He was very upset after the guy collapsed, and when this Birdman guy came round and started asking about it, like what we saw and all that, it seemed to trigger him. He freaked out. Went off on his motorbike in a right state.'

'Poor guy.'

'Yeah, and poor Cynthia,' Dylan said. 'I suppose this whole legal thing is her problem, seeing as she's the owner now.'

One of many problems, Julia thought. And potentially not even the most serious. She hadn't told them about her earlier conversation with Hayley about Cynthia, and the information she'd shared with the detective inspector.

'You like her, do you?' she asked Dylan. 'Cynthia?'

'I do, yeah. She's a really nice person. Understanding. Like, if you needed to change a shift, or borrow a few quid advance until the end of the month, you'd go to her, not Desmond. Not to speak ill of the dead, but Desmond was intense. He was brilliant with the food, really creative, but could be a tricky one. Cynthia was the calmer of the two. She's a trained chef, she knows food, but doesn't have his, like, *passion* for it. And she's good with the clients, the suppliers and the staff. They complemented each other well and made a good team. Poor Cyn will have a tough time without him – the last thing she needs is a lawsuit.'

'Well, if it's any consolation, it looks like if anyone's going to be at the sharp end of a lawsuit, it'll likely be the seed mix supplier, not the caterer,' said Sean. 'Assuming it was sold as nut-free.'

'I can tell you, whatever happened, it wasn't Candy Catering at fault,' Dylan said defensively. 'There's this whole system for allergies. They take allergies very seriously.'

'I'm sure it'll all be sorted out. Richard is alive and healthy, that's the main thing. Thank goodness you were there, Sean, and he got the pills quickly,' said Julia. Sean ducked his head, deflecting the praise.

When everyone had had second helpings, and every drop of soup was finished, Jess said, much to her mother's surprise, 'Who's up for a game of cards? What was that game we used to play, Mum?'

'There were so many. Rummy? Spite and Malice?'

'Rummy. We can all play. Spite and Malice is only for two. Let's play that tomorrow though, Mum.'

The others cleared the table while Julia fetched the cards. Jess had loved card games when she was little, and they had played many an evening. Occasionally Peter – not a games lover – submitted to being roped in, but mostly it was just the two of them. Julia's own mother had taught her Spite and Malice. It was a good game but an odd name – strange to name a card game after ill feelings.

There seemed to be a fair amount of ill feeling surrounding Desmond. The wife. The fight with Cynthia. She did wonder who else didn't like Desmond Campbell.

Jess handed her two packs of cards, interrupting her thoughts. 'Come on, Mum! You set the cards up, I've forgotten how.'

Julia took the packs and shuffled, watching with satisfaction as each card fell, slotting neatly into its place between its neighbours and hitting the table with a little click.

20

Julia's finger hesitated over the little record icon. Was she crossing the boundary between helpful and interfering? Or was she simply giving a friend an appropriate warning of a potential problem?

The latter, she hoped. She tapped the screen and spoke into the phone: 'Hi, Hayley, just letting you know that there's a lawyer in town asking questions about the allergy incident at the wedding. The victim is going to sue. But there's talk of bringing a charge against whoever was responsible. Something criminal. Not sure what, but, if that happens, it means this thing will likely land in your lap. Or your desk. Anyway, it might not happen, but I thought a heads-up might be handy.'

Minutes later, a voice note arrived back from Hayley. 'Hi, Julia. Gosh, it seems there's no end to the wedding drama. Thanks for the warning. It doesn't sound like a matter for the police, so it might not come my way.' She sounded wistful rather than confident on this point. There was a small hesitation, which might have been a sigh, then she said, 'Hope not. I've got my hands full with Desmond Campbell's murder. Anyway. Thanks. Oh, and thanks for your info on Cynthia

Skinner. It's been very helpful. She definitely seems to have been the last person to see him alive. It's looking bad for her.'

'Hi, Mum.' Jess was at the kitchen door still in her pyjamas, her hair tangled from the pillow, her dear face puffy from sleep. Julia felt a swelling of love at the sight of her. She looked so young and vulnerable. She was wearing Julia's big sheepskin slippers, which make a swish-swish noise on the tiles as she padded across the kitchen towards the kettle. 'Want tea?'

'No thanks, love, I've just had a cup.'

'Dad phoned,' she said, her back to her mother, her voice muffled. The running of the tap, the clicking of the gas catching, the sound of the heavy kettle on the stove. 'They're leaving today. Going back to London. The police said they don't have to stick around. Which is good news, obviously. It means Christopher's not under suspicion now.'

'I'm pleased to hear it. Of course, we knew it would come to nothing, Christopher didn't do it, but it was a worry. And they have a strong suspect now, I believe.'

'Good. I'm meeting Dad and Christopher for a last breakfast at the Buttered Scone.'

Her voice sounded flat. Julia knew that tone, it meant she was keeping her emotions in check.

'Ah, I'm sorry, love. You'll be sad to say goodbye.'

'I will. I'll see them again in London on my way through, but it still feels too soon. It's less than two weeks before I leave Berrywick. And England.'

Julia had been trying to keep that thought at bay for some days. The idea of her daughter leaving the village and then the country gave her a funny lurching feeling in her gut. She got up and walked to the stove, and gave her daughter a hug. 'I'll miss you, my darling.'

'I'll miss you too, Mum.'

Jake, flustered by all the emotion, came over and sat next to them. His kind brown eyes moved anxiously between them as his doggy brain tried to work out what was wrong, and how he could help.

'And I'll miss you too, Jakey,' said Jess, squatting down to his level. A fat tear dropped onto his head. 'I'm being silly,' she said sternly. 'Gosh, I don't know what's got into me. Hong Kong is great, only... I don't know. You're here. And Berrywick is starting to feel like home.'

Julia spoke gently. 'It's okay to be sad, darling. It's hard, being away from the people you love. Even when you're happy where you are.'

'It is.'

Jess switched off the stove and wiped her eyes on her sleeve. 'I'm going to be late for breakfast if I don't get a move on. I want to walk. Better hit the shower. I'll have tea there. Oh, Mum, can I take Jake with me?'

'Of course. He'd love an outing with you, especially if there might be a bit of bacon in the offing.'

'There might be indeed. Get yourself ready, boy. Leaving in twenty!'

The house was eerily quiet without the two youngsters. Julia washed her mug and side plate and tidied the kitchen. She fed the chickens and fetched the eggs – a rather lonely business without Jake, her constant companion in these activities. She even rearranged the contents of the fridge, which Jess always took out and put back willy-nilly, with zero respect for her mother's sensible system – dairy on the door, fruit in the top drawer, veg in the bottom, condiments at the top, and so on.

Her household chores complete, Julia did the Wordle – got it in two! – and an online crossword. She felt oddly ill at ease. She'd become used to the company of her dog and her daughter. She dreaded saying goodbye to Jess. It was all she could do not to join in her daughter's crying.

'An outing, that's what I need,' she said, addressing herself in her most no-nonsense voice. 'I need a few things from the shops. I'll go to Edgeley for a change. The drive will be nice, and I can pop in at the new cheese shop.' Usually, these observations were addressed to Jake. Speaking to herself seemed somehow sadder and madder than speaking to a chocolate Labrador. But she was happy to have a plan and a little mission.

Julia couldn't recall the name of the new cheese shop that had received glowing reports on the 'We Love Berrywick and Edgeley' Facebook page for its variety, quality and service – and the free tasters they generously gave out to customers. She knew the name was something cheesy, but couldn't remember what. The Big Cheese? The Big Wheel? Brie-zee? No, none of those, although she did make herself smile.

She parked in the first parking place she came across on the main road. She didn't know where exactly the cheese shop was, but it was best to walk along until she spotted it. She had walked a few blocks when she saw the signage: Cheese Louise. How could she have forgotten such a cheesy name? She went in cheeseless, and emerged with five different types of local cheese. Cow, sheep, goat, hard, soft, she covered all the cheesy bases. And the Facebook people didn't lie; she felt as if she'd had a meal by the time she'd finished all the tasters.

'Now, pop by the baker's shop a few doors down, and pick up a good loaf to go with it. They do a good sourdough, and a fine seeded rye,' said the shopkeeper, who was dressed as an actual milkmaid, and whose name – if her tag was to be believed – was indeed Louise.

As it turned out, the bakery was right next door to the Village Pie Place. It was only a few days since she'd last been, on a snooping errand. And here she was again, on legitimate business. There was no sign of the van this time, and the pie shop looked as if it might be closed. There seemed to be a note in the window, and Julia went a bit closer to read it. 'CLOSED FOR PERSONAL REASONS. WE APOLOGISE FOR THE INCONVENIENCE' shouted the sign, in bright red caps. Was Cynthia in custody, Julia wondered? Or with her lawyer? Whatever was going on, it was obviously serious enough for Tim to close the pie shop for the day.

Would Tim be able to make a go of the pie shop if his wife was put away for murder, wondered Julia, as she turned to the small bakery from which the most wonderful smells of freshly baked bread were drifting. And as for the Candy Catering business – was there any hope for that if Cynthia turned out to have murdered Desmond? Julia sighed. One stupid and evil decision, and two local businesses would probably close.

The man behind the bakery counter did not look at all bothered by any worries for his business. He looked, it had to be said, like a baker from a storybook – with ruddy cheeks and a wide smile.

'What can I help you with?' he asked. 'We've got sourdough, sourdough rye, a wholewheat, and our special seeded country loaf with linseed, sesame, pumpkin and poppy seeds.'

'What is it that I can smell?' said Julia. 'It smells absolutely delicious.'

'Ah, that would be our seed loaf,' he said, indicating a tray of fresh bread that was still steaming slightly. Next to the tray was a small sign saying, 'Try our fresh juices and a slice of cake'.

'Then I'd like a seed loaf, please.'

He put the loaf in a paper bag and handed it over.

'Anything else?'

She glanced at the little sign. 'I'm not hungry enough for cake, but a juice sounds nice.'

'We've got orange, apple and strawberry, all freshly made this morning,' said the baker.

Julia could seldom resist a freshly pressed apple juice. 'I'd love an apple juice, please.'

'Take a seat, love, I'll bring it over.'

Julia sat at one of the tiny tables, enjoying the warmth and the yeasty, bready smell of the shop. A small laminated menu listed the available cakes. Each one sounded delicious, and Julia wondered if she perhaps did have a little bit of space for a coffee cake, or perhaps some lemon tart.

The shop phone rang and the baker answered it. 'Oh, Tim,' he said after a moment, 'I've been worried about you, with the shop closed this morning. You've never closed it in the time you've been there.'

He listened a bit longer.

'Of course, of course,' he said. 'I can do that. And anything that I can do to help you or Cynthia, give me a shout.' His smiling face now looked much sadder, and less like a caricature of a cheery baker.

Not wanting to be caught eavesdropping, Julia turned her attention back to the menu, flipping it over to studiously peruse the history of the shop. She diligently read the not-very-interesting story – the baker, whose name it seemed was Jeremy Chapman, started the bakery ten years ago, using only the best local ingredients, and so on and so on.

At the bottom of the menu were the logos of the suppliers – Argyle Farm, Halo Mills, Westlake Juices, Seedy Business.

'Sorry for the wait. I had to take that call. A friend in need, as they say.' Jeremy put a small glass bottle and a glass in front of her. 'Here's your apple juice.'

'No problem. That apple juice looks good.' It did indeed; cloudy, and a rich golden colour. When she opened it, it smelled as if she'd cut into an apple. 'Westlake Juices?' she smiled, putting her finger on the logo on the menu.

'Yes. They grow and press the apples not far from here.

Freshest, tastiest apple juice you'll find. All our suppliers are local and sustainable.'

'What's Seedy Business?'

'Also local. They specialise in seeds and seed mixes.'

'And nuts?' The question slipped out, almost of its own accord.

'No. Seeds only. In fact, the owner's kid is allergic to nuts, so there are no nuts on the premises. It's one of their selling points, being safe for people with allergies.'

He indicated a shelf to the side of the tables, filled with prettily labelled brown paper bags. 'You can buy the seed mixture separately,' he said. 'It's used by all the best caterers in the area.'

'Like Candy Catering?' said Julia. Jeremy looked at her for a moment, perhaps wondering how much she knew about his neighbour's wife's business.

'Indeed,' he said after a moment. 'They use it for all their bread.' He gave a big laugh at that point. 'I'm always telling them to buy their bread from me. But that Desmond, he was a purist.' His face fell again. 'Terrible business,' he said, shaking his head. 'Terrible.'

Before Julia could agree that it was, indeed, a terrible business, a mum came into the store, struggling with a double pushchair and two tiny, sleeping babies in matching beanies, one yellow and one orange, each with a soft spray of back curls peeking from them.

'Excuse me,' Jeremy said, hurrying off to help his customer navigate the pram through the small shop.

Julia sipped her drink and wondered where, given what she had just learned, those nuts had come from.

21

The weather turned on Thursday. The day started off bright and mild, but the clouds came in and the temperature dropped, and by the time Julia arrived home from a shift at Second Chances, it was frigid. A mean little wind crept down her collar and between the buttons of her too-light coat as she walked briskly to her front door. She was pleased to see light in the windows and smoke coming from her chimney.

The sitting room fire was blazing. The large brown mass of Jake rose and fell in front of it, emitting a soft, wheezing snore. He was fast asleep. Jess and Dylan were so absorbed in their conversation, they didn't hear her come in.

'Oh my lord, I just cannot believe it,' Dylan was saying. 'The shrieking! And all the breakages. That'll cost a penny.'

Jess was a quivering, giggling heap next to him on the sofa. They looked up and noticed her.

'Oh, hi, Mrs Bird.'

'Hi, Dylan. What's going on?' Julia asked.

'Tell Mum about the tail!' Jess managed to get the words out, and fell back, gasping.

'It's really not that funny, Jess,' he said solemnly. 'The whole event was ruined. And poor Cynthia...'

Jess composed her face momentarily, and tried for seriousness. 'I know, it was terrible for the poor bride-to-be. And her mum and the guests. And Cynthia. But...'

'And there's health and safety to consider, you know... You can't have a rat running about in a food service area.'

Jess lost the battle and dissolved once more. As a child, she'd always had this same tendency – once a fit of laughter took her she was unplayable. It had gotten her into trouble at school on more than one occasion.

'Tail!' she instructed, with a gasp, pointing to Dylan and then Julia.

He tried to look stern, but couldn't help but smile at her hysteria.

'What on earth are you talking about?' asked Julia. She was bemused by the whole scene – Jess completely undone with giggles, and Dylan in a state somewhere between aghast and amused.

He took up the story. 'There was this bridal shower, right? There was a cake, under a silver dome thingy. And a rat... I don't know how it happened, but somehow it got into the dome. And the tail...'

The mere word set off another spate of laughter, but weaker now.

Jess wiped her eyes and caught her breath enough to speak. 'Here, Mum, watch the video. It's all over social media already. Poor things.' She handed over her phone and pressed play.

Julia recognised the function room at Stag's Manor, a stately home turned upper-end wedding venue, just beyond Edgeley. A fire burned in the grate. A couple of dozen young women sat at a long table heavily decorated with flowers and what looked like antique birdcages encasing inexplicably unlit candles. Balloons floated above the chair at the end of the table, where a shiny, willowy blonde – the bride, presumably – presided. Seated next to her was an older woman with the same fine features, pale eyes and thin lips, her hair expensively highlighted to approximate the younger woman's natural golden streaks. There was no mistaking the relationship; they must be mother and daughter.

At the furthest end of the table the room's huge windows looked out over a magnificent garden. Standing next to the window were two women in heated conversation. 'There's Cynthia,' Julia said. 'And that's the florist woman.'

'Angela.'

'Oh yes. She doesn't look very happy. Is this the bridal shower?'

'Yes,' said Dylan. 'Properly posh, isn't it?'

'And here comes the cake.' The plummy voice came from whoever was holding the camera and providing the narration.

There was a lot of cheering and excited shrieking, and a huge tray covered by an enormous silver cloche wobbled into view on the outstretched arms of a waiter. The cloche was so big that only a few gelled-up blonde spikes on the top of his head were visible.

'The waiter is Braydon,' said Dylan. 'The guy I work with. Remember, he was at Peter and Christopher's wedding.'

Cynthia turned sharply away from the conversation with Angela and followed the waiter over to the table. She looked even thinner and paler than when she'd last seen her. Hardly surprising, considering she'd spent quite a bit of time in the police station, being quizzed by DI Hayley Gibson as a suspect in Desmond's murder. The fact that she was out and about meant that Hayley didn't have enough on her to keep her. Yet.

'Oh yes.'

'Ssshhh, Mum – watch, or you'll miss the best bit.'

The waiter approached the bride and her mother, with

Cynthia hovering nervously behind and to the side. She helped him place the domed tray on the table in front of the bride.

'Will you do the honours, Lady Wellmouth?' Cynthia asked.

The older blonde woman – presumably Lady Wellmouth – smiled and reached for the handle. She looked proudly at her daughter and turned her regal gaze to the rest of the table. She paused for dramatic effect. When all eyes were on her, she looked down, ready for the reveal.

The camera zoomed in to catch the moment. It wavered. Zoomed in further. Something long and thin and dark emerged from beneath the dome, which Lady Wellmouth had lifted half an inch in anticipation.

'Let's have three cheers for Penelope Wellmouth, the soon-to-be Mrs Brotherton!' shouted one of the guests. 'Hip hip...'

'Hooray!'

The camera stayed on the silvery cloche, and the pink thing snaking out of it. The photographer zoomed in further. The pink thing seemed leathery, and alive. A voice – the photographer's presumably – said in disgust, 'Gosh, that's not a... Oh my, is that a—'

Her question was drowned out by the second and the third cheer, and then a good deal of whooping.

The thing lashed about. It was undoubtedly alive. It was undoubtedly...

'... a tail? Oh my God, it *is!* There's a—'

Half the table was still cheering, and half were following the photographer's gaze. Lady Wellmouth lifted the dome further. One by one, the cheerers were beginning to realise that there was something wrong. They turned their attention to the head of the table. The scene was suspended in time for a long and disbelieving instant, but the next word broke the spell:

'—RAT!'

The tail whipped round like an earthworm on a hot pavement and disappeared into the dome. A nose appeared in its place. It was a dark shiny nose, followed by a white face with pale whiskers and beady black eyes. Lady Wellmouth pulled off the dome to reveal the cake, a magnificent confection, at least four layers tall, covered with creamy, buttery icing, and with tiny macarons in delicate pastel colours. There it was, a fat rat with rather attractive brown and white markings, crouched next to the cake, its tail lying pink and scaly across the macarons. The screaming ratcheted up a notch.

'That's a fancy rat,' said Dylan, prompting a gulping snort from Jess.

At this point the camera filled with freckled cleavage and a sky-blue silk bust, and then went momentarily blank, clutched to its owner's chest in horror. But fortunately for thousands of YouTube viewers, she regained her composure in time to record the absolute chaos that was to follow.

Lady Wellmouth tossed the cover aside and shoved the cake, trying to get the rat as far away from her as possible. The rat made a run for it, scampering down the centre of the table as the cake turned over – it felt like it happened in slow motion, watching it – and slid onto Penelope, who leapt to her feet, scattering mini macarons. Her escape was thwarted by the ribbons that affixed the balloons to her chair, which now acted as a net, preventing her from making a quick exit. She flailed her arms about, becoming ever more entangled in the ribbons, the balloons bobbing merrily above her head. Trying to disentangle her arm from the ribbons, she managed to fall over her chair, somehow knocking her mother over with her and the two of them landing heavily on the floor. The *pop, pop* of the bursting balloons punctuated the mayhem. Cynthia went to their rescue, while Braydon stood rooted to the spot in horror, the tray dangling at his side.

The photographer swung round to the sound of a shriek. A particularly loud shriek that managed to rise over the general noise level, which was, itself, quite intense, and above the voice of the furious Lady Wellmouth. The rat had made its way to the far end of the table, and was sitting in one of the birdcage ornaments, surveying the scene from a position of relative safety. It seemed remarkably calm, perhaps stunned by the cacophony. Not so the shrieker, a porcelain-skinned redhead, who seemed to be in some sort of hysterical state, her eyes fixed on the rodent. The two of them were rooted to the spot in a strange challenge where neither could look away first, while all around them chaos reigned.

Arabella the wedding planner, presumably summoned by the noise, rushed into frame. She could be seen trying to calm the scene, but it was an impossible task. The panic had reached a tipping point and there was no going back. The guests were fleeing the table like, well, like rats from a sinking ship. The women shoved their chairs back and scrambled to get away, pushing and falling over each other. A tough-looking brunette in a severe bob had somehow attached herself to the tablecloth, and pulled it with her when she exited the table, scattering glasses and cutlery, upending flower arrangements, and pulling over neighbouring guests. Braydon tried ineffectually to catch things as they fell, lunging at ornaments and breakables. The tablecloth woman tripped, and crashed to the ground in the tangled cloth, like a fallen angel. Braydon grabbed the birdcage in which the rat had taken shelter, but it was too late to stop the chaos. It continued, even in the absence of the rodent.

'Lucky it's Braydon there, not me,' Dylan said with a shiver. 'He likes rodents. I'd be one of the shriekers knocking everyone over to get to the door.'

The photographer could be heard muttering, 'Oh my God... Oh hell... The cake!... Oooh Delphinia, that must have hurt.'

'*Delphinia!*' gasped Jess, and let out a strangled shriek of laughter. '*Oooh, Delphinia!*'

Dylan nudged her.

'Sorry,' she said. 'I know, but I just can't help it.'

On the phone screen, a final act of destruction was in motion. The table lurched to one side after a particularly emphatic shove of a chair. Everything on it began to slide, the remaining table covering gathering it all up, slowly at first, and then surprisingly fast. It reminded Julia of those videos of icebergs calving, the giant chunks of ice cracking and creaking and then sliding surprisingly elegantly into the sea.

The photographer swung around and back – left, right, left – giving a panoramic view of the carnage – the broken decorations, the upended flower arrangements, Braydon clasping the birdcage to his chest, and inside the cage the little brown and white rat that started it all. The camera came to rest on the cake-covered, balloon-strewn bride and her furious mother, who had managed to get to her feet and was standing like a warrior queen amongst the chaos and the groaning fallen. Lady Well-mouth pointed to Cynthia, and then to Arabella, and shouted above the noise.

'You are finished, do you hear me? *Finished*. Both of you. You will *never* work in this village again. Not in this county! Not in this *kingdom*. I shall see to that.'

And the screen went blank.

22

'There's so much to do in Gloucester,' said Jess, turning round in her seat to face Dylan, and waving a small sheaf of papers, some printed out from the Internet, others scrawled with her still childish handwriting. 'I've done mad research.'

It was true that, once she'd recovered from her hysterical laughter at The Rat's Bridal Shower, as she called it, and Dylan had gone home, she had indeed spent the evening lying on the sofa in front of the fire, googling on her laptop.

'Would you like to hear my suggested itinerary?'

'Sure,' said Dylan eagerly. 'Go on then.'

'So first we're going to go to the cathedral, which is more than nine hundred years old and has a stained-glass window as big as a tennis court.'

'Cool,' said Dylan.

'And then we will have lunch at the docks, which are apparently the most inland...'

Julia let their chatter wash over her as she drove, and her mind wander. It went to Desmond Campbell, rather unsurprisingly, seeing as they were on their way to his place of work.

'Thanks for going past the Candy offices, Mrs Bird. I'm

sorry to put you out. I'd forgotten that I'd left my bag with my raincoat there.'

'No trouble, Dylan, it looks like the weather's coming in, and you might need it. Besides, it's hardly out of the way and we've got plenty of time for the train.'

'When Mum's in charge of getting you to the station, you can be sure you'll be standing on a platform freezing your butt off for a good long time.' Jess said it in a teasing but loving way. 'Anyway, I'm interested to see where you work. Is it a big industrial kitchen?'

'Yeah. State of the art. Gas hobs. Big freezers. Plating station. And all built to strict health and safety requirements.'

Julia drew up outside the premises.

'Do you want to come and have a quick look?' he asked Jess. 'It's a bit early, there won't be much going on, but you can see the place.'

'Have we got time, Mum?'

'Yes, if we're quick.'

'You come too, Mrs Bird.'

'Julia.'

'Julia,' he said, with an awkward duck of his head.

The front entrance to the office was closed, but Dylan led them round the side of the building, to the parking area, where two Candy Catering vans were parked. 'The office staff come in at nine, but depending on the jobs we have booked, the kitchen staff are often in earlier to prep,' he said.

Julia rather hoped there was no one there. She imagined the mood at Candy Catering would be pretty bleak after the rat video had gone viral. She thought back to the promise Cynthia had made to Arabella at the funeral – 'Penelope Wellmouth's bridal shower will be perfect. It will be the talk of the town.' One of the two sentences had certainly been proved true. The bridal shower was indeed the talk of the town – although not in the way Cynthia had intended.

The big double doors into the back of the building were closed, but not locked. 'Looks like someone's here, probably Cynthia. She likes to get an early start,' Dylan said, pushing them open to reveal a large kitchen with gleaming white floors and walls and stainless-steel counters and shelves packed with equipment. To one side was the cooking section with a line of gas burners, and two big ovens.

'Wow, it's really cool, Dylan,' Jess said. Julia was surprised too, she'd imagined something a lot less professional.

'Like I said, state of the art. And at the back there, that big door is the walk-in fridge, the one next to it the pantry, and then the room where they keep all the serving platters and such. Catering is big business, especially now the Cotswolds is such a popular wedding destination.'

Julia was reminded of Peter and Christopher's wedding, and the mysterious nut incident, the first of the disasters to befall Candy in recent days. 'When you said the caterer takes allergies seriously the other day, what do you mean? What would they do?'

'Well, like, if the client tells us there's an allergy issue, the kitchen is informed, and they inform the suppliers they are using, to make sure they are aware. There's a prep area that's isolated, and a special bleach for wiping down surfaces. We're not even allowed to bring our own food into the kitchens, like a chocolate bar or whatever, in case it contaminates the food with an allergen. That's why I was so sure the nuts didn't come from the Candy Catering kitchen. Anyway, we'd better get a move on. Have a look around while I pop into the office and get my bag.'

They snooped around a bit while they waited, wandering over to the pantry.

'Look at that giant bag of flour, Mum. And the big tins of tomatoes. Aren't they funny?'

Julia laughed. 'Yes. It's like something from *Alice in Wonderland* when Alice drinks the potion and gets very small.'

'Okay, got it.' Dylan came in, swinging his backpack from one hand. 'Funny, I didn't see anyone about, but the place is open, so there must be someone here.'

'Right, let's get you two to the train to Gloucester.'

As Julia turned away from the engrossing selection of very large items, she caught sight of something sticking out from behind a stainless-steel counter. Something not very large, but completely out of place. A shoe. A running shoe. How odd, she thought for a second, before her brain caught up with her eyes, and she realised that the shoe was in fact on a foot, attached to a leg. She stepped closer, calling to the others.

'There's someone here, it's...'

Jess, right behind her, followed her mother's gaze and whimpered, 'Oh no. Oh, Dylan. Look!'

He was next to them in a few steps. They looked down in horror at the shoe and the denim trouser leg, and the face-down body of Cynthia Skinner. A large carving knife was stuck in her back, and beneath her pooled a crimson lake, stark against the white tiled floor.

It was blood, and she was most certainly dead.

23

'This is not good at all,' said DC Walter Farmer, rather redundantly, Julia thought. And then again, for good measure: 'Not good at all.'

He bent over the body and shook his head sadly from side to side. 'Definitely dead.'

Another helpful observation from the detective constable.

'Yes, Walter. About as dead as you can get,' said Hayley Gibson irritably. 'And no, it is not good.'

'There goes our prime suspect for the Desmond Campbell murder,' he muttered glumly. 'Just think, if we'd got the warrant a day earlier, she'd be alive right now. Not very happy, but in custody and alive.'

'Indeed.'

'You were about to arrest Cynthia?'

Hayley looked at Julia in surprise when she spoke, as if she'd forgotten she was there. 'Yes. We got the warrant yesterday afternoon. We were going to bring her in this morning. This makes things a whole lot more complicated.' Hayley looked grimly furious.

'Well, we can't interview her now.' Walter seemed insistent

on stating the obvious. 'And also, we have to solve her murder. As well as the other one.' He sighed at the burden of it all.

'Yes, thank you, Walter.'

'You're welcome, DI Gibson,' he said, oblivious to her sarcasm. In fact, he looked rather pleased with himself.

'DC Farmer, could you please go outside and take statements from Jess and Dylan? I asked them to wait there.'

'Of course, DI Gibson.'

When he had trotted off eagerly to do her bidding. Julia asked Hayley, 'So you think Cynthia definitely killed Desmond?'

'She had motive and opportunity. She was the person who had most to gain from his death. She got his share of the business when he died. We interviewed Desmond's wife Goldie and she's already spoken to a lawyer. The will was watertight, apparently. It had all been left to Cynthia. Goldie wasn't at all happy. She was livid with Cynthia. Said it was all her fault.'

Julia remembered how angry Goldie had been when she saw her at the charity shop, tossing out Desmond's things just a day after the funeral.

Hayley continued. 'We know Cynthia was at the scene of Desmond's murder – she lied about her whereabouts at the time of the murder. She changed her story, like I told you. It seems she might have been the last to see him alive.'

'I see, it does look like it was her.' Although Julia had proposed Cynthia as a suspect, she felt sad to know it was likely her that killed Desmond. And now she, herself, was dead. What a sad mess. What a waste.

'According to her, she left and Desmond was still alive. But I'm not convinced.'

'Motive, opportunity and method.'

'You've been paying attention to your cop shows on the telly, I see.'

'I have. The three things a murderer needs to have to be a

suspect: the "how", the "when" and the "why". So, what about the how – the method?'

'Method of death? Anyone could pull that off.' Hayley shrugged dismissively. 'Just shut the door. It's hands-off, not at all bloody. Not like this,' she said, gesturing to the body that lay at their feet. 'No, this is another matter. This is someone with an axe to grind. Someone very angry with Cynthia. So now I have to find someone who fits that description.' But from the look on Hayley's face, Julia could see that she already had a very good idea.

Jess and Dylan had given their statements to Walter Farmer and were free to go, but they dithered and hung about, not knowing what to do. It seemed almost disrespectful to the dead woman to go ahead with their cheery tourist plans, and besides, they were hardly in the mood for larking about the Gloucester docks with a gin and tonic.

'Perhaps you should go,' Julia said, when the three of them got to the car. 'There's nothing you can do to help Cynthia and you won't have another chance to go to Gloucester. Dylan will be back at uni on Monday and you'll be returning to Hong Kong soon.' Her heart lurched at the thought of Jess leaving.

Dylan and Jess looked at each other for a moment and they both nodded. 'Okay,' Jess said.

Julia started the car. 'Okay then, I'll take you to the station.'

The three of them sat in stupefied silence, Jess in the front passenger seat, Dylan behind, staring out of their respective windows, deep in their respective thoughts. Julia was thinking about what Hayley had said: '*someone with an axe to grind. Someone very angry with Cynthia.*'

Who had an axe to grind? Goldie, of course. *She* was the obvious suspect. In fact, when she'd come into Second Chances with Desmond's clothes, she'd been furious with him for not leaving the business to her. And furious with whoever killed him. Her small angelic person had been filled with anger at the world.

Julia remembered Goldie's response when she'd expressed hopefulness that the police would find his killer: 'If I don't find them first.' Had she found Cynthia first? Had her anger got the better of her?

Julia couldn't help herself. 'Dylan, do you know Goldie, Desmond's wife?'

'A bit. She used to work at Candy Catering, running the office and the ordering and stuff. Came round from time to time. Popped in when we were setting up for a function. Seemed nice enough, although...' There was a pause, in which Dylan was presumably considering the etiquette around speaking ill of the dead. The women waited. 'Desmond wasn't the easiest fellow. Intense, like I said. Could be moody. And, I would have thought, not the easiest chap to be married to.'

'What, did he mess around?' Jess was not one to mince her words.

'Not that I know of, but I know the ladies liked him. He had that brooding creative genius type vibe, you know? Girls seemed to dig it. He got a fair bit of attention, and I would say he liked it.'

And Goldie didn't, Julia thought as she pulled up at the station and Jess and Dylan got out.

'Thanks, Mum.'

'Have fun!' she shouted after them as they walked away.

Julia was pleased that Jess and Dylan had gone to Gloucester; there was nothing to be gained from moping about the place. They'd managed to catch the train after the one they'd planned – it seemed impossible that so little time had elapsed when so much had happened – and they would still have a full day of exploring. And she had the day to herself.

As soon as she'd dropped them off, she phoned Sean and told him about Cynthia's death. He was shocked and the car filled with his questions, relayed in stereo from the phone to the car speakers.

'Come over,' he said. He didn't work on Friday afternoons unless there was a patient in urgent need, and there were no emergencies, so he was about to leave for home.

'Go and fetch Jake,' he said. 'We can have a late lunch at mine, and we'll take the dogs for a walk. You can tell me everything.'

She had said goodbye to Sean but not yet ended the call when Peter phoned. She felt a bit like a character in a farce, juggling two phone calls coming in simultaneously, from two different men. Of course, the set-up for such would require that the second man hadn't married someone else a week or so earlier. And that he wasn't phoning about their daughter's Christmas present. And that she wasn't, herself, preoccupied with matters of murder rather than love.

Julia could hardly concentrate on what he was saying – that money seemed impersonal, but it was always useful... there was jewellery... did Jess wear scarves?

'Peter, can I ask you something? It's a legal thing. About wills.'

'Of course. Always happy to help you, Julia.'

'Not mine. Desmond. The caterer that was murdered.'

She explained about the will, leaving everything to Cynthia. And Goldie losing out. And now Cynthia was dead days after him.

'Goodness,' he said. 'That's complicated.'

'Yes. So, what would happen to the business? Would it go to Cynthia's heirs then? Or what?'

'If the lawyer who drew it up was worth his salt, there

would be what's usually called a pre-decease clause. It's very common between business partners or spouses. There's a special set of circumstances that applies if they die at the same time, or within a certain time frame, usually a couple of weeks, or a month. It's to avoid a situation where the inheritance is entangled in two different estates.'

'You mean that if Cynthia dies, the business might revert to Goldie?'

'Goldie being the wife?' Understandably, Peter was a little confused by the cast of characters.

'Yes. Desmond's wife.'

'Yes. If *I'd* drawn up the will, there would have been a clause to that effect. Presumably, the two partners agreed to leave their half of the business to each other. If both of them were to die – in a car accident, for instance, or if one were to die and then the inheritor were to die within, say, a month, the inheritance would revert to someone else. In this case, the spouse seems the next logical choice.'

'Right, thank you, Peter. Got to go.'

And then she phoned Hayley Gibson.

24

One of the things Julia liked about Sean was his quiet competence in the domestic sphere. With minimal fuss, he served up a roasted vegetable lasagne he'd made and frozen the week before and popped it in the oven when she phoned to say she was on her way. While their lunch settled, they watched the rat video, Sean being seemingly the only person in the whole of Great Britain who had not seen it.

The video of the rat-ravaged bridal shower was a lot less funny the second time around. In fact, it was sad and creepy. Julia couldn't get her head round the fact that Cynthia was alive then, and now – less than two days later – she was dead. Sean watched it straight-faced and remarked that he felt sorry for the bride, having her lovely event ruined.

'But at least the rat was rather a pretty one,' he said, closing his laptop and leaning back into the sofa. 'I've never seen one with such cute markings before. If you're going to have your bridal shower ruined by a rat, you'd want a fine-looking fellow like that one.'

'I doubt she was thankful for that particular blessing, under the circumstances, Sean. It's not there in the bridal magazines,

"Pay particular attention to the little details of your special day, like making sure the rodent on your cake is a handsome one".'

He laughed. 'No, poor girl. And I feel sorry for the poor rat, too. Imagine being stuck in the dark under that dome, and then emerging to all that screaming. It must have been terrified.'

Julia loved this about Sean – his ability to see things in a different way, and feel sympathy for a rat stuck under a dome. She tried to think like Sean – imagine herself as the rat, with the dome coming down on her. Frankly, if she was the rat, she would have made a run for it.

Julia felt that whoomp that always hit her when she'd missed something important or obvious, then suddenly realised it. 'How did it get in?'

'What?'

'How did the rat get into the cake dome? Sean, a rat couldn't open that heavy thing and climb in under it and close it. And it's hard to imagine someone shutting the animal in there by mistake. Surely they would have noticed? It's not a fly or a cockroach, it's a fairly plump rodent. And wouldn't it have run away? But this one apparently sat there, calmly allowing itself to be trapped.'

'I suppose there's a chance the caterers weren't looking. Maybe the rat was hidden by the cake. Maybe it was asleep.'

'Hhhmff.' None of those explanations seemed at all plausible to Julia, and Sean hadn't sounded very convinced by his own theories.

Still suffused with admiration for the rat, he went on: 'It was remarkably calm, really. Clever little things, rats. Sitting out the chaos from the safety of that birdcage ornament was a good idea.'

'It was. In fact, I wonder...'

Sean turned his attention to Julia, recognising her tone. It was the tone that meant her brain was whirring around, putting the pieces of a puzzle together. She continued, after a pause: 'I wonder if there's more to this than meets the eye. What if that's not an ordinary rat that found its way into the cake? What if it was put there? Deliberately.'

'But who would do such a thing? And how?'

'Sean, can I have your laptop?'

He opened it, put in his password and handed it to her. It didn't take long for her to find all the information one could ever need on rats, wild and domestic.

'This isn't a wild rat,' she said, turning the computer towards him so he could see the screen, on which Google Images had served up an array of rodents. 'Look here. Here's your basic wild rat. Brownish grey. Skinny. Now look here. This one looks very similar to the rat in the video. Brown and white markings, like a skewbald pony, the smaller rounder ears. It's a special domestic breed. Sean, it's a pet rat. That's why it was fairly calm around humans. That's why it climbed into the cage.'

'You think that this was a pet rat someone put in there to disrupt the bridal shower?'

'That's exactly what I think.'

'Do you have any ideas on who the perp might be? A competitive bride? A disgruntled employee? A rival country lady who wanted her daughter to marry the groom? A cake baker determined to make the opposition look bad?' He was joking, but not entirely.

She didn't answer. She played the video again. She saw how carefully Braydon raised the dome. She saw the nervous look as he did so. She saw the way he dashed to the end of the table to grab the rat as the table began to list, and the way he hugged the decorative bird cage and its rodent inhabitant to his chest. His actions seemed careful. Protective.

'I don't know who or why, Sean. But I think I know who can answer that question.'

. . .

Julia hesitated to phone Jess – she didn't like to bother them on their outing – but she couldn't let the matter go. She called.

'There's nothing to worry about, everything's fine,' she said quickly, when her daughter answered, her voice wary and uncertain. 'I have a question for Dylan and I don't have his number. I wouldn't disturb you, but it's urgent. Could you put him on?'

'Hello?' Dylan sounded just as wary.

'Dylan, how well do you know Braydon?' she asked.

'Braydon Winter? From work?'

'Yes.'

'Not very well. We've worked together for about six months, but he'd been at Candy for a while when I started working there. We get on fine, but we don't socialise or anything.'

'What do you think of him?'

'He's a nice guy. Does his job well. He's a few years older than me, and he does this for a living. Not studying or anything. It must be quite hard.'

'You mentioned that he likes rats.'

'Yeah, he's got loads of pets. All sorts of things. Bearded dragons. Fish. And a few rats. He talks about them a lot. I guess that's why he didn't freak out.'

'I see. Dylan, do you have a phone number for him?'

'I don't, sorry.'

'I don't suppose you know where he lives?'

'Not the exact address, but it's somewhere near Candy's offices. Very close. He often walked the few blocks to the kitchen, and then got a lift to the venue with Desmond or Cynthia. And sometimes back again, if they were returning to the office.'

'Thanks, Dylan.'

'Is anything wrong? Do you need us to come home?'

'No, not at all. I just have a question for Braydon. But not to worry. You two have fun in Gloucester. Let me know when you want me to fetch you from the station.'

'Will do, Mrs B— Julia. Thanks.'

Sean had been watching with a quiet admiration as she set about putting her theory together. 'So you think that Braydon put the rat there on purpose?'

'I think there's a good possibility that that's the case.'

'Watching the video again, I can see why you say that. But why?'

This was the part that Julia was struggling with. After a year or more of working at Candy Catering, and it being his primary source of income, why would he cause this kind of havoc? Did he know the wedding family somehow, and have a grudge? It seemed unlikely. Was there some dispute with Cynthia, and he was messing up the event to get back at her somehow?

'This video has gone viral. It's been watched over a million times in two days. This is the kind of exposure that could sink a company,' she said. 'Why would he jeopardise his job?'

'I doubt the company will survive. First Desmond's death... or rather, Desmond's *murder*. Then within a week or two there's this video. And they're facing a lawsuit over the nut issue. And now Cynthia's murder. They've been battered by a series of catastrophes.'

'It's not a coincidence, I'm sure of it, Sean. Think about it. I believe the rat was put there on purpose, to cause havoc. The same could be true of the nuts. The supplier actively doesn't use nuts, and Candy Catering has rigorous allergy protocols in place. The only explanation left is that someone planted them. It could have been the first deliberate attempt to get Candy Catering into trouble.'

'You think there was some kind of sabotage?'

Julia nodded. 'I do. And if I'm right about Braydon and the rat, then it seems likely that he was the perpetrator with both the nuts and the rat. And then Cynthia ends up murdered. I don't know how, but it's all tied up, somehow. We need to find out how and why.'

Sean looked at her with a grin and a twinkle in his blue eyes – another of the things she liked about him. In fact, she liked his twinkle even better than his domestic competence – and he said, 'Well, let's get to it then, shall we?'

She didn't have a phone number, but she did have the Internet. She did a quick search for Braydon Winter on all the usual channels. Really, social media made it so easy. There he was on Instagram with his pets.

'There he is. And look, he's holding the rat from the video!' she exclaimed triumphantly. 'Look, Sean. It's the very one!'

The rat's name was Bella, apparently. She discovered, too, that Braydon was a skateboarder. There were photographs of him flipping and tricking against a backdrop of concrete waves and graffitied walls, surrounded by a chain-link fence. In the distance, incongruously, green fields and a dense stand of trees.

'I recognise that skatepark,' Sean said. 'It's over towards Edgeley. I drive past it when I go that way to the pet food supplier to get Leo's food, and to the Wolsey Woods.'

'That means it's not far from the Candy Catering offices. Which, as we know from what Dylan told us, is not far from Braydon's house.'

She checked the dates on the pics, and found that most of them were tagged #FridayFlippers and posted on Friday evening.

'It seems to be a regular event, the Friday afternoon get-together at the skatepark,' she said.

'Are you thinking what I'm thinking, Ms Bird?'

'I think I'm thinking exactly what you're thinking, Doctor.'

'I was thinking that an outing might be nice. Seeing as it's Friday.'

'And I was thinking – in addition to what you were thinking – that I've never really watched skateboarding, live.'

'And I was thinking that the dogs might enjoy a ride in the car, and a stop at the Wolsey Woods on the way back to Berrywick.'

'Well, in that case, I think we should get going.'

It did seem rather a mad outing, and rather a long shot, heading off to a skatepark in search of a rat-owning waiter skater who might, just might, be able to shed some light on a mystery. But she was ready to embrace uncertainty, and risk disappointment.

If they were very lucky, they'd bump into Braydon himself.

Second prize, they'd find someone who had his number or who could point them in the direction of his house.

Third prize, they would be no closer to finding Braydon, but they would get to see the skateboarders, and the dogs would have a lovely walk in the woods nearby. And she'd find some other way to get in touch with him.

Julia noticed how much more accepting she'd become since her retirement, more able to take things as they came. She'd almost given herself an ulcer in the last two years of work. She had been so stressed and tired, and taken on all the troubles of everyone she met or worked with. Now she took one step at a time, doing what she could, philosophically accepting the limitations of the world.

'Well, that was easy. There it is,' said Sean, as Julia pulled into a parking space next to the small skatepark, which seemed to have been fashioned from a disused parking lot. It was indeed the same one they'd seen on Braydon's Instagram account. 'And there he is.'

Braydon's long, slim figure could be seen leaning against the fence on the far side, his board under his arm. His blonde spikes caught the late afternoon sun behind him, and gave him a golden halo, like those mediaeval pictures of saints. He was watching a gangly teenager go through his moves. The boy was wearing the T-shirt and lumberjack shirt combo that Dylan favoured, the shirt-tails flapping in the wind as he flipped and turned his body and his board in space. He came to a clattering halt in front of Braydon, spinning his board up and catching it.

Braydon nodded and launched himself onto his own skateboard. He raced up the curved wall, flipped the board, landed on it, and raced back down to complete a similar move on the far wall. The wheels spun noisily against the hard concrete. It looked lethal. Julia felt sure she would break both hips and at least one wrist if she so much as stood on the board, but the young man was graceful and seemingly untroubled by the possibility of brutal injury. He swooped up and round and down with an easy rhythm, circling back at each peak, and after a few minutes, came back to the fence. The two boys bumped fists, and the younger took off, hurtling towards the ramp and taking flight, leaving Braydon leaning against the fence, awaiting his turn.

Julia, having left Sean at the car with the dogs, walked over and positioned herself near Braydon.

'Aren't you Braydon?' She was going for casual, but she missed it. She came off more like a social worker and the Head of Youth Services, which is exactly what she had been until her retirement and her move to Berrywick a couple of years ago. Chatty sixty-something women were presumably not regular visitors to the skatepark. Braydon eyed her with suspicion.

'Why d'you want to know?'

'I'm sorry, I should have introduced myself. I'm Julia Bird. I'm a friend of Dylan's.'

He waited.

'I recognise you. Didn't I see you working at a friend's wedding?' she said.

She had sworn off the term 'husband's wedding', which only sowed confusion and resulted in awkward detours into personal matters. 'Peter and Christopher. Last week.'

'Yeah. You look sort of familiar.'

He said it grudgingly. He wasn't exactly an eager informant. She gave up trying the soft approach and went straight in with, 'I saw the video.'

He looked at her, his face determinedly impassive, and turned to look back at the skaters. He said nothing. A vein pulsed against the frayed neck of his sweatshirt. In the background, the sound of wheels hitting concrete. A board clattering to the ground. A cheer. Sean had both dogs on their leads and was taking a slow walk along the far end of the park, in the direction of the woods. Jake looked back to her, his head cocked in that quizzical way he had, no doubt wondering why she wasn't coming, and what she was up to with that young man and – most importantly – what it all meant for him, The Dog.

Julia turned her attention back to Braydon, keeping her tone calm and friendly, 'I saw you in the video of the bridal shower, and I remembered you from the wedding.'

He winced at the mention of the video, as if in pain.

'Your rat is very pretty, Braydon. Is he all right after all that drama?'

A storm of emotions played over Braydon's face as his brain tossed up his options – deny the connection between him and the rodent, pretend he didn't know what she was talking about, or own it.

He chose a fourth. Confrontation: 'Why are you here? What do you want?'

'I want to know why you put the rat in the silver dome with the cake. Listen, Braydon, no one knows but me. I worked it out. But I need to understand what was happening and why.'

'It was just... I would never have done it, but she... It wasn't meant to get so crazy. People... And the damage...'

'I'm sure that's true, Braydon,' she said calmly. 'I'm sure you didn't mean to cause such chaos. Or for it to be captured on video and shared, what is it now, half a million times?'

'A million views,' he said miserably. 'Last I looked.'

'And your rat? Is he okay?'

'She. Her name's Bella.' For the first time, his face softened. 'She's okay, thank goodness.'

'I'm pleased to hear that. She was quite graceful under pressure, I thought.'

He allowed himself a small smile at that, and said earnestly, 'I would never have put her in danger if I'd thought—' He stopped himself.

'Of course not. As soon as I saw you on the video, I knew that you cared for her. I realised that she was your pet. I don't think anyone else has made the connection. I haven't told the event organisers, or the police.'

'The police? Why would you?'

She waited.

'It's not a matter for the police!'

'You're right, Braydon. It probably isn't. Not the rat.'

He looked relieved. She continued. 'But I'm afraid the nuts are a different matter.'

'Nuts?' the tone of surprise was weak and unconvincing. 'What's that got to do with me? I'm just a waiter...'

He started off in blustering denial, but when he saw the look on her face, he gave up. His shoulders slumped and he seemed to deflate. He chewed on his lip.

'That man is all right, I saw him,' he said, his tone somewhere between hopeful and defensive. And then with a desperate edge: 'He's fine, right? After the nuts?'

'He is. He got the pills in time and he recovered.' She didn't mention the threat of the lawsuit, fearing it would only push him further into denial.

'Look, Braydon. I'm not trying to get you into trouble. From what I hear you're a decent, hardworking guy. I have no interest in this beyond trying to find out what happened, because I think there might be a link between these incidents and the deaths of Desmond, and then Cynthia.'

'The murders? No! Oh no, no, no. That's got nothing... I had nothing to do with that. I promise on my life.'

The teen skater came over with a slouching, easy grace. Braydon stopped talking. 'You're up, Braydon,' he said, pulling off his cap and digging his fingers into his wild curls to scratch his head.

'Thanks, I'm gonna sit this one out. You go ahead. You're looking good out there, Alice.'

Julia looked closer, and discovered that the teen boy was indeed a teen girl.

'Cool, thanks, Braydon.' She put her cap back on her head, tucked in the mad curls, and pushed off again. Julia had seen a lot of stressed and unhappy young people in her life. It cheered her to see this one in her baggy khakis and big sneakers, strong and healthy, owning the skatepark.

With Alice gone, Braydon leaned against the fence in despair. He patted down his pockets for a vape, found it and sucked at it hungrily. When he exhaled, the air smelled of fake berries, and he looked somewhat calmer. He put the Vape back in his pocket and said, 'I don't know what to do. I had nothing to do with the deaths, I promise. I made a mistake. But not... Not that... I wouldn't...' His words caught in his throat and he bent double, breathing heavily with panic.

Julia spoke calmly, as she had so many times to so many troubled young people. 'Braydon, I believe you. I don't think you had anything to do with the murders. Or not deliberately, anyway. But we need to find out who did. Tell me who put you up to the nuts and the rats, and why. Then we'll decide together what to do next. Let me help you, Braydon.'

Braydon straightened up, steadying his breathing. He faced Julia with a look of cool assessment, as if deciding whether he should trust her or not. Either he decided he could trust her, or he realised he was out of options, but after a long moment's silence, he started to talk.

25

It being Saturday, Hayley Gibson was in her weekend
wardrobe, which was very similar to her work wardrobe, with
some slight adjustments. Instead of trousers, she wore rather
formal dark blue jeans. Her usual well-pressed button shirt was
replaced with a somewhat softer white cotton shirt. On her feet
she wore sneakers rather than sensible black or brown shoes
with good grip.

Julia was surprised to hear from the detective. The two
women were friendly, but the friendship had its limits. Hayley
was a private person, and besides, it wasn't easy to socialise
when you were a small-town police officer. She didn't trust
easily, but she was coming to trust Julia, both for her common
sense and good instincts, and for her discretion. Julia didn't
gossip. At least, not about important things, like police matters.

Hayley had invited Julia for breakfast at the Buttered
Scone. The invitation specifically included Jake, who was
sitting quietly at Julia's feet, trying to look like the sort of dog
who was deserving of a piece of bacon but wasn't going to make
a big fuss about it. Biding his time, he was. He really was
growing up, Julia thought, both pleased and a little sad.

'I wanted to thank you,' she said. 'The information you got from Peter about wills was very helpful.'

'I'm pleased to hear it. In what way?'

'Between you and me...' Hayley looked around the tearoom, which was a known gossip mill, constantly absorbing and releasing local intel, almost as if it was an organism breathing in and out. The table closest to them was empty. The next one along was occupied by a group of five women, clearly out-of-towners, wearing sensible outdoor gear and engaged in lively conversation. They were in high good spirits ahead of some imminent adventure, and couldn't be less interested in wills and pre-decease clauses.

Hayley opened her mouth and snapped it closed again when she saw Flo appear at Julia's elbow. Flo had a famously silent tread, enabled by white plimsolls, which made her a masterful eavesdropper.

'Hello, Hayley. How are you both? Out for a bit of crime-solving of a Saturday morning are you?' she laughed at her own joke.

'Oh yes, I never rest,' Hayley said lightly, and picked up the menu. She was eager to move off the topic, given Flo's husband's own recent incarceration.

'Well, you certainly have your work cut out for you. Two deaths in as many weeks. Tragic.'

'Yes,' Hayley nodded, and focused pointedly on the menu, running her finger down the options as if she – and everyone else in Berrywick – didn't know the whole thing off by heart. 'I'll have the full English please. Julia?'

'French toast and bacon. Thanks, Flo.'

When Flo was well out of earshot, Hayley continued, leaning forward: 'Between you and me, after you told me what Peter said, I took another look at Desmond's will, and Peter was right. That's exactly what they had. I didn't notice it at the time, because Cynthia was still alive. It was one clause in a whole lot of legal bumf, and it wasn't relevant. But with Cynthia dead, it is relevant. In fact, it's a crucial piece of information – it means the business goes to Goldie.'

'Gosh, well that does change things, doesn't it?'

'You're right, it does. It gives Goldie a strong motive for killing Cynthia – and fast. The waiting period would be up in a week or so. She would have known that, having seen the will. Plus, we know that she spoke to a lawyer, so he would have explained the will to her in detail.'

'So you're saying Cynthia killed Desmond to get the business, and then Goldie killed Cynthia to get it back again?'

'There might be other contributing factors, but that's what it looks like.' Hayley nodded.

'It's hard to believe, isn't it? Two people dead over a small-town catering company.'

'Our forensic accounting team took a look at the books when Desmond died. It's a very profitable business. You would be surprised at the turnover. The margins are good, especially when it comes to weddings.'

'People go mad with weddings. It's like some sort of crazy arms race – bigger, better, more elaborate. And then you factor in the pressure and the emotions...' Julia thought about how even mild-mannered and perfectly reasonable Christopher had gone a bit Groomzilla over their big day.

'Right. And companies like Candy Catering are the beneficiaries of the madness. They are doing an average of one a weekend, more in spring, apart from all the other business, the birthdays, a bit of corporate work, and so on.'

'So have you brought Goldie in? Is there a warrant?'

'No, no. Not yet. We have to tread carefully. She is Desmond's grieving widow, after all. We are following up on a few things, and the forensics should be finalised by Monday. I spoke to her when Cynthia died, but I didn't interview her as a suspect. When Cynthia died Goldie was home alone, of course

– heaven forbid anyone should have an alibi that is easy to check, that wouldn't do at all.' Hayley looked personally affronted by this turn of events.

'Well, to be fair, Hayley, Goldie did live alone, seeing as her husband recently died. And it was early in the morning. Rather an unlikely set of circumstances for a solid alibi.'

'Yes, it would have been very early in the morning. Early forensic results indicate that Cynthia had been dead an hour or two when you found her.'

'We got there a little before eight, if I'm not mistaken.'

'Yes. So that means she would have died between, say, six and seven o'clock in the morning. And Goldie lives in that row of modern houses on Greenside Way.'

'I know the place. The young families seem to like it. Nicky and Kevin just moved there. It would be a good fifteen- or twenty-minute drive to the Candy Catering offices. She'd have to have been up very early if she had killed Cynthia.'

'Well, if she was, there'd be no one there to see her,' Hayley said grumpily. 'Still, poor old Walter will have to knock on doors.'

A good-looking thirty-something fellow with a tousled, wind-swept look passed them with a nod and a 'Morning' and joined the five cheery women. Their cheer only increased at the sight of him, and the conversation ratcheted up in volume to be sufficiently loud and revealing that Julia knew they were meeting there to go foraging. The young chap was their guide.

She heard him promising 'delicacies like wild garlic... sorrel... young stinging nettles... mushrooms...'

'Glad I'm not going to any of them for dinner tonight,' Julia said in an undertone. 'Best-case scenario, you're eating weeds; worst-case, you're in the ER.'

Hayley made a sound between a grunt and a laugh. 'Give me good old bacon and eggs any day.' And as if on cue, Flo did just that, putting a plate full of greasy deliciousness in front of

Hayley, and French toast in front of Julia. They smiled at the coincidence, and in anticipation of their breakfast.

'Thanks, Flo.'

Jake had apparently had enough of biding his time. He leaned his velvet muzzle on Hayley's knee and rolled his limpid chocolatey eyes imploringly.

'Not at the table. I'll save you something,' the detective said. She was plain-spoken and direct, which worked well with humans and with dogs. Jake removed his snout and settled down with a resigned sigh.

After a few bites, Julia rested her knife and fork on the plate and said, 'I know you like Goldie for the murder, and it makes sense, but there's something else you should know. Something that might have a bearing.'

Hayley's full attention was on Julia, her breakfast forgotten. 'Go on.'

Julia told Hayley what Braydon had told her – that the two recent events catered by Candy Catering had been disrupted – 'sabotaged', she called it. Braydon had been paid to sprinkle ground-up nuts into the food. He had described it to Julia as a moment of weakness, a lapse of judgement. There had been £200 in it for him, which he sorely needed as he was skint, and the person who'd made the request had sworn that no one would be in any danger.

Hayley looked disbelieving. 'That's a hard thing to promise.'

'As it turned out, it was true.'

'Lucky for him – and for Richard who ate the nuts.'

'You're right, of course, he did a very stupid thing.' Julia sighed. 'More stupid than he realised, because after that, he was compromised. The next time the same person came to him with a request to disrupt the bridal shower, he wasn't able to refuse.'

'How about a simple no?'

'I imagine there was an additional two hundred in it for him the second time. And now they had something on him. They threatened to tell Desmond and Cynthia what he'd done if he didn't help again. He would lose his job.'

'And who is this mysterious person with ill intent and hundreds of pounds to splash around on dodgy waiters and rats?' asked Hayley, taking out her notebook and pencil.

'He wouldn't give me a name. I'm assuming it's someone in business who has a grudge against them. One of the suppliers. Or a competitor of some sort.'

'I'll look into it. Luckily for Braydon, we looked at Richard's complaint and he's not going to get anywhere with a criminal case. With both partners dead, he'll probably drop his civil suit. So your ratty little friend – and whoever put him up to it – might be off the hook for this one.'

With that, Hayley turned her attention back to cutting her sausage and pulling it through a mildly off-putting pool of saucy baked beans and egg yolk. Julia went back to her own, rather more aesthetically pleasing breakfast. She was relieved. She didn't think Braydon was a bad man. Rather, someone who'd made a poor judgement in the moment. He'd done something stupid and dangerous, and it was only by good fortune that it hadn't turned out worse in several possible ways. But something else was bothering her.

'Hayley, the sabotage – you don't think it has anything to do with the murders? It seems a strange coincidence that all these disasters should happen within weeks of each other. I wondered how they might be connected.'

Hayley chewed slowly. 'I was thinking the same. It is a strange coincidence. But remember, Desmond was not particularly well liked on a number of fronts – he was difficult with suppliers, and staff; he was a flirt. And then there were his competitors. Any one of them could have wanted to make trouble for him. But to kill him? And presumably Cynthia? It's quite a stretch. Goldie seems to have a clearer, stronger motive than some business enemy. At least when it comes to Cynthia. Her very livelihood was at stake.'

Hayley put her knife and fork together with a sharp clack of finality, and picked up a piece of bacon she'd saved for Jake. He sat up still and quivering. She held her arm out and dropped the bacon, which he snapped out of mid-air, like a trained seal with a fish.

'Good boy.'

Julia waved to Flo and made the international sign for the bill – a squiggling hand movement, fingers and thumb pressed together, as if she was signing a bill with a pen. In a few years' time, would they all be making a swipe gesture, Julia wondered.

Hayley picked up her table napkin – the Buttered Scone provided fresh white linen, no paper – and patted her lips. 'I'm going to have to bring Goldie in. There's nothing else for it. I'll pop by the office after breakfast, make some calls, and see if I can get a warrant today.'

'You're probably right. You need to talk to her.'

'As I said, the optics aren't good, her being the grieving widow. I only hope it doesn't backfire.'

'I hope not, Hayley. You go, I'll get the bill. Let me know how it goes.'

'I'll keep you posted. Thanks for breakfast.'

Jake and Julia were taking a slow walk home along the river path when the quiet of the Cotswolds countryside was shattered by an ear-splitting shriek.

'Jake, Jake, Jake!'

It was young Sebastian, running towards them as fast as his small legs would go. His mother followed behind, talking into the phone tucked between her ear and shoulder.

'You a good boy?' Sebastian asked, taking Jake's face

between his hands and staring lovingly into his eyes. 'Who's a good naughty boy? You. You smell like bacon.'

Jake nudged the boy gently with his head. He was, after all, a chocolate Labrador, which is to say, a bottomless pit when it came to affection. And food. Sebastian took the hint and played with his silky, floppy ears, murmuring sweet words to the happy dog. Nicky had caught up with them. 'Bye, Mum. I've got to go. Sebastian is asking me to read to him,' she said. She might have gotten away with the fib if not for the noise. Jake freed himself from Sebastian's attentions and made a lunge for a large goose that was emerging from the river onto the bank. His excited bark was followed by a furious hiss and a great flapping of wings, and then a terrified wail from Sebastian.

Nicky killed the call and came to her son's rescue, while Julia grabbed at the lead trailing behind Jake. It took her a few goes, as he was bounding around like a mad thing. The goose was long gone, back to the safety of the water, paddling serenely away from them.

'Good heavens, my beating heart.' Nicky held her hand dramatically to her chest. 'I suppose a quiet morning walk is too much to expect with a kid, is it?'

'Or a dog,' said Julia. 'I think Jake was responsible for starting that particular drama. Sorry.'

Nicky waved the apology away. 'Oh, I'm a bit edgy. Bad night's sleep. Bad month's sleep, actually. Sebastian's been waking me up most nights ever since we moved house.'

'How is the new house? Are you enjoying Greenside Walk?'

'Oooh, yes. It's nice, having a bit of garden. You know, we were in a flat before. It had its advantages, but with this little ball of energy, the extra space is nice. And it's convenient for Kevin, he can get to The Swan in no time. But Sebastian's not happy about the change. He's got into the habit of waking at four or five and getting into our bed and squirming and kicking like a cat in a sack. And of course it's too late for me to go back to sleep, so I'm up and about in the dark while Sebastian and Kevin go straight back to sleep for a good couple of hours. Dead to the world, they are.'

'That must be hard for you. Moving house is a big change, but Sebastian will get used to it. I hope he settles soon.'

They looked over at the boy, who had calmed down and was playing tug-of-war with the dog and a stick. Sebastian managed to wrestle it from Jake and toss it a foot or two. Jake made a show of running for it and bringing it back. A tussle ensued, which Jake let Sebastian win.

'So do I! It's been five weeks already.' Nicky rolled her eyes, and then patted at her face. 'Look at me! I've aged years. I tried a face serum, never had one of those before, cost a bomb, I can tell you. Have you ever tried one?' she peered closely at Julia, and presumably decided that she had not, because she shook her head and explained. 'It's like a special oil, with special ingredients, and it's supposed to take years off. Skin like a baby. But it made me break out in a rash. And then the neighbour died, poor Desmond. Murdered, apparently. Not at home, thank heavens, but anyway, that didn't help my peace of mind.' Once Nicky got talking, the words came tumbling out of her, chasing each other in a continuous stream without the customary pauses used to indicate a change of topic. You had to have your wits about you, or you found yourself still thinking about face serums when murders were now under discussion. Another thing about Nicky was that she was not easily halted. Not that Julia had any interest in stopping her once the conversation had turned to Desmond. She kept one eye on the dog and the child, and fed Nicky a small encouraging question to set her off again.

'So very sad. Did you know Desmond and Goldie at all?'

'Kev knew him from work. Candy Catering did a lot of functions at The Swan. Weddings and whatnot. Well, you know that, of course. Your husband's... Anyhow, we said hello when we moved in. They're right across from us. Their house is, like, a mirror image, you know, our kitchen faces their kitchen. They were friendly enough. They said they'd have us over for a meal to welcome us to the neighbourhood, which would have been nice, what with him being such a good chef and all, but of course that didn't happen because before we knew it he was dead.' Nicky paused for a microsecond to take a restorative breath and to honour her neighbour's death, before ploughing on. 'So, to answer your question, I don't know Goldie really, but one thing I do know is that she hasn't been getting a good night's sleep and a lie-in either, not since Desmond passed. When I'm up and about, on account of young wriggle-bum here, and sitting at my kitchen table having my morning tea, she's up drinking her tea and fretting about her poor dead husband, or so I imagine. It's so sad. The other day, she was wandering about the garden, looking lost. And only yesterday morning I saw her sitting there in the window, crying, poor lamb.'

'Are you sure it was yesterday? Friday?' Julia asked.

'Yes, definitely.'

'What time, do you think?'

'Oh, very early it was. It was still dark and she had the light on, which is how I knew she was up, and why I could see her. She was sitting at the little kitchen table by her window. It must have been about six or six thirty, I'd say, and there she was in her dressing gown – rather a pretty one, soft grey and fluffy, but not too fluffy. You know, some of those gowns, you look like a polar bear in its winter coat. One wash and they're all matted. Not attractive. I'd like to ask her where she got it, but it might seem a bit, you know... Nosy. Watching her in the mornings like that. Not that I was watching. But...'

'Nicky, this is important. Are you absolutely sure Goldie was at home yesterday morning?'

Nicky's gabbling ceased, finally, and she considered the question before answering, firmly and calmly: 'Yesterday morning she was right there at her kitchen table in her grey robe, crying. I kept checking, and she didn't move for ages.'

'Thanks, Nicky, I—'

'Sebastian! Put that down!' Nicky bellowed, and then stomped off towards him, muttering. 'Lord above, give me strength. You can't take your eyes off them for a second, can you?'

Sebastian had found a large cup – one of the giant ones they give you at the takeaway, and which he had likely found in a nearby dustbin – and was scooping up river water to create a small patch of wet mud. He had his shoes off, despite the chilly autumn weather, and was splashing about in his socks. Jake was patting and lapping at the water as it fell, and bounding around encouragingly. Needless to say, he was covered in mud a few shades lighter than his fur. Julia sighed at what she knew would be an afternoon of wrangling and washing the muddy beast.

But first, she had to get hold of Hayley Gibson. Right away. Goldie could not possibly have killed Cynthia at the same time as she was seen weeping in her kitchen, but Hayley was about to arrest her for just that.

26

As luck would have it, Julia got hold of Hayley Gibson as the detective was leaving the police station to drive to Greenside Way and bring Goldie in to answer some tough questions. She had the warrant she needed, but Julia's call stopped her in her tracks.

'You happened to bump into Nicky, just after our breakfast?' Hayley asked. 'Just after we realised she lived on the same road as Desmond and Goldie?'

'Not just on the same road. Directly across the road from them, as it turns out.'

'And you're telling me that Nicky was spying on her neighbours on the very morning that Cynthia died?' she asked, incredulous. 'That's rather a remarkable coincidence.'

'Most mornings, I suspect. So perhaps not quite such a coincidence.'

'Right.'

There was silence on the line. This new piece of information would have set Hayley back significantly. If Goldie was at home at the time of Cynthia's murder, Hayley had lost her key suspect. Julia could almost hear her brain whirring away on the other end of the phone line, thinking about what this meant, what to do next.

'It looks like my whole theory has gone out the window, Julia. If Cynthia killed Desmond to get the business, and Goldie killed Cynthia to get the business back and take revenge on his killer, it all made sense. The murders were linked. But now I'm not even sure that Cynthia did kill Desmond. And even if she did, if Goldie didn't kill Cynthia, and someone else did, what's the connection?'

'There has to be something linking the murders,' Julia agreed.

'Of course. It's too much of a coincidence for the two partners to have been killed unless it's related. I think we're back to the drawing board, but it seems safe to assume that they were killed by the same person.'

'Hayley, you need to speak to Braydon.'

'My thoughts exactly. Whoever put him up to the nuts and the rats has moved up to poll position in this murder investigation. In fact, with Goldie out of the picture, I don't have another strong suspect for Cynthia's murder. I've left a message for Braydon to get in touch with me. If I don't hear from him in an hour or so, I'll send Walter Farmer to his place.'

Having passed on the information she had gleaned, Julia had no further distractions to delay the inevitable and unenviable task of cleaning Jake. While she had been on the phone, the mud had dried, and she was hopeful that it might be brushed off, so she wouldn't have to get a hosepipe or a bucket of warm water and dog shampoo. It all seemed rather exhausting, and she found herself gazing around the kitchen looking for a task to further delay the dog cleaning. If she left him outside long enough, maybe the mud would fall off on its own. He would be a self-cleaning dog, like those mysterious self-cleaning ovens.

She was pondering the likelihood of this when Jess came padding into the kitchen in her pyjamas, looking rumpled. 'Oh, hello, love. Goodness, you slept late. I thought you must be... Oh...'

Dylan walked in after Jess, properly dressed, thank goodness. It was a bit of a surprise, but Julia regained her composure quickly. 'Good morning, Dylan. Lovely day.'

He greeted her seemingly without a trace of awkwardness, but Julia found herself oddly flustered by the situation. Jess was a grown-up, after all, living an independent life on the other side of the world. She didn't need Julia's permission to have a friend stay over. Nonetheless, Julia was grateful when Jess started rummaging in the fridge and giving a running commentary of her discoveries, seemingly oblivious to her mother's awkwardness.

'Tomatoes, a nice bit of cheddar. That would be good. Those last three droopy mushrooms need to be thrown out. How long has this bacon been here?' She opened up the butcher's paper and stared at the contents suspiciously. 'Have you had breakfast, Mum? I'm going to make us omelettes.'

'Not for me, Thanks, love. I had breakfast. I've been up for hours! I've already been out to the Buttered Scone with Hayley. Flo's French toast will keep me going until supper time. And that bacon is fresh. I bought it on Thursday.'

Julia's phone vibrated noisily on the kitchen table. She'd switched it to silent at breakfast, and forgotten to turn the sound back on, but it rattled against the wood. Dylan passed it over, 'Speak of the devil,' he said. 'It's Hayley Gibson.'

Julia answered, and Hayley did not even give her a chance for the usual niceties. 'Braydon's not answering his phone and he's not at home. Walter went round to see if he was there and the place was deserted except for a lot of cages and tanks in a big sort of shed out back with all his animals.'

'What are you thinking? That he might be' – she turned away from the young couple at the stove, and spoke quietly into the phone – 'in trouble?'

Hayley didn't answer the question. Instead she asked one of her own. 'When you spoke to him, he wouldn't give you the name of the person who put him up to causing that trouble for Candy Catering. Why did you think that was?'

'I got the impression he didn't want the person to know he was the one who got them into trouble. He didn't want to be linked to it. I suppose he thought they'd be cross if they knew it was him.'

'Julia, how did he seem when he spoke about them? What was his manner?'

She thought back to the previous afternoon at the skatepark, and his flat-out refusal to name names. She conjured up his face, the anxious frown that furrowed his brow, the determination in the set of his jaw.

'He seemed worried. Maybe even...'

'Scared?'

'Yes.'

'I'm going to go and help Walter look for him.'

'If I—'

But Julia didn't finish her sentence. Without so much as a goodbye, Hayley Gibson was gone.

'Where do you keep the grater, Mum?'

The question took a moment to sink in. Julia was preoccupied with the question of what had happened to Braydon, and – more importantly – how it was related to Desmond's death.

'What? The grater? Oh, for cheese.'

She opened the big pot drawer, took it out and handed it to her daughter, who was at the stove, melting butter in a pan, her hair now tied back in a rough ponytail. Dylan was whisking eggs.

Jake arrived at the open back door, accompanied by Henny Penny. Two pairs of eyes watched curiously, but the animals remained in the doorway. They obeyed Julia's 'No chickens in the house' rule, but only just. The doorway was, by silent agreement, an inter-species no-man's-land.

'Do you think she knows we're eating her future babies?' Dylan asked.

Jess nudged him hard with her elbow. 'Why did you have to say that? Horrible! Ugh!'

He laughed, and they pushed and jostled in a touchy, flirty sort of way. Jake edged closer, eager to be part of the fun.

'Oh no, you don't,' Julia said, flapping a tea towel at him. There had been so much going on, she'd forgotten all about the muddy dog. 'You're not coming inside until you're clean. In fact, Jess, do you think you two could give him a good brush when you've had your breakfast or lunch or whatever that is? He got himself covered in mud and it should brush out once it's dried. Hopefully.'

'Sure, Mrs B. Will do.' Dylan sounded surprisingly enthusiastic at the prospect of brushing dried mud off a dog – presumably because he would be doing it with Jess.

'Thanks, Dylan. And Dylan, there's something else I wanted to ask you. It's about Desmond.'

He nodded, sombre now. Jess took the bowl from him and poured the eggs into the bubbling butter.

'When you said Desmond had fought with lots of people, what did you mean?'

'Honestly, he was a difficult guy. He was always in a beef with someone. He was always in a row with his neighbour – the most recent one was something to do with a tree, I think. The vet, something about his prize Labradoodle. And everyone at work, at some time or another. It can get stressful when there's something big on, and he had a short fuse. Arabella can be very demanding, but that's the job of the wedding planner, I suppose. To get the best out of everyone. The two of them could get snippy on occasion. He and Cynthia had their moments, too, although they mostly got on well. Oh, and the suppliers. Not Angela, she was never in his bad books, I guess because her flowers are always wonderful. But the food suppliers heard all about it if the lettuce wasn't perfectly crisp or the tomatoes juicy. Have to say, they did their best for Desmond because of it.'

'Enough chatter, omelettes are ready,' Jess said, proudly holding up the skillet with her creation. It smelled richly of melted cheese and butter – and they knew for a fact that these eggs were organic.

Julia left them to their breakfast – or more accurately lunch, as it was well after noon. The animals followed her outside, where she took an amble around her garden. It wasn't large, and she knew every single plant. What was coming into bloom, or going to seed. Which plant needed water, or a bit of pruning. It was a happy sort of paying attention that she hadn't known before she moved to Berrywick, and that she had come to love. She was behind on her gardening tasks. Packets of bulbs – tulips, crocuses and daffodils – awaited planting, and she needed to mulch the beds with compost. She'd been so busy with Jess, and the wedding, and the awful murders, she hadn't spent much time in her garden. 'Gardening day tomorrow, chaps. We'll spend Sunday doing autumn clean-up and getting things ship-shape. I'll see if Sean wants to help.'

Jake looked at her adoringly. Her plans were all simply fantastic as far as he was concerned. He was totally there for whatever she suggested. Henny Penny, being a chicken, had little interest in Julia's hopes and dreams.

As she walked around her small estate, she wondered if Hayley had had any luck finding Braydon. She felt sure that once the police came calling, he would spill the beans on whoever put him up to his troublemaking, and Hayley would have a new line of enquiry.

Julia bent down to check the leaves of her spinach for whatever it was that was snacking on them. She thought about the list of people that Dylan had named. Could one of them be the murderer? Could a falling out of the type that Desmond seemed rather good at possibly have caused his death, and his business partner's?

Arabella, the wedding planner, had been around on the night of Peter and Chris's wedding, and at the bridal shower, but it was hardly in her interests to disrupt an event that she herself was organising. Far from it, it made her life extremely difficult. A rival made more sense. There was the rival caterer, the woman who owned In Good Taste. What had she heard Cynthia tell Arabella at the funeral? Something like *'Don't phone Henrietta. You know she's been awful to him.'* Or something along those lines.

Jess came out of the kitchen door, wielding the dog brush, and shouting, 'Beautification time, Jakey! Come on, boy!'

'I was saying that I'm going to be working in the garden tomorrow. Join me if you feel like it.'

'Saying to Jake, I take it?' Jess said, her eyebrows raised, and gave her mum a squeeze. 'Mad old lady vibes, Mum. Discussing your plans with the dog. Sure, I'll help you in the garden. Dylan's got to work.'

'Yeah, I would have liked to garden, but I'm working. Arabella has a fortieth-birthday brunch booked. I was booked to work the gig for Candy Catering, but obviously, without Desmond or Cynthia... Anyway, she phoned to say it was still on, she wants me there. She must have had to scrabble around a bit, but she got it sorted – probably gone to In Good Taste, I should think. Henrietta Simmons will be pleased.'

'Dylan, at Desmond's funeral, I overheard Cynthia talking

to Arabella about something bad Henrietta had done to Desmond. Do you know what it is?'

'No. Don't know anything about that. Before my time, probably. I don't know her personally, but I know there was fierce competition for business. I can ask around tomorrow, if you like.'

'Thanks, please do, Dylan. And let me know if you hear anything.'

27

Julia's finger hovered over the send button. She hesitated. It was really none of her business. But when did that ever stop her?

She sent the message.

Even though it was Sunday, DI Hayley Gibson messaged back almost immediately: *No sign of Braydon. Not answering his phone. Walter went back to his house this morning. I'm worried. Escalating.*

Julia felt the prickle of fear run up her throat and into her jaw. She phoned Hayley.

'Do you think he's in danger?' she asked. In her worry, she'd adopted the detective's habit of cutting to the chase without even a greeting to ease the way.

'Let's just say I don't like it when I want to talk to someone – a witness, a source – and they mysteriously disappear. It could mean they're avoiding me. Or it might mean something's happened to them. It could be nothing, but it could be something. I'll get Walter working on it today. See if he can find friends. Parents.'

'Okay, you could also go to—'

Julia's suggestion – that they try the skatepark – was cut short by an incessant beeping, and Hayley's clipped tone. 'Walter on the line. I have to go.'

The phone went dead.

'I know I said we're going to be gardening today, and we will, but there's something we need to do first.' Jake looked expectantly up at her, indicating that he was cool with whatever she had planned, as long as he was included. He was ready to go and awaiting further information. 'We're going to the skatepark. I'll get your lead.' The word 'lead' sent him into a frenzy of excitement, spinning circles and barking madly. 'Car,' she said, at which he hurtled over and sat next to the back door like a very, very good boy, waiting for the next exciting phase of what was turning out to be a very good day.

At the skatepark, Julia opened the car door to be greeted by the now familiar whizzing sound of the wheels, and the clattering of the skateboards, and the young people shouting to each other. A speaker was playing *doof doof* music, but at a volume that wouldn't bother the neighbours. It was a mild and pretty day, and the park was fuller than previously, the atmosphere busy and friendly. There was no sign of Braydon, unsurprisingly, but she did see Alice. The girl was leaning against the fence, watching the skaters. Her skateboard leaned against one leg, and the other leg was bent, her sneakered foot resting against the fence. Her golden curls were imperfectly restrained by some sort of bandana. Julia thought she looked as if she could have been in an advertisement for some very cool product, not that Julia knew what that product might be, of course.

She got Jake out of the back of the car, clipped on his lead and walked over to where the girl was standing.

'Hello. You're Alice, aren't you?'

The girl looked at her with a squinty frown that indicated she vaguely recognised her but couldn't place her. It was a look that Julia noticed she had gotten increasingly often from young people as she marched through her middle age and into her early sixties.

'Oh yeah, I saw you the other day. You were talking with Braydon.'

It was nice to be recognised – even if the recognition was a little delayed. Better than complete invisibility.

'That's right. I'm Julia. I was here on Friday with him. In fact, I'm looking for Braydon. Has he been here today?'

'No. Not here and he won't be. Not today.' She looked around as if deciding whether Julia deserved more information, and then added, 'He said he was going somewhere. He'll be gone a few days. He asked me to feed his animals.'

'That sounds like a big job,' Julia said with a laugh. 'There are a lot of them.'

The girl responded warmly. 'I know, right? And they all eat different things. Crickets for the reptiles, can you believe? At least they're dead. And dried. But still. Crickets. And then there's the rodents. Lots of those, but I like them. Clever little things, and at least they eat pellets. Anyway, he said he'd pay me for my trouble.' She sounded pleased at the prospect of payday.

Julia gazed over at the skaters, and said with a casual tone, 'Ah, well, sorry I missed him. He didn't mention he was going away. Nice that he's having a break, though. Where's he gone, do you know?'

'He's camping. Weird, really, he doesn't seem like the camping type.' It sounded to Julia as if he might be hiding, rather than camping. 'Anyway, I dunno where he's gone. Probably somewhere local cos he doesn't have a car. He would've gone on his bike.'

'Any idea when he'll be back?'

'He said he wasn't sure. It was very last minute. He asked me yesterday. Said there's enough food for the animals for a week or two.'

As soon as she got back to her car, Julia phoned Hayley and relayed the news.

'Well, that's a relief. At least he's not dead,' the detective said brusquely. The very mention of it gave Julia a horrible feeling in her tummy.

'He left in a hurry, Hayley. The day after Cynthia's death. The day after I spoke to him. It seems as if he was running from something.'

'Or someone.'

'Hayley, I think what I said spooked him,' Julia said. 'I was there on Friday afternoon, asking about the sabotage at Candy Catering. I think that's what made him leave town the next morning.'

Was it possible for a silence to have a tone? It wasn't clear, but there was a definite tone of anger and frustration in the uncomfortable period of quiet emanating from DI Hayley Gibson. The detective took a deep breath – Julia could hear the air whistling gently as it entered her nose and exited her mouth in the form of a sigh. 'Well, it looks like he's scared of something. Or someone. And if you're right about the timing, he's scared of whoever paid him to sabotage Candy Catering.'

'Hayley, we need to find him before whoever he's scared of finds him. We need to get to him first.'

'I'll have Walter start phoning the campsites, see if he can find him and have a little chat. He unearthed the parents. Parent. His dad was widowed a few years back. He lives with his new wife and two little kids. No space for Braydon, so he rents a room in that house – a right mess, according to Walter –

with three other students, and they all keep to themselves. No one knows anything much about him.'

It sounded rather sad: the ramshackle house, the pets, the absent parents, the disinterested roommates. Julia hoped that Braydon was okay. But she had a horrible, sick feeling that maybe he wasn't.

Sean was pulling up at her house as Julia arrived home.

'That's good timing,' he said, opening the hatchback for Leo to jump out. 'Where have you been?'

'The skatepark.' Julia freed Jake and the two dogs greeted each other delightedly and ran to the garden.

'Interesting hobby choice for your retirement.' His eyes narrowed and gleamed when he teased her, a little smile twitching on his lips.

'Just keeping life interesting,' she said. 'New experiences. New challenges.'

'New hips, if you're not careful.'

'You underestimate me.'

'I assure you I do not, Mrs Bird,' he said in his rumbling burr, his blue eyes locking on hers. They stood like that for a long minute. Her heart pounded a little faster in her chest.

'I was on a mission for information, not a new hobby.'

'And did you find it?' He loved her interfering ways, and her good instincts, and welcomed new information with glee.

'I did. Come on in, I'll tell you all about it while we get going on the garden.'

'I can't wait.'

They decided to start with the pruning. Julia had a good sharp pair of long-handled pruning shears which she employed with a satisfying crush and snap, feeling the muscles in her arms working. As she cut, Sean grabbed the branches and pulled them into a pile on the lawn. The chickens retreated nervously to the far side of their coop, with the exception of Henny Penny who watched from the other side of the garden, where the dogs were lying in the wan autumn sun after a chase. Leo followed Jake's lead and accepted the bossy chicken as some kind of feathered doggish equal; small, but not to be messed with.

In between grunts of exertion, Julia told Sean about her early morning investigation. 'And now Walter Farmer has gone to look for him.' She paused to bear down on the handles and cut through the thick stem of the laburnum which had been dripping with yellow blossoms a few months back, and was now straggly with dead flowers. The stem gave with a sharp snap and fell to the ground. She continued. 'He's checking on all the campsites nearby.'

Sean pushed his fists into his lower back as he straightened up. 'You're not going to believe this, but I think I know where Braydon is.'

'You do? How?'

'My neighbourhood WhatsApp group was all in a tizz this morning. Nothing new there, of course. They're decent people, but they do like to get worked up about things. But this time it sounded rather more serious than the usual complaints about dustbins and dogs. Someone had spotted a person – a young man – in the allotments down the end of the road. He had a backpack, and the person who saw him reckoned he might have slept there overnight.'

'Did they say anything about him? What did he look like? How old?'

'Lucky for you, the chap took a photograph and sent it to the group. Hang on.' Sean fished his phone from the pocket of his windproof jacket and pulled up the message. 'Here you go.'

The nosy parker in question was no paparazzi, but they had managed to get a blurry shot of the rear view of a lanky fellow with spiky blonde hair and a backpack pushing a bicycle out of a field of allotments. He gazed over his shoulder in what looked like a furtive gesture. His face was out of focus, but she was sure.

'It's him, Sean. It's definitely Braydon. I'm going to phone the police.'

28

Julia was on her way indoors to phone Hayley and send the photograph and the location to her and DC Walter Farmer, when Dylan arrived back from work with more news. He came out of the kitchen door looking very proud of himself. 'I got the low-down on Henrietta like you asked, Mrs B.'

'Julia.'

'Julia. I asked Arabella. Casual like. You'd have been proud of me. So, turns out In Good Taste was catering the function today. They stepped in at the last minute, because, you know, Candy couldn't do it, obviously. Henrietta wasn't there herself, she had another job on, but her people were there. They did the food. Arabella thanked me for coming to work, said she knew it must be hard, losing Desmond and Cynthia, and now working with the opposition. After all the bad blood between them.'

Julia nodded patiently, letting him tell the story at his own pace, even though she really wanted to chip in, *Just tell me what she did to Desmond, for heaven's sake!*

'Seeing as she brought it up, I asked her what the beef was between Henrietta and Desmond. She said they were rivals, obviously, but that it got out of hand when Desmond discovered

Henrietta was leaving bad reviews about Candy Catering on all these websites. You know, the ones where you get recommendations. She was clever, created false accounts, a few different names, but one day she did it from her own account by mistake, under her own name. She said something bad about Desmond personally, and he confronted her, and then he discovered she'd written all the others.'

'That's a terrible thing to do,' said Jess, with all the indignation of youth. 'Completely unfair.'

'It was. A really low blow. Arabella said Desmond and Cynthia were furious. They were talking to a lawyer about suing her. They wanted to close down her business for good.'

They fell quiet for a moment, as the same question passed through all of their minds. Was Henrietta worried enough to kill them both?

Jess was the first one to voice it. 'So, is she the murderer? Did she kill Desmond and Cynthia, do you think?'

'Maybe. But wait, there's more. I spoke to this guy who has worked for Candy on and off for a long time. Norm, his name is. He was working the bar today. He said that about six months ago, Henrietta offered him money to slip a little something into the soup at a graduation dinner Desmond was catering.'

'No!' Jess said, somewhere between horrified and excited. 'Did he do it?'

'No. He refused. Told her to take a hike. And then she said she was only kidding. Didn't mean it. Tried to make out it was a test or a joke or something, but he said he reckoned she was serious.'

'My God, what an evil woman!' Julia thought about this new information. 'Dylan, you've done great. This is really helpful. I'm going to phone DI Gibson and tell her everything you've found out, and she can take it from here.'

. . .

Hayley was astonished by what Julia had uncovered in her day's work. 'You located Braydon, and you got all this information about this rival caterer woman?'

'Henrietta Simmons. Yes.'

'All in one morning?'

'It was Dylan and Sean, really. I just put things together.'

Hayley made a noncommittal grunt on the other end of the phone. She didn't encourage Julia's amateur sleuthing efforts, but on the other hand, she was the recipient of some useful information as a result.

'The main thing is that Braydon is okay. I was worried when he went missing, I must say.'

'I was too, Julia. But it's definitely him in the picture. I'll give Walter the location. He can't have gone far. Let's see what he's got to say for himself.'

'I'm fairly sure he will say that Henrietta put him up to the nuts and the rats.'

'Indeed. And I wonder if maybe sabotage wasn't enough for her and she stepped up to murder. I'm going to her office now. It's in Hayfield, I should be there in twenty minutes. I hope she's still there. Henrietta Simmons has some questions to answer.'

'Good luck. Be careful!'

'Will do.'

Jess and Dylan had moved into the sitting room and were sitting close together on the sofa, watching something shouty with very loud music on her phone and laughing.

'Hayley is on it,' she said.

'That's good, Mum.' Jess didn't look up from her phone. 'Dylan, look at this one, it's so funny.' More noise.

She retreated to the garden, feeling mildly annoyed. Her peaceful little house felt full and noisy, and Jess was distracted by Dylan. She immediately felt guilty for feeling annoyed. She'd been longing to have Jess around, filling the place with her youthful energy. Now she was irritated by the noise. And as for the constant presence of Dylan, they were young, and seemingly in love. Or in something. It made Jess happy. Julia should be happy. And she was. It was silly to feel excluded and grumpy.

'Hayley is on it,' she said to Sean.

'Pleased to hear it. You might have given her the information she needs to finally solve these horrible crimes. Speaking of which, the neighbourhood nosy parkers have spotted the so-called squatter – your friend Braydon is back.'

Sean was a more communicative audience than the youth.

'Really? I had better tell Hayley. It's getting chilly out. I think we're done with gardening for the day. Shall we move inside? It'll have to be the kitchen, the kids are in the sitting room making a noise.'

'I should probably be getting back to my house. Why don't you come over for the afternoon? Give the young a bit of space.'

'You know what? I will.' Julia surprised herself with her spontaneous acceptance. 'That's a fine idea. I'm always a bit mopey on a Sunday afternoon. A change of scene will do me good. Let me tell Jess, quickly.'

Jess looked mildly taken aback at her mother's plan, but her eyes slid over to Dylan with a little smile. 'You two can have the place to yourselves,' said Julia, in what she hoped was not a voice that suggested either approval or disapproval at anything that might happen while she was out.

'Can you leave Jake?' Jess reached down for the dog. 'I'll miss you too much, Jakey boy.'

Julia tried not to be hurt that her daughter would miss the dog more than her own mother, but she agreed.

. . .

Julia rang Hayley while Sean drove. 'I'll put it on speaker so you can hear.'

Hayley answered brusquely.

'Julia, what is it? I'm at Henrietta's office.'

'I wanted to let you know that Braydon is back at the allotment. Sean got a message on the neighbour group.'

'Right, I'll let Walter know.'

'Have you seen Henrietta?'

'No. The staff are unpacking from the morning function, but she's not here.'

'Oh, where—'

'Listen to this, Julia: the manager said she's gone to her allotment in Berrywick to pick her parsnips, or potatoes, or maybe it was pumpkins.'

'Her allotment? In Berrywick? Could it be the same one?'

'I think so. They said it was north of the village. There's only one on that side. I'm leaving now.'

'Hayley, if Braydon is there, she might find him. Or perhaps she went there *to* find him. He could be in danger.'

'Exactly. He's the one who knows she was behind the sabotage.'

'She might even be going because she knows he's there,' said Julia, feeling a wave of anxiety. There had been so much violence. It would be too terrible if any harm were to befall Braydon.

Sean chipped in. 'Hayley, Sean here. We're right here. Literally driving past. We'll head in there and see what's going on.'

'She's a dangerous woman, Sean. I don't want you two confronting her.'

'We won't. We'll just keep an eye, see if we can spot Braydon. If we find him, we'll take him home to my place.'

'I don't like it, but... Just until I get there. Julia, you be very careful.'

'Will do. Got to go.'

Sean put his foot on the accelerator, going a little faster than his usual speed, which was always precisely on the speed limit, no faster, no slower. In almost no time, he drew up at the allotments. Julia had walked and driven past many times, and admired the little gardens that the allotment holders had created. Each one was different. Some were neat and symmetrical, with seedlings planted precisely in rows. Some were wild and unruly, a jumble of flowers and vegetables. Some had sheds. A couple had chicken coops. They were visions of industriousness and care, and the world somehow seemed the better for them.

It struck Julia that she didn't know what Henrietta looked like. She'd never met her. Neither had Sean. She needn't have worried. There was only one person working on the allotments. She was wearing a large straw hat that covered her face, and a pair of gardening gloves. She carried a pair of sharp, shiny shears in one hand and a large garden fork in the other. She was walking down the path between the rows of cabbages and carrots, looking left to right, right to left.

'She's looking for him!' Julia whispered, even though the woman couldn't possibly hear. 'Come on. We need to find him before she does.'

Sean hesitated, but Julia was out of the car in seconds, closing the door quietly behind her. He followed her lead.

Henrietta turned left and disappeared from view behind a shed. Julia and Sean picked up speed. Julia stumbled over a piece of uneven ground. Sean reached out and took her arm to steady her. They turned into the path Henrietta had taken and stopped to catch their breath and decide what to do next. They caught a glimpse of her between two trellises that were covered with some sort of creeper. The creepers were dense in places, and Julia couldn't see clearly, but she seemed to be bent over.

'There you are,' Henrietta said. Her voice was oddly tender;

it gave Julia the creeps. 'I thought you'd be here, and here you are. It's time.'

She straightened up and raised her fork high.

'Stop! Henrietta, no!'

The woman turned at the sound of Julia's voice, but didn't stop the plunge of the fork towards the ground.

Sean leapt forward, Julia right behind him. She hesitated a moment – she couldn't bear to see what damage Henrietta had wrought on the skater boy's lanky body with the garden fork. She took a breath and gathered her courage. She stepped to the side, to see what Sean was seeing – Henrietta standing open-mouthed in shock and confusion, her big straw hat askew, her fork stuck in the ground. At her feet was not Braydon's body but a potato plant. A small hole had been excavated a few inches from the stem, revealing a clutch of baby potatoes, nestled like eggs in a nest.

Henrietta had regained her composure sufficiently to speak, her clipped posh voice icy with anger. 'Who are you and what do you want? You nearly gave me a heart attack.'

'Where's Braydon?'

'What are you *talking* about?' she seemed genuinely confused, her brow furrowed. She was older than Julia had expected, although her hair was artfully and expensively coloured, and her make-up was carefully if lightly applied. She had the very fancy wellies that the very fancy people had – Julia forgot the name.

'Braydon. The waiter.' Julia spoke weakly, as the realisation came to her that they'd made a terrible mistake.

'That Braydon? How would I know where some part-time waiter is? And why do you care?'

'I know you were behind the rat.'

'Behind a rat? What rat? Are you actually insane?' Henrietta brushed her cheek, leaving a smear of mud. When she spoke again, it was with calm authority. 'I must insist that you leave. I'm here on my own allotment, harvesting my vegetables. I will not be harassed by some strange woman.'

'The rat at the bridal shower. You sabotaged Candy Catering. First by planting the nuts at the wedding, and then with the rat on the cake at the bridal shower.'

Julia wasn't sure, but it seemed like a shadow of understanding flitted across Henrietta's face, before her eyes grew hard.

'I've no idea what you're talking about. Now leave.'

They had reached something of a stalemate. It was true, there was no sign of Braydon. There were potatoes. It seemed Julia had jumped to conclusions and made a terrible mistake. Perhaps he had not been in danger at all. And as for the sabotage, well, there was no proving that in the absence of Braydon.

Sean broke the silence. 'Julia.' She followed the tilt of his head. Hayley Gibson exited her car, slammed the door, and hurried over the uneven ground towards them. It was a relief to see her. Perhaps she could sort this whole mess out.

'Where's Braydon?' she said.

Julia and Henrietta spoke in unison. 'Not here.'

Except that he was. He had come in from the top end of the allotments, and was loping towards them, a backpack on his shoulders, bewilderment on his face.

29

Far from being a day of rest, Sunday had been a long and exhausting day, the challenges of which stretched into the evening. After the confusion and embarrassment of the confrontation with Henrietta at the allotment, the whole group had decamped to the Berrywick police station, where Braydon spilled the beans on Henrietta. It was – as Julia had suspected – Henrietta who had paid him to sabotage Candy Catering, like she had tried to convince Norm to. Braydon had been spooked by Julia's questions, and his admissions, and the possibility of legal action over the incident with the nuts. He explained that he was worried that Henrietta might come looking for him – 'She's not a very nice lady,' he said, looking at her, and then quickly away. He explained that he 'took himself off for a bit of a wander', in the interests of safety, and in the hope that things would blow over.

Henrietta denied everything, of course. She went straight on the offensive, telling them all in a most imperious tone that she was a respected and respectable businesswoman, and very well connected in Berrywick and in fact the whole county and she didn't appreciate these unfounded accusations from a young hooligan and they would be well advised not to tangle with her, and so on and so on. She hadn't noticed the muddy smudge on her face, and its presence rather spoiled her high-handed performance. Henrietta responded to all evidence and accusation with such indignation that Julia wondered whether she was merely arrogant, or actually so delusional that she believed the story she was dishing out. It wouldn't be the first time Julia had come across such a thing.

To her credit, Hayley Gibson was having none of it. She wasn't cowed for a minute. She told Henrietta firmly but politely that there would be further investigation into the matter of sabotage, but she would like to turn to the more serious matter, which was of course the murders.

The word stopped Henrietta in her tracks. Her imperious-ness deserted her, replaced by pure, abject terror. The differ-ence between this Henrietta and the one that had been on display a moment before was remarkable. She was pale and shaken and stammering: 'No, no, no... I had nothing to do with that... I would never... How can you even think...? Please, you have to believe me...'

Before, she had been acting. But now, Julia didn't think she was. Either she was telling the truth, or she was a very good actress. Julia suspected the former.

Sean agreed. 'I think your friend Hayley Gibson still has a killer to catch,' he said dryly, when they finally left the station in the dark.

'So do I, Sean. So do I. And I'm all out of ideas as to who it might be.'

Julia felt that given the busyness and stress of her Sunday, she deserved an additional day of rest, but it was not to be. Diane's husband, Mark, was still wearing a big orthopaedic boot, which meant that Diane had to drive him to work, and Julia had agreed to help Wilma out at Second Chances. She messaged Wilma to tell her that she would be coming in a little late – it wasn't as if there was usually a queue of customers gathering outside the charity shop at nine on the dot – and allowed herself a bit of a lie-in and a slow start. Jess and Dylan had baked a carrot cake (and, importantly, they'd cleaned up the kitchen meticulously, even mopped the floor). Julia treated herself to a big slice of the cake for breakfast. She placed it on a side plate, which she put down next to her giant mug of tea. She sat down and surveyed her breakfast with pleasure, shooing away any lurking guilt. It was basically vegetables, she told herself, cutting off a generous mouthful with the side of her fork. Vegetables with walnuts and cream cheese icing. Almost the same as fruit and yoghurt and granola, if you think about it. She speared the cake and put it into her mouth. Delicious. A good start to a good day.

Wilma greeted Julia's arrival as if it was all that stood between her and complete disaster. 'There you are! Excellent. Gosh, there's so much to do.'

'Is there?' Julia looked around the shop for evidence of a huge workload. There was a single customer – an ancient fellow perusing the bookshelf at the back of the store – and a single small zip-up carrier bag of clothes at Wilma's feet.

'Goldie brought those in. They're Desmond's. The actual clothes he had on the night he died. This is what he wore to work, apparently, before he changed into his whites. They were in the bag and the police took them. They released his things this morning and she brought them straight here. Said she couldn't look at them. Even said she'd pay for the dry cleaning or whatever was needed.'

'Poor Goldie. So hard for her. I'll unpack them, shall I?'

'Thank you. If you don't mind. Gives me the shivers. I'll take care of the till and the customers.'

Julia refrained from asking exactly which customers were going to keep Wilma so busy, and took the bag to the little back room where they sorted things and made tea. She opened it with a feeling of sadness and trepidation. They were only clothes, of course. The clothes of a dead man. A pair of black jeans. A long-sleeved black cotton undershirt. A soft wool pullover and thin windbreaker jacket, both black. A pair of thick-soled, comfortable trainers. So ordinary, and so poignant.

There was no use in sitting there moping over an old jumper, Julia told herself. She pulled herself together and went through the routine they always followed when people donated clothes. Check the condition – anything damaged or not suit-able would be sent away. Check for cleanliness. Check the size. Check the pockets.

Julia slipped her hand into the pocket of the windbreaker, nothing. In the second pocket, her fingers met paper. She fished out a scrap, probably a sweet wrapper or a receipt or a shopping list or some such. It was a folded piece of white paper, a receipt as she'd expected. She recognised the logo of The Swan, which was – unsurprisingly, a simple line drawing of a swan floating on three wavy lines representing the river. She glanced at the receipt – three beers, two burgers – and felt sad all over again. She noticed a scrawl showing through and turned over the paper.

D. Well done on great wedding food as always. Had to go. Will be back at 10pm. Meet me out back. Need to talk... Love. A xxx

A sweet sketch of a flower followed the row of kisses. The sketch was of a simple little flower, a daisy, perhaps. It was familiar, somehow, but Julia couldn't place it.

Her brain went into overdrive, her heart too. It galloped in her chest and her hands shook with the hit of adrenaline that was pumping into her body. The note, with its kisses and plans, put a whole new spin on what might have happened that night.

So many thoughts, so many questions. D *must* be Desmond, but who was A? Julia thought through the people that had been linked to the wedding. Arabella! Could it be the wedding planner? Was he having an affair with Arabella when he died?

And assuming, for the moment, that that's what was going on, did that mean she was involved in his death? Julia thought about the timing. The note said she'd be back at 10 p.m. That was around the time of Desmond's death. Did Arabella come back and kill him? It certainly didn't sound as if whoever wrote the note wanted him dead. It looked more like a love letter than a threat of murder.

Did she arrive to find him dead? Or not arrive at all? Or was the note merely a ploy to lure him out to the parking lot to kill him?

She tried to calm the flurry of questions that were swirling around in her head. She tried to remember everything she knew about Arabella Princeton. There was very little. She had never even spoken to her, as far as she could recall. She'd seen her at Peter and Christopher's wedding, where she'd been presiding over the preparations. She'd sat behind her at the funeral, where she'd been seated on the pew next to Cynthia.

Arabella was a surprising match for Desmond. She couldn't imagine her drawing that heartfelt line of x's, and the loopy little daisy. She was the best in the business, by all accounts, stylish and efficient – Julia had heard her described as having nerves of steel. She was the one who employed the caterers and all the other suppliers – the decorators, the furniture renters, the personalised balloon bouquets and the party gift providers, and the florist.

The florist, Angela! Julia felt a fresh wave of chemicals flood through her. A for Arabella, or A for Angela? Could Angela be the A who signed the note?

She thought of the fresh-faced blonde with her love of flowers. She thought about how tenderly she had touched the potted hydrangeas outside her pretty shop. The way she removed a dead leaf. The care and attention she gave to her arrangements. The way she had been so sweet to her rather demanding partner at the funeral. She seemed as odd a match for Desmond as Arabella was, but in a different way.

She remembered how Braydon had described Desmond's many fights and fallouts with staff and suppliers and colleagues 'Not Angela,' he'd said. 'She was never in his bad books.'

If Angela and Desmond were in love, she might well be the one person who escaped his fiery temper.

The drawing of the daisy! She remembered where she'd seen it. It was almost identical to the drawing on the side of Angela's van. She remembered that van, driven by Angela's rude aggressive husband. And his sense of entitlement at the funeral. That might explain the affair. He was horrible, he had driven her into the arms of Desmond. The more she thought about it, the more likely it seemed that it was Angela who wrote that note. Everything seemed to fall into place.

Except that she couldn't imagine Angela killing anyone. Julia knew that the most placid, gentle people could be surprisingly violent. But Angela? She didn't know her at all well, but she couldn't see it. Not even in a jealous rage, or in the aftermath of rejection. Julia sighed, disappointed once more in humanity. She'd been wrong before, imagining this or that person could *never* have done this or that awful thing. Maybe this was one of those times. Or maybe she was completely mistaken and Angela had nothing to do with Desmond's death.

Fortunately, this wasn't her problem to solve. It was a problem for DI Hayley Gibson. Except that DI Hayley Gibson wasn't answering her phone or reading her messages. As soon as her shift at Second Chances was over – at 1 p.m. on the dot – Julia would go to the police station and deliver the evidence in person.

The minutes passed like hours. Occasional customers drifted in and out. Someone dropped off a big box of CDs, which Wilma thanked him enthusiastically for, while they both knew they were as good as worthless. A South African family came in to see a classic English charity shop and poked around delightedly at the crockery and decorative odds and ends, before deciding, with great sadness, that they couldn't take the two porcelain Staffordshire terriers back to Johannesburg.

Finally, the moment arrived. Julia gathered up her handbag and her jacket from the back room, checked that the note was in her pocket, and fled the shop, waving cheerfully at Wilma as she did so.

Hayley was in a meeting, Walter Farmer told Julia, his eyes wide. He lowered his voice to a stage whisper: 'It's Superintendent Grave. After that story in the Sunday paper, the pressure is on. Big time.'

Julia looked at him blankly. She hadn't even seen the papers the day before. She'd been too busy gardening and looking for Braydon and getting into a muddle with Henrietta.

'A country wedding murder, they're calling it.' He handed her the Sunday paper and there, above the fold, were those exact words, as well as a picture of The Swan all decked out for a function, and a professionally taken photograph of Desmond looking young and dashing, his chef's whites pushed up at the sleeve to show his tattoos. His dark hair was glossy, and his eyes shining. Walter opened the paper, and there was a picture of Cynthia, looking happy and beautiful in an ivory lace shift, at her own wedding to Tim. Both of them alive, so alive.

Julia felt horrible, thinking about the awful loss of life and love.

'The whole district is up in arms about it now. If the papers are to be believed, people are too scared to go out. It's affecting tourism – people have cancelled their bookings for the weekend. There's a lot of talk about how useless the police are, which isn't fair, really. I must say. It's not easy. I mean, if only Henrietta Simmons had been...'

His wish that Henrietta had proven to be a cold-blooded murderer was interrupted by the arrival of Hayley. She came through the door from the offices, holding it open for Grave, who swept through with an air of great self-importance, which he somehow combined with fierce disappointment. He nodded to Julia. His slight frown indicated that he vaguely recognised her from the investigation into the pub quiz murders, but couldn't place her, or dredge up a name. He ignored Walter Farmer completely, but turned to Hayley and said in an almost threatening tone: 'I shall be expecting progress. Rapid progress.'

Hayley waited for him to exit, and let out a defeated sigh. 'Shallow Graves. Back again.' Then, as if only now realising that Julia was standing there, she added, 'Oh, Julia. What are you doing here?'

'I've got something for you. Something that might be useful to the investigation.'

'Well, that would be God's own miracle. Right now, the investigation is all dead ends and disappointment. And, today, a good old butt-kicking, as they would say in the States.'

'Sorry about Graves. But this might cheer you up.'

Hayley jerked her head in the direction of the office door, and started walking. Julia followed her in. A pile of files occupied the visitors' chair so she remained standing. She reached into her pocket and brought out the receipt with its note. One tiny little piece of paper to add to the collection of paper already resident in Hayley's space. 'Gloria brought in Desmond's clothes, the ones he was wearing the night he died, and this was in the jacket pocket. I think I know who wrote it.' She held it out to Hayley.

Hayley's face relinquished its tense frown. She looked, if not happy, at least surprised, in a good way. For a detective, a new piece of evidence was like a gift handed down from the gods.

'You're saying that you think the A is for Angela, the florist?' she said, minutes later, when Julia had taken her through her own thought process. 'I must say, the daisy, it seems... Possible.'

'That's what I'm thinking. But the note is so loving, it's hard to imagine what happened to go from that to murder.'

'Oh, there are a hundred reasons,' said Hayley, who was cynical in matters of the heart and took a rather dim view of human nature, generally. 'Maybe he broke up with her. Or he cheated. Or she wanted out, and he was hanging on too tight. Or there was a passionate lovers' quarrel. Whatever. It could be that she slammed the door on him on the spur of the moment, not meaning to kill him. It isn't impossible.'

'You're right. Any of those things might be true, Hayley. But what's harder to explain is Cynthia's death. Did Angela kill Cynthia as well? And if so, why?'

'You're right. That's a tougher nut to crack. Julia, what do you know about the two women's relationship? Friends? Enemies? Colleagues?'

'They would know each other from work, of course. They were the top picks for the top events. Best food, best flowers. They'd be working the same functions, every week, most likely. In fact, they were both at the bridal shower, now that I think about it.' Julia was fairly sure she remembered Angela and Cynthia on the now infamous video. They were talking, if she remembered right.

'Let me see.' Julia pulled out her phone, and found what she referred to in her head as 'the rat video', but which, on YouTube, was billed as 'Giant RAT ruins posh hen party!!!'. She hit play and muted the sounds so that she wasn't subjected to the additional trauma of all the shrieking and breaking glass and crockery. 'Here look...' The two women came into frame. She unmuted the phone, but whatever they said to each other was too far away for the microphone to catch and besides, the shrieking and smashing soon rose to an unmanageable volume. What was clear was that the two women were in conflict. The angry faces. The words spat out of tight lips. The flashing eyes. The clenched hands. It was brief, a second or two, but undeniable.

'Angela and Cynthia are fighting. How could I not have seen it?' Hayley said, bringing her fingers to her temples. 'And the next day, Cynthia was dead.'

Julia ran the video again. There was one brief moment where they were both turned to face the camera, their lips moving. She squinted, trying to imagine what words they might be uttering. 'If only we knew what they were saying.'

Hayley slapped her hand against her own forehead, like a cartoon character having A Grand Realisation. 'You know what, Julia? I think I know someone who might be able to help.'

'You do? Who?'

'Believe it or not, Walter Farmer. He's an odd fellow, with some splinter interests. He's interested in lip-reading. He did a course recently. They offer loads of strange things through the police training unit. He practises the whole time. Drives us nuts. Walter!'

He must have been hovering or lurking nearby, awaiting a summons, because he was in the room in mere seconds. 'Here I am, Inspector.' He stood up straight, as if to attention.

Hayley turned to her PC and pulled up the video on the bigger screen.

'We need your lip-reading skills, DI Farmer.'

He nodded solemnly. Julia felt a bubble of laughter rising within her, the murderous circumstances notwithstanding. Lip-reading skills? She'd never imagined she'd be involved in a situation that might require such a thing.

'Well, I'm still learning, but I'll do what I can.' He sounded like he had been waiting for this moment his whole life.

Julia gazed determinedly at the wall for a few moments, willing the giggles to pass, while Hayley showed Walter the couple of seconds of video. The waves of latent hysteria rose and fell, but she kept herself in check while Hayley spoke.

'There's Cynthia, see? And the blonde one is Angela. They're talking, but you can't really see... Now, she's cross, right... Doesn't she look cross? And here, Angela shaking her head, mumbling, and now Cynthia turns. Wait... Let me pause it here. You ready? There...'

Julia felt it safe to move her gaze from the wall to the phone screen, where Cynthia was moving to face Angela. As Cynthia's face was directly in front of the viewer, her eyes narrowed, and her mouth moved, forming distinct words. Words that Julia didn't recognise, frustratingly. She dared a glance at Walter, who was a picture of rapt concentration, his lips moving soundlessly with Cynthia's. Julia quickly looked back at the wall and gathered herself.

'Are you all right?' Hayley asked.

'Perfectly,' Julia answered, with all the self-control she could muster. The laughter was in danger of overtaking her at any moment.

'You look...'

Julia closed her eyes and shook her head gently. Hayley's lip began to twitch. The situation was in danger of getting out of hand.

'I've got it!'

The giggles were gone. Both women turned to DC Farmer. His lips had stopped moving, and he was nodding slowly to himself.

He took a moment to enjoy their full and eager attention, and then he spoke.

'Cynthia is saying, "I saw you, you were there later that night." What night do you think she means, DI Gibson?'

Julia looked at Hayley. The laughter left as suddenly as it had arrived.

'I can't be sure, of course, but it could be...' She looked at Julia. 'It could be the night of Desmond's murder. A secret rendezvous that ended in tragedy.'

'And after this conversation at the bridal shower, Angela knew Cynthia saw her there, so.'

The two women looked at each other, recognising what it all meant.

'Inspector!' Walter cried, processing the facts a beat or two after them. 'I do believe Angela might have killed Cynthia, to stop her talking!'

30

The machine that answered Blooming Marvels' number had said, regretfully, that there was no one to take a call right now, but to please press 1 to place an order, or 2 to request a call back in connection with an event. Or to please leave a message after the beep.

There was no number 3 to press 'if you are investigating a murder', so Hayley left a message asking Angela to phone her as soon as she got this message.

'You could try the shop?' Julia asked. 'She might be there.'

'Come on,' Hayley said, grabbing her jacket and walking towards the door.

Julia and Walter trotted obediently after her without so much as a question. Julia wondered if the DI had forgotten she was even there; it wasn't like her to invite Julia along, but she was not about to argue. They pulled up outside Blooming Marvels to find the door closed and locked. It was Monday mid-afternoon; the florist should have been open. The place looked sad and empty. Even the flowers in the pots – the ones Julia had seen Angela attend to so carefully only days before – looked a little less perky, as if they could do with a drink of water and the tender brush of Angela's fingers. The three of them stood outside staring at the building, wondering what to do next.

'We could try her home,' Walter said.

'Yes. Please call in and get the desk sergeant to see if she can find the address.'

'Oh, I know where she lives.' He was quite casual about it, and looked surprised that she didn't know he knew. 'We drove past it on the way. It's on the same road as my aunt Ally. You know, Sally's mum, Ally?'

Hayley didn't comment on the Farmer family's genealogy or geography. Or their naming conventions. Julia suspected that she was rolling her eyeballs behind the closed lids and silently counting to three, before she said, 'Thank you, Walter. Why don't you drive us there, okay?'

Angela's house was exactly what you'd expect – barely visible behind a lush and varied garden. Julia realised that she'd admired it on her walks without knowing who the owner was. It truly was a delight. A stone path went from the little wooden gate to the front door, painted the same sage green colour as the shop's. To either side were deep flowerbeds of huge dahlias in shades of red and orange and purple, and snapdragons in all colours of the rainbow, and little blue asters, and white Japanese anemones. Trees had been artfully planted and pruned to screen the fences along either side, and they were in their full autumn finery. There was very little grass, but what there was, was long and wild and scattered with little flowers that would, in the old days, have been persecuted as weeds, but were now a safe home for bees and butterflies and other small beasties.

Even Hayley, who was usually not one to remark on matters of a decorative nature, said, 'Well, this is pretty.' She rang the bell.

They waited a long moment in silence. No sound came from inside the house. Hayley rapped her knuckles sharply on the door and shouted, 'Hello!'

Walter stepped back from the front door and looked up, squinting into the wan afternoon light. 'Doesn't look like anyone's home. Maybe they're away. The upstairs windows and curtains are closed. Strange, it's only three thirty.'

Before they could decide what to do next, there was a sound from inside. Footsteps coming down wooden stairs, faint at first, and then louder and closer. The footsteps came towards the door and stopped. The door opened.

Julia recognised the man who answered as the person who had pulled up in the Blooming Marvels van to collect Angela from work. He looked completely different without the angry scowl. He was dark-haired and good looking, his full lips and even teeth shaped into a welcoming smile. 'Hello. Sorry to keep you waiting. I had something on the stove. Can I help you?'

'Detective Inspector Gibson. I was hoping to find Angela at home. I have a question for her. Is she here?'

'She's not, I'm afraid. She's gone to visit her mum for the day. Took the train to Oxford. That's why I was busy at the stove. Making dinner for her when she gets back tonight. I'm her fiancé. Can I give her a message?'

'Could you give me her number? Sorry, I didn't get your name.'

'Ben. Ben Roberts. Here's her number.' Walter scribbled the numbers on his notepad as Ben read them. 'She might not answer, though. She usually puts her phone on silent when she's with her mum, so she's not disturbed.'

'Right. Would you call her for me? She'll likely answer for you.'

Ben pulled his phone from his pocket and dialled. The phone rang and rang, and went to voicemail. 'Sorry. It seems she's not picking up.'

'Will you tell her I came by, and ask her to call me, if I haven't got hold of her?' Hayley handed over her card.

'Of course, Detective. I'm sure she'd be happy to help with whatever you need.'

'Thank you.'

They made to go, but Hayley turned back. 'Mr Roberts?'

He faced her with a helpful, eager expression.

'What is Angela's mother's name?'

He hesitated, and in that brief moment, Julia thought she saw his solicitous smile falter, but she couldn't be sure. It was back in an instant.

'Geraldine Camwell.'

'And her phone number?'

He quickly searched his cell phone and then read it off, Walter scribbling on his pad, and checking back.

Hayley nodded. The three of them walked back through the beautiful, fragrant garden, to the car.

'Walter, are you sure you wrote it down right?' Hayley asked. They had driven back to the station, and were gathered in the shadow of her piles of files. 'It's not going through.'

Walter looked affronted. 'Absolutely sure. I was very careful.'

'Okay, read me the mother's number. I'll give her a try.'

This time, the number rang, but nobody answered. There wasn't even a message to say whose phone it was and invite the caller to leave a message.

Walter was sent off to consult the various databases, and check whether these were the correct numbers.

'There's something odd about this. I don't like it,' Hayley said, while they waited. 'It looks like we have the wrong number for Angela, and her mother's not answering. I've got a friend up in Oxford. We started our training at the same time. I'm going to give her a call and see if she might be able to pop in on Mrs Camwell.'

'I'm going to head home. You don't need me here.' More to the point, Julia had spent the whole morning on her feet and had not eaten anything since breakfast. She wanted to sit down in her own kitchen with a cup of tea, and possibly a cheese sandwich. 'Will you let me know if your Oxford friend finds Angela? I'm a bit worried.'

'So am I, Julia. So am I.'

Julia arrived home to find Jess lying gloomily on the sofa, flicking through a magazine with a picture of a violet-eyed, dark-haired beauty on the cover, who looked familiar, but whom Julia could not identify. This wasn't unusual. It turned out that this was one of the unexpected things that happened in middle age – you simply ceased to know who anyone was. The detritus on the table next to Jess – a plate scattered with toast crumbs and a smear of honey, an apple core, a half-empty water glass, a mug with the dregs of coffee and a raft of souring cream floating on the top – indicated she had been there a while.

'You okay, Jess?'

Her daughter sighed out an unconvincing, 'Yeah.'

Julia waited.

'I was just thinking about leaving. It's only a few days till I go to London. And then back to Hong Kong.'

'I know, love, I feel the same. I'm dreading you going.'

'I'll miss you. And Dad. And Jake.'

'And Dylan?'

Jess smiled coyly. 'I guess. I mean, it's a new thing, but it's been nice. He's really nice.'

'He is. You seem to get on so well and have fun together.'

'Well, I'm not doing long distance. It never works.'

Jess spoke with such finality that Julia assumed she was convincing herself, rather than her mother.

'You don't have to decide on everything now. You will have

finished your degree in six months or so. You might be back in England. Who knows?'

'You're right. And maybe you could visit me before then? It would be fun to show you around.'

'I'm going to do that, Jess. I'd love to.'

'Maybe Sean...'

'We'll see.'

Jess had sat up and stretched, letting out a loud groan. 'I should take a walk or something. I've been lying around all day.' She stood up and gathered her empty plates and cups. They went through to the kitchen, feeling better now that they had a sort of plan to see each other again.

'Well, Jake might be willing, if you ask nicely. I'm going to put my feet up.'

'I'll see if Dylan wants to come. He was going to come over anyway.'

Jess went off to phone Dylan, and Julia's own phone rang.

'Angela is not at her mother's house,' Hayley said. 'My copper friend who went round there said the mother seemed surprised at the suggestion that she might be. His impression was that they didn't see much of each other. That they weren't close. Maybe even estranged. What did his note say?' There was a pause, in which Julia imagined Hayley scrabbling through the bits of paper on her desk. 'Here it is, he says that Geraldine said, and this is a quote, "We don't really see each other since she got engaged."'

Julia felt sad for the mother. And for the daughter. She wondered what had happened, why they had fallen out. Whatever the cause, it must be so painful for both of them. She felt a rush of gratitude for her good relationship with Jess, and the precious time they'd had together on this visit.

'Are you there, Julia?'

'Sorry.' She pulled herself back into the conversation. 'I was thinking, there's something about Angela's fiancé that doesn't add up. Don't you think it's odd that he didn't ask why you wanted to talk to Angela? What it was in connection with? You'd think he would wonder – a police inspector arriving at the house.'

'Now you mention it, yes, it is a bit unusual. Although he would probably assume it was something to do with the investigation into Desmond's death. We've spoken to Angela before, as a possible witness. He might have thought that it was a follow-up question and not been that bothered.'

'But then why would Ben lie about her being with her mother? Especially when you were bound to check.'

'Either he genuinely thought she was there, or he wanted to get rid of me. Temporarily.'

'Which would be because...'

Hayley jumped in to finish the sentence, 'Because he knows she's the killer and he knows why I was looking for her!'

Julia nodded, even though Hayley obviously couldn't see her.

'That adds up. She's on the run, or hiding out somewhere, and he's sending you off on a wild goose chase. Although, you've got to wonder why he's protecting her. If he knows that she's the killer, he must know that she was having it off with Desmond. Would you still cover for your fiancée in that situation?'

Hayley sighed. 'It could be that Ben thinks that Angela killing Desmond is the ultimate proof that she's over him, that she loves Ben. I don't know, love does strange things to a person. Relationships... that's your speciality, not mine, Julia.'

Julia wasn't sure that Hayley's suggested explanation held water, but she wasn't wrong about love. 'You'll have to go back and talk to Ben.'

'And I would do that, except he's gone AWOL too. He's not answering his phone.'

'So what are you going to do?'

'I'll put out her description to all local police, see if anyone sees her. And Walter and I will go back over all the footage and all the statements from the night of Desmond's murder. Tomorrow we'll re-interview people from that night, as necessary. Starting with Arabella; she might remember if and when Angela was there.' Hayley sighed.

'Well, we know Angela *wasn't* there when Christopher was looking for the rose petals. Because he looked for her, and her van, and didn't find them.'

'I'll check my records, but as far as I recall, that was at about nine thirty. Which means that the timeline *could* work, but it doesn't mean it did. We need to place Angela on the scene at ten.' Another sigh. 'An evening in front of some gripping CCTV for me, it looks like.'

And Hayley was gone.

31

It seemed impossible, but Julia woke up more tired than she'd gone to bed. She had slept badly, her unconscious mind busy with tales of husbands and wives, and mothers and daughters, and a confusing dream sequence of hiding and seeking and finding and losing. Angela's fiancé, Ben, made an appearance just before she woke up. The Ben in the dream was the angry, scowly Ben she had seen in the car outside the florist shop, not the charming Ben who had met her and Hayley at the door.

It left her with a tense, unsettled feeling. She didn't trust Ben. Her gut told her that he wasn't a good man, and he wasn't telling the truth. It struck her that Angela's mother might have had the same response. Perhaps it wasn't coincidental that her relationship with her daughter had taken a turn for the worse at the time of Angela's engagement to Ben. It could be that Geraldine didn't like Ben, that she didn't think he was good for her daughter. Or it could be that Ben wanted to alienate mother and daughter. Julia phoned Hayley with her theory.

'It's a well-known element in controlling or abusive relationships. The man tries to alienate the woman from the people closest to her, the people who love and support her and boost her confidence. He wants to have her to himself, and he wants her dependent on him. It gives him more power over her.'

'Disgusting.' Hayley spat the word out.

'It is. And dangerous.'

'I shall phone the mother again, and see what she has to say about the relationship.'

'I think that's a good idea. But, Hayley, go gently. She'll be defensive of her daughter, and she might feel guilty that she hasn't been able to help her. If you go in too hard, she'll probably shut the conversation down.'

'Gently, right. I'll be... yes... Gentle.'

Julia could hear the doubt in Hayley's voice. Gentle wasn't exactly her go-to position. She tended to be very direct, blunt, often to the point of brusqueness.

The same worry had obviously occurred to Hayley. 'A thought, Julia. Perhaps you could phone and talk to this Geraldine person. You're good at that sort of thing, being a social worker and all. You're more, I don't know, more diplomatic. More gentle, as you say. And besides, if I phone and say I'm police, it might spook her. Julia, I think you're the person for the job.'

This was something of a surprise to Julia, who knew that in addition to being diplomatic, as Hayley said, she was also nosy, and interfering. She knew that, on occasion, she had overstepped appropriate boundaries and found herself on the wrong side of DI Hayley Gibson. Yet here Hayley was, asking for her help. That was a turn-up for the books, as Julia's mother would have said.

Hayley took her hesitation for reluctance, and spoke persuasively. 'It's perfectly legitimate, the police working with other professionals. We do it all the time. So why not with you? You would be doing me a service.'

'Well, in that case, yes. I'll do it. Send me the number.'

'I thought, if you don't mind, we might phone her together.

You can put her on speaker. If you come to my office, we can record the call. Would you mind? Do you have time?'

It was settled. Julia would give herself, the hens, and the dog breakfast, and make her way to Berrywick police station. And they would phone Geraldine Camwell.

Geraldine Camwell had a brisk efficient tone, which Julia hadn't expected. She'd been expecting a dithery old dear, and now she felt guilty for making ageist assumptions.

'A social worker? That seems unusual.' The woman was canny, too.

'It is a little unusual,' Julia said, then echoed Hayley's earlier words. 'The police do sometimes bring in other professionals when they think it might be helpful.'

'I don't see how it will help you find my daughter. Or that so-called fiancé of hers.'

'The detective thought if we understood the relationship a little better...'

'Well, as far as I'm concerned, since you asked, I don't think the relationship between them is bad. As long as he's getting his way.'

'That sounds like it might be unpleasant for you to witness.'

'It is. He's so...' She seemed to run out of words at this point.

'Controlling? Possessive? Self-involved?'

'All of the above. He doesn't like her to have friends. Or see her family. He alienated her from me, drove a wedge between us with his lies and interfering. She phones me every week or so, but we don't visit. It's too hard.'

'That is very sad. It must be upsetting.'

'It broke my heart.'

In the silence that followed that simple sentence, Julia thought how bereft the woman must be.

'I'm grateful that she has her work. He tolerates that,

because she makes the money. I know she gets a lot of pleasure from it. She's adored flowers since she was a little girl. And at least she has those hours to be herself, to do what she loves, without him around.'

And in those hours she fulfilled her creative passions, and her romantic ones – she met and fell in love with Desmond, thought Julia.

'Why do you think she stays with him?'

'I think she loves him. Hard as it is to imagine. He can be very charming. Charmed the socks off me when he first arrived on the scene. I'm no fool, and even I thought he was delightful. He treats her like a goddess. As long as she plays by his rules.'

Hayley pushed a piece of paper across the desk. *Violent?*

'Mrs Camwell, was he ever violent towards her, as far as you know?'

'Oh God, I hope not. I don't think so. But he can be very angry, very aggressive to other people. If he thinks they're a threat to him. He's been, well, very blunt with me. I think he would do anything to keep her. But violent to her? Oh God, you don't think anything's *happened* to her, do you?' Her voice rose in panic.

'No, no,' Julia said quickly. 'I've got no reason to think that. None at all. I'm just asking generally.'

'I think he adores her. But in an unhealthy way. And I think she can't see it clearly enough to get away.'

The call ended after a few more questions, and Julia and Hayley were both silent, thinking about what they had heard, putting it together.

Julia looked over at Hayley and saw in her face that she was likely thinking the same thing: that there was the problem. Ben adored Angela. In an unhealthy way. He was possessive. And could be aggressive to other people.

And then there was the one thing they knew that Angela's mother did not know: that Angela had written a love letter to another man. How would he react if he had known that?

Hayley tapped her pen against the desk, deep in thought. Her sharp, clever face bore a slight furrow of concentration. Julia's gaze was fixed on the scrawl on the piece of paper.

Violent?

Julia spoke first. 'We know from the note and from what Cynthia said on the video that Angela was there that night,' she said.

'That's why we thought it could be Angela who killed him.'

'But what if Ben had also known that Angela would be there that night. With Desmond.'

'He wouldn't have been happy about it, that's for sure.' Hayley frowned. 'He'd have gone after her, I think.'

'I think so too,' said Julia.

'It wasn't Angela,' Hayley said slowly.

'Hayley, it was Ben!'

'Right. Come on, Julia, let's go.'

Hayley interrupted DI Walter Farmer's tea break, summoning him with a curt instruction as she swept past his desk and out of the door, Julia a pace behind her. Walter slurped a last gulp of tea, which must have been too hot because he gave a small, repressed shriek as he swallowed it and went after the two women.

'Not you, Julia,' Hayley said as she reached for the car handle. 'You can't come on a police investigation of a possible murder suspect. Absolutely not.'

'I don't need to come, but I do need to tell you something. It's important. I've got a theory, so I was thinking that if Ben—'

'I can't stop. We need to find Angela.'

'That's what this is about. If you'd just let me tell you.'

'Oh, get in then. You can talk on the way. I'll drop you off.'

'Fine, that's fine,' Julia got into the back seat, the two police officers up front. The car was already on the move by the time she put on her seatbelt and continued. 'Do you remember, when we went to Angela's house yesterday, we waited a while for Ben to come to the door?'

'Yes. A few minutes. I thought he wasn't home. Then we heard his footsteps coming down the stairs.'

Hayley spoke curtly, her eyes fixed on the road. She drove fast, but not dangerously so, holding the corners tightly.

'Exactly. But remember, he said that he'd been in the kitchen, cooking supper and Angela was supposedly with her mum, except that she wasn't. Unless they have a most unusual design, the kitchen would be on the ground floor. There would be no need for clomping down the stairs, now, would there?'

Hayley took another corner before she spoke again.

'So he was upstairs. Not in the kitchen at all.' She briefly caught Julia's eye in the rear-view mirror and said, 'The curtains were closed, remember? We remarked on it. The place looked deserted.'

'Yes, we thought they must be out, or have gone away.'

'But they weren't out. He was there.'

'And maybe she was too,' Julia said.

'I was thinking about the numbers,' Walter said. 'The number he gave for her mum was wrong. Two of the numbers were transposed. Maybe he did that on purpose. So we wouldn't find out that Angela wasn't there.'

'Hayley,' said Julia. 'I think Angela might be in real danger.'

'So do I,' said Hayley. 'Hopefully we'll get there in time.'

Hayley pulled the police car over, blocking the driveway where the Blooming Marvels van was parked.

'Stay here,' she told Julia.

She and Walter jumped out and walked past the van and to the front door. They disappeared out of sight. Julia was tempted to get out, to see over the impressive display of dahlias peeping over the low wall, but she decided against it. She surveyed what she could see, which wasn't much. Beyond the van was another path, presumably leading to the kitchen door, but it wasn't visible from where she sat. By craning her head forward, she could see the upstairs of the little house. The curtains were still closed, and the place looked as empty as it had the day before.

A minute ticked past. Another minute. After a couple more, Julia reckoned that Hayley and Walter must have gained entry, or they'd be back at the car by now. She tried to imagine what was going on inside the house. Was Angela there? Was she being held against her will? Was she even alive?

Julia sat staring at the headrest. It had only been a few minutes, but she was unsettled. Not for long. There was a bang, like wood against brick, and from the direction of the kitchen door came Ben, pulling Angela behind him. Julia moved behind the headrest and peered out from behind it, largely hidden.

Where was Hayley? She and Walter must be in the house. She didn't let herself wonder what was keeping them or if they were all right.

She watched Ben. Keys at the ready, he lunged for the passenger door of the van, pulled it open and pushed Angela in. Only then did he notice the police car parked across his driveway. His face clenched with fury. He slammed his hand down on the roof of the car and shouted something, a harsh monosyllable that Julia couldn't make out. He grabbed Angela's arm and pulled her out.

He was only a few feet from Julia, moving fast. She slid down in her seat, wondering what to do. She felt she couldn't confront him, a big, angry man decades younger than herself. But she didn't want to let him get away.

Where was Hayley?

He was almost level with Julia now, coming up alongside the car, pulling Angela behind him, not looking where he was going. More on instinct than by decision, Julia opened the car door as fast and hard as she could. He crashed into it. She had her weight against it, but he was heavier and moving. He crumpled, his knees buckling, his face momentarily at her window with an expression of shock. She had the advantage of surprise for a moment. She got out, and held the door open, blocking the gap between the side of the car and the brick post of the driveway.

'I'm so sorry, I didn't see you there. Are you all right?'

Ben was on the ground, but already getting to his feet. He didn't answer.

'Hello, Angela, we met at the shop, I think. I'm Julia Bird. Are you all right?'

Angela looked confused, which wasn't altogether surprising under the circumstances. She looked down at Ben, and back at Julia, and said, 'I... I think so. But I must be going, I think.' She took a couple of tentative steps, edging past Ben, who was bent over, hands on his thighs. He stood up and took her arm. 'We will go together.'

Julia smiled in what she hoped was a reassuring, non-threatening way. 'I think it would be wise to stay. The police are here, and it might be better to have a chat with them before you go anywhere.'

Angela looked to her husband. 'Ben—'

'No. We can't...' He moved towards Julia, and tried to squeeze by in the narrow space between the police car door, Julia and the gatepost. Angela stood behind him.

'Come on Angela,' he said angrily.

Julia edged herself forward. He could have shoved her out of the way, and for a moment she thought he would, but he hesitated.

'The thing is, there's quite a lot to sort out, and you're the only one who knows what really happened to Desmond. You can explain. Tell your side of the story.'

At the mention of his name, Angela made a sad little noise, somewhere between a sob and a gasp. Ben tightened his grip on his fiancée's arm.

'That's just it. I can explain. They've got the wrong idea. I was the person who was wronged – *me*! Tell her, Angie. Go on, tell her.'

'I keep telling you that you've got it wrong. I wasn't having an affair with Desmond. He was a friend. A friend when I needed one.' Her voice was quiet and slow, and she had a sort of dazed look about her. Julia wondered if she might be drugged, although she'd seen similar responses to shock and grief. She sounded like someone who had given up on being listened to or understood.

'I know when I'm right, Angela. I know what I saw, and you can't play mind games with me.'

'That's why you should stay and have a conversation with Hayley Gibson. Hayley is a very reasonable person, you know. She'll listen to your story, truly listen.'

'The police?' he sneered. He looked at the car. 'I heard them come in and we slipped out the back. They're bashing about upstairs now, calling and looking for us. Idiots. They're certainly not going to help with anything. Fools.'

Julia was relieved at this news. Presumably it meant that Ben hadn't harmed Hayley and Walter. She glanced back down the path. Behind Angela, Julia saw the top of Walter's head, and caught a glimpse of Hayley behind him. They were moving low and quietly towards the police car. Julia quickly shifted her eyes back to Ben, but he must have seen something flicker in them.

He turned, saw the police and, pulling Angela towards him, shouted, 'Stay back!'

Hayley and Walter stopped in their tracks. 'It's okay, we only want to talk,' Hayley said calmly.

Julia could see Ben's shoulder shaking under his cotton shirt. The man was scared. He put his arm round Angela, pulling her back to his chest, his forearm across her collarbone. He wasn't strangling her, but his forearm was snug against her, resting at her throat. The position could have been tender, a hug, but it was a little too tight, too rigid. Angela looked at Julia, her eyes wide with fear and pleading.

Ben's eyes darted from the police, to Julia, to the exit behind her, weighing up his options. 'This is all a mistake. It's not what you think.'

Julia kept her voice calm and neutral, as if they were having a regular conversation about ordinary matters. 'Ben, I know you're frightened. This is not an ideal situation we're in here, but the thing is, it's a situation that could get worse, or it could get better. I think we all want it to be better, not worse. I know that you want that, too.'

Angela spoke for the first time. 'Please, Ben, she's right. You've made mistakes. Don't make things worse.'

'It wasn't supposed to be like this. I just want to get away.' He sounded so sad that she felt a tiny bit sorry for him.

'I'm sure you do,' Julia spoke in her most understanding tone. 'But running isn't a good idea. It doesn't make you look good, and to be honest, Ben, you won't get far. The only way you can make this right, and move on, is to talk.'

He nodded. His arm loosened around Angela's throat. 'All right then,' he said to Julia, and then lifted his head and said louder to Hayley Gibson, 'I'll talk.'

32

For a sad occasion – a farewell for Jess – it was a surprisingly happy one. For a start, it was one of those sparkling autumn days that almost convinces you that winter is still months away.

Secondly, there were dogs. Julia had originally chosen a fancy gourmet restaurant, glowingly reviewed and heartily recommended, for Jess's farewell, but Jess had vetoed it.

'Oh, Mum, that sounds lovely, and I'm sure the food is brilliant, but they won't let Jake in, I'm sure!' she said, when Julia presented her plan. 'We can't have my farewell without Jakey. Let's go to The Swan. The food is super and they allow dogs on the terrace.'

So it was back to the scene of the crime – literally – they went, and with *two* dogs, as it happened. Jess had insisted that Sean bring Leo. 'We can't leave him out, the dear boy.'

'If I'd known it was a bring-your-own-pet party, I would have brought Too, too,' Tabitha said with a twinkle in her eye. 'Handy to have a cat around, just in case of, you know... *rats*.'

There was laughter from the assembled guests. Not from Hayley, who looked grey at the mere mention of *that* mess. Henrietta had taken extreme umbrage at the intimation that she might have killed Desmond, and threatened to sue the police department and get Hayley fired. A judicious reminder of her potentially criminal activities as a peanut poisoner and rat releaser had encouraged Henrietta to pipe down, but Julia knew that Hayley had had a grim few days of it.

'I can't believe it's nearly over,' said Jess. 'So much has happened. I was expecting rather a dull time in the country – no offence, Mum – but I have to say, it's been the most eventful holiday I've ever had.' She looked at Dylan and they both blushed.

'This was *not* a regular few weeks in Berrywick,' Tabitha said, ignoring the little spark that had flown across the table. 'The most dramatic event of the previous month was when someone picked Pippa's prize chrysanthemums in the middle of the night.'

'Now, Tabitha, you're not telling the truth. There was that drama over the planning permission for Mr Garner's shed.' Sean made air quotes with his fingers around the word shed. Everyone laughed uproariously, except for Jess, who said, 'What? What happened?'

'Ah, well, it was not so much a shed as a games centre, and right on Margie Mansfield's boundary fence. She had a sign made 'I'm Mad in the Shed', and she put it up in front of his house. Mad in the shed, mad in the head, get it?'

More laughter, and tutting, and shaking of heads. Jess continued to look bewildered.

'Don't remind me.' Hayley put her head in her hands in mock despair. 'I had both of them down at the station trying to bring charges against each other. In fact, fully half of the complaints our desk sergeant hears are related to planning permission disputes. That and trees.'

Jess looked none the wiser.

'Sometimes a tree from one side of the fence hangs over a neighbour and... Honestly, never mind. Take my word for it.'

'Better than murders, though,' Julia said. And immediately regretted spoiling a bit of harmless fun and laughter.

'I heard Angela's fiancé has been charged with Desmond's murder,' said Dylan.

'Yes. And Cynthia's,' said Hayley. It was, after all, in the public record.

'I don't understand. Why did he have to kill them?'

Hayley looked uncomfortable and didn't answer. Julia, who wasn't an official, said, 'It was all very sad and unnecessary. From what Angela told me, she and Desmond were close. Good friends. Nothing more than that. She'd confided in him that Ben was controlling, emotionally abusive. Desmond said she should leave him, she went backwards and forwards, didn't know what to do. Until the night he arrived at The Swan.'

'The night of Dad's wedding?' Jess asked.

'Yes. Ben was out with his mates. He always stayed out late, early hours. Angela went back to The Swan to talk to Desmond. She thought she was ready to leave Ben, she wanted his advice. But Ben had got it into his head to go home early. When Angela wasn't home, he went a bit crazy. He came to The Swan and saw Desmond and Angela together. They didn't see him.'

'*Together* together?' Tabitha's eyebrows arched impressively.

'No, not like that. Talking. Desmond's arm around her shoulder. Angela saying she thought her relationship was finally over. Desmond listening, supporting, encouraging her to do what was right for her. Of course Ben was furious. He hid until she left, and then he confronted Desmond.'

'Did he think they were having an affair?'

'Yes. He lost his temper. Locked Desmond in the van and went home. He claims it was pure impulse. He didn't mean to kill him. And because it was so late, and everyone had left, nobody would have heard Desmond in the van.'

'But the temperature was turned right down,' said Sean. 'It was deliberate.'

'That's certainly how it looks,' agreed Hayley.

'Mum, did Angela know then? That he killed him?' Jess asked.

'No. She didn't even know that he had been there that night. He carried on as normal, she said. Quite lovey-dovey, didn't want any waves, or to draw attention. For a while it looked as if he'd got away with it.'

'What changed?' Dylan asked.

Knowing it would come out anyway, Hayley continued the story. 'Unbeknownst to Angela, Cynthia had seen her with Desmond on the night of his murder. As we deduced from Walter's lip-reading, Cynthia told her that she knew she'd been there. It seems at first she'd kept it to herself because she knew what sort of man Ben was, and she knew that Angela had been having troubles with him. Desmond had told her. But on the day of the great rat debacle, she told Angela that she needed to tell the police that Angela had been there, because we thought that it was her – Cynthia – who was the murderer. And now Cynthia was wondering if maybe it was Angela. Angela didn't know what to do. She knew she wasn't the murderer, but she had lied to the police about being there.'

'Why did she lie?' asked Jess.

'Because she didn't want Ben to know she went back. How would she explain it? Better to keep quiet. Obviously, she didn't realise that Ben already knew she'd been there, that he'd seen her and that he'd murdered Desmond. And now, with her friend Desmond murdered, she was having second thoughts about leaving Ben. Ben was being kind and attentive – and remember, she had no idea that he was the murderer.'

'But after she spoke to Cynthia, she was scared that she was going to tell the police she'd seen her there that night,' said Dylan thoughtfully.

Hayley nodded. 'Exactly. Angela was scared. She went home and told Ben that she had gone back to The Swan that night. She told him that she'd left something behind, some of her florist tools. She explained that she hadn't mentioned it because, after Desmond's death, she thought it best to be quiet. But now that Cynthia was throwing around accusations that she was the murderer, she was going to go to the police and explain. Go to them before they came to her.'

'Ben panicked,' said Julia, taking up the story again. 'He didn't want to draw police attention to the fact that Angela was there that night. Remember, he thought there was something romantic between Angela and Desmond, that if it came out, it would draw attention to him as a suspect. He told Angela not to worry, that he would take care of everything. And the next morning, Cynthia was dead.'

'Surely she realised then,' said Jess, clearly feeling that she would have been smarter than Angela in this particular situation.

'She said that she wasn't sure,' said Julia. 'That she couldn't quite believe it. But she knew he'd left the house early that morning. And she knew that he was behaving strangely. He didn't want her to go anywhere, and kept the curtains closed. She hadn't realised that he was actually keeping her locked in the house until the police arrived.'

'When we knocked on the door, and he saw through the upstairs window who it was, he panicked. He knew that if we questioned Angela, the truth would come out. So he shoved her in the bedroom, took her phone, locked the door, and told us she was out of town. And the rest, as they say, was history,' said Hayley.

'Hello, all!' Kevin came over with a bottle of champagne and a tray of champagne flutes. 'On the house, Mrs Bird. A little gift to say goodbye to your Jess. Dylan told us it was a farewell.'

'How kind of you, Kevin! Thank you.' She was pleased to have an excuse to move on from the subject of murder.

'Our pleasure. I'll pour, shall I?'

He divvied the bottle up among the glasses.

'Thanks, Kev,' Dylan said, accepting a glass.

'We need a toast!' Julia raised her glass. She looked at her daughter, sitting there, the light coming in from the window, making her hair shine like the autumn chestnuts they had collected, and the bubbles glinting in the champagne flute in the girl's hand. Her heart was so full of love and happiness and sadness that she didn't trust herself to speak.

Jess stood up. 'Okay if I say something, Mum?'

Julia smiled and nodded. Jake misinterpreted Jess's intent, and leapt to his feet, hoping for a walk. Jess patted his head.

'Good boy, Jakey. Hello, everyone.' She giggled, a little nervous now that she'd grabbed the spotlight, then cleared her throat. 'Have to say, when Mum told me she was moving to a village in the Cotswolds, I thought it was a crazy idea. I was worried she'd be lonely and bored. I should have trusted my mum's instincts – as you all know, they are often spot on. I'm happy to say, I couldn't have been more wrong. She's found friendship, purpose, love, even. I've experienced the same. You've made me so welcome and I've felt so at home here. I want to toast you all, and to thank you. To friendship and to Berrywick.'

She raised her glass. Jake, who was still waiting for the chat to wrap-up and the walk to begin, let out a sharp bark, just to hurry things along.

'And to dogs!'

A LETTER FROM KATIE GAYLE

Dear reader,

Katie Gayle is, in fact, two of us – Kate and Gail. We are so grateful to those of you who have read all of the Julia books so far, and to those who have just discovered her. We always love an adventure in Berrywick with Julia and Jake, and we hope that you do too. If you are a new friend of Julia Bird, please grab a copy of *An English Garden Murder* to read about Julia's first adventures in Berrywick, and then follow her on her subsequent adventures.

We've still got more adventures planned for Julia and Jake and the characters of Berrywick. If you want to keep up to date with all Katie Gayle's latest releases, please sign up at the following link. Your email address will never be shared and you can unsubscribe at any time.

www.bookouture.com/katie-gayle

You can also follow us on social media for regular updates and pictures of the real-life Jake! (What a Good Boy he is!).

We would be very grateful if you could write a review and post it on Amazon and Goodreads, so that other people can discover Julia too. Ratings and reviews really help writers!

You might also enjoy our Epiphany Bloom series – the first three books are available for download now. We think that they are very funny.

You can find us in a few places and we'd love to hear from you.

Katie Gayle is on the platform formerly known as Twitter as @KatieGayleBooks and on Facebook as Katie Gayle Writer. You can also follow Kate at @katesidley and Gail at @gailschimmel. Kate and Gail are also on Insta and Threads, and Gail, for her sins, is trying to figure out TikTok!

Thanks,

Katie Gayle

 facebook.com/KatieGayleWriter
x.com/KatieGayleBooks

PUBLISHING TEAM

Turning a manuscript into a book requires the efforts of many people. Katie Gayle and the publishing team at Bookouture would like to acknowledge everyone who contributed to this publication.

Audio
Alba Proko
Sinead O'Connor
Melissa Tran

Commercial
Lauren Morrissette
Jil Thielen
Imogen Allport

Cover design
Lisa Brewster

Data and analysis
Mark Alder
Mohamed Bussuri

Editorial
Nina Winters
Sinead O'Connor

Made in the USA
Coppell, TX
27 March 2024

30608892R00142